To Andie,

It has been a real
pleasure to
meet you.
May Sam steal
your heart!

Sam
Destiny

SAM DESTINY

AJ's Salvation

By Sam Destiny

also by
Sam Destiny

Romances

Tagged For Life (Tagged Soldiers Book 1)

Forever Girl (Tagged Soldiers Book 2)

Tagged For A New Start (Tagged Soldiers Book 3) (Coming Spring 2018)

Call Me Michigan

Morningstar Series

Set In Flames (Book 1)

Set In Sparks (Book 2)

Set in Burns (Book 3)

Set To Start (A Morningstar Novella)

AngelBond Trilogy

Raise The Fallen (Book 1)

Raise The Hopeless (Book 2)

Raise The Damned (Book 3) (Coming Fall 2018)

Dedication

For here I lie completely broken,
And you came with your healing touch,
Not many words between us spoken,
Yet you made me smile and such.

To my best friend Yvi, who always makes me feel better.
Together forever, never apart,
maybe in distance, but never at heart.

Prologue

*A*lessia looked at the guy who wanted to change her life forever. She was packed and ready to leave for college and start her new adventure, yet right now, she was hesitating.

"You never bothered to speak to me," she accused, her heart breaking at all the times she had looked at her brother's best friend and longed for him just to acknowledge her.

"You never planned to come back here, Aly. You're the perfect choice. Just go. You already told everyone bye! Everyone who matters knows you're leaving. And everyone who matters knows you and I never had anything going on. Ever. Please."

Alessia couldn't get herself to look at what he was carrying, so she focused on the face she had seen so many times during the day and touched so many times during her dreams. The bundle in the carry-on babbled quietly and she watched as Jam placed it on the floor. A baby. Aly had just turned eighteen, and her life was supposed to begin for real now. She wanted to leave since her heart couldn't get over being in love with Jamison, and there he stood in front of her with a plea like *this*.

"Jam, you have no idea what you're asking," she pleaded, her throat feeling dry.

"You know Collene. She'll never stop treating him as she does now. And you know her father. I can't take him anywhere because they'd forever hunt me. You, on the other hand... you're the only logical option for me."

"Treating him how?" Alessia asked, almost afraid of the answer.

Jamison knelt next to the carry-on, opening the light green blanket before carefully pulling up the baby boy's shirt. The sight of the black and blue little body made Alessia gasp. "No," she almost sobbed, her heart breaking. She knew Collene had a violent streak, but she never thought the woman would hit her own child.

"They're going to say I beat him. Her whole family will attest to it. You need to take him far away."

"You're asking me to kidnap a child," she accused, outrage clear in her voice.

"I'm asking you to save his life," Jam insisted, and she shook her head, hugging herself. She should have kept going once she had spotted him on the side of the road.

She should have told herself not to care when he had flagged her down in the middle of some forest, but it was Jam and she hadn't been able to ignore the bag and baby at his side, either. Her heart had started a wild rhythm. In her mind, she had told herself that maybe, just maybe, he had finally realized he loved her and now wanted to come with her.

She would have taken him in a heartbeat.

Collene Karmison was the mayor's daughter, and they ruled the city as if they were kings and queens. Corruption was rich in their hometown of Townsend, but Alessia had always stayed out of Collene's way. Being a nice girl and just average looking had kept her safe from attacks, but she had heard about them and had seen the victims, too. It had always been a mystery to her why someone like Jamison had slept with Collene. A mistake, which had ended badly for him, if she considered where they stood now.

"They can't lock you up for that. You don't even love her."She tried to reason with him, but he just choked out a cold laugh. He knew just as well as she did that they'd be able to do whatever they wanted to him. It was the only reason she considered this craziness at all. "Do they know you have him?"

"The nanny left him on the doorstep to get his bottle of milk. No one knows where he is. I need to get back soon or they'll know something's off. Make a decision now, Aly," he pleaded.

"My life is over if they ever realize where your child is," she argued, and finally, the green eyes clouded with unsheltered grief.

"I know. I'm sorry for asking. You don't deserve having to clean up my mess for me," Jam agreed, and it was what made Alessia move forward and reach for the baby boy. She wasn't even sure the little guy had a name yet since Jamison and Collene had fought over it for the last four months.

"Did you decide on a name yet?" she questioned, and Jam kissed the little boy's forehead before taking the tiny bundle out of his carry-on and giving it to her.

"He's yours. You name him. It doesn't matter what Collene called him. It doesn't matter what I'd call him. He's your boy now." It was more than obvious how much it hurt Jamison to let his son go, but that didn't matter. What mattered was the infant's life and they both knew it.

He put the bag in her car, another addition to fill the last spot she had left before he placed the carry-on as a car seat in the front. "Ditch it and buy a new one tomorrow. You should be far enough by then to switch the seats. Make sure to keep him safe and warm," Jam demanded, his request without much heat, though.

"Come with us," she pleaded. There never had been an ounce of hope for them, but she was desperate now. A child would keep them together. Maybe she could get her chance with Jam finally. Then another thought occurred to her. "How in the world will I be able to afford a child?"

Finally, the smallest of smiles lifted the corner of his mouth. "You'll figure it out. Leave now, or you'll never go."

She nodded. He didn't even bother to take her in his arms as a thank you or as a way of saying good-bye. Instead, he just held open her door and watched as she slipped behind the wheel.

Aly started the car after strapping in the little boy. Driving was something she knew how to do, so her body needed no real input. Her mind was racing. She needed a name for the boy and a story to go with it.

In her rearview mirror, she saw Jamison shrink away. He looked like a broken man, and as much as Alessia wanted to go back, she forced herself to move forward. She knew this could ruin her life faster than a Ferrari could get to a hundred, but he was her weakness and the boy next to her actually gave her a reason to go through with leaving. No kid ever deserved to be beaten.

No person ever did. Period.

"Oh God, Jam, please tell me you didn't lie to me," she whispered as the thought hit her. Now it was too late to turn back, though. She had more or less kidnapped a child, and she knew returning would not change anything at all.

≈

*J*amison ran a hand through his blond curls, feeling relief like never before. His son was out of harm's way. As much as he felt guilty for forcing the only girl he'd ever loved to commit a crime, the boy was all that mattered to him.

Turning away, he walked back to his car, which he had hidden in the forest. He had waited for quite some time for Aly to appear, so he was freezing by the time he slipped back inside, but he was sure it had been well worth it in the end.

His beat-up truck was just as cold as he felt as he sank back into the seat. His hands were shaking, and he wished it were because he had handed over his only child. Deep down, he knew it was because it had taken everything in him not to kiss Alessia at least once in his life.

"You did the right thing."

Even though Jamison had known he wasn't alone, he still jumped.

"Greg," he murmured, watching Aly's brother and his best friend from the corner of his eye.

"Still here. I was with you when we got here, remember?" Of course, Jamison remembered since Greg had been his plan B. Just then, something hit him.

"You didn't bring a bag. You were ready to run with my son without anything but the clothes you're wearing?"

Greg shrugged. "Alessia has loved you for as long as I can think. I had no doubt she was going to take him from you, especially not after seeing the little boy's injuries."

Jamison wasn't surprised. After all, that was, too, what had convinced Greg to tag along.

"How exactly did those happen anyway?"

Jamison closed his eyes, still seeing the way Collene had grabbed the baby and shaken him until Jamison had feared his son would end up dead. Taking him from her without hurting him anymore had almost been impossible.

"She used to hit him when he wouldn't stop screaming. And I told her she needed to stop that, so she started to shake him. I can still see her fingers digging into his tiny body, and..."A shiver passed through him, and Greg interrupted him with a gesture.

"He'll have the best home any boy can get. Be sure of it," he promised, reminding Jamison he had just saved his baby more pain.

"No doubt about that," he agreed. "Collene will be pissed... immensely so."

"You finally can move out. She no longer has any leverage on you," Greg commented, and Jamison only nodded.

"Good-bye," he whispered, then he started his car and headed back into hell. But now, it had become just that tiny bit more bearable.

chapter

*A*lessia Rhyme pulled her dark hair back in a ponytail while standing on the porch of their little house. She had worked hard to get her own safe haven, and finally, after nearly a decade of nightly hours and having to put Alessandro in the care of a neighbor, she had reached her dream. Or what had turned into her dream after she had run away with a tiny baby boy. Now, he was hers, and she would never ever give him up again.

Running had been surprisingly easy, and five years after she had taken him, no one had come looking for the boy. In fact, no one had ever even bothered to contact her about the kidnapping, either. She had hidden the baby away and then had vanished. In the end, she simply pretended she had birthed him in some tiny country hospital. The people in her new town didn't know any different.

Sunrow was a small-town like any other coastal town in the continental US. Tourists were equally loved and hated, but Aly didn't mind them. She had a small café, and since it gave her the chance to spend a lot of time with Lesso, she adored it more with each passing day. Her son usually came over right after school, giving her the most beautiful smiles ever.

"Mom, can I please, please, please go for a swim?" Alessandro stepped out onto the porch next to her.

It was early summer, with June just presenting its most impressive sunshine. Still, the weather wasn't nearly warm enough for her to be comfortable with letting him out in the water.

"Nope, Lesso. Stay away from the water's edge or your afternoon outside will rapidly end," she threatened, laughing as she saw him grin at her. Whenever he looked over his shoulder at his mother, he reminded Aly so much of his father that her heart was aching.

She had tried the dating game, but in her first year here, she had been too busy to pursue anything lasting. Then afterward, she had been a mother mainly. No matter how young she appeared on the outside, she knew she had left behind a girl and arrived a woman.

No guy was able to capture her heart. People who told you that you couldn't lose your heart while you were young had never met Jamison. Or grown up watching a guy who was probably as unique as a snowflake.

"Sweet girl, you have that pensive look again." Aly shook her head, clearing Jamison from her thoughts to focus on the new arrival. She hadn't even noticed her elderly neighbor walking up to her porch.

"Dorly." She smiled, kissing the old woman on her papery cheek. She had been like family ever since Alessia and Alessandro had arrived.

"Will you tell an old woman what kept your thoughts busy this time around?" the lady inquired, and Aly started to collect Alessandro's towels and clothes. She had made him change earlier since, like all boys, he hadn't been able to resist getting his feet wet no matter what she'd said.

"I was just enjoying the view," Aly explained, lowering her eyes since she had a feeling the old woman could read her better than all the cheesy novellas she usually carried around.

"Okay, let me tell you what you've been thinking about," Dorly said, drawing a beach chair near. Aly sat down on the porch steps as she always did, turning to look at her neighbor without losing sight of her son.

She had to hide a grin as she arched a brow. "Sure, share your wisdom," she teased, and Dorly shook her head.

"Don't make fun of me, young lady," she scolded gently, and Aly laughed. It was weird, but she felt as if she only could be her true self around that woman. The smile vanished from the older neighbor's face, though, as she looked out at the ocean. "You were thinking about the kid's dad."

Okay, she wasn't watching the ocean. Dorly was watching Alessandro.

Aly decided not to reply anything, so she stayed silent instead. She didn't even try to deny it because she knew Dorly would see right through her.

"He looks so much like his dad. It's incredible," the woman went on.

"Yeah, he has nothing from me," Aly agreed, swallowing as Jamison's face came back to her. She didn't even think about the comment closer since she had heard it a lot over the years. Alessandro's teachers always asked about his father since they obviously guessed he must be a handsome guy. Aly no longer had any idea if that was true, but he sure had been a looker back when she had still seen him daily.

"How long have you lived next door?" Dorly asked, confusing Aly with the sudden change of topic. She had started renting the house before Dorly had actually sold it to her for a bargain. Alessia knew it was because she was helping her out and Dorly had no children of her own, but that didn't matter. Aly would forever be indebted to her.

"Nine years? Give or take," she finally replied, and Dorly nodded.

"Not once have you been back home. Not once has anyone visited you. I never asked about where you're from, but let's be honest, an old woman has to be curious. A young lady like you and a handsome boy like he without any family? I can't believe that."

Aly had always avoided answering questions like this one, but she figured she owed Dorly some explanation. "I have a brother. My parents died when I was still young. My aunt raised us until she ran away when I was sixteen. My brother took care of me after that. Not that he needed to. I was pretty independent by then." She paused for a moment, wondering how to go on.

"Independent enough to be a mother? You were just a child when you came. You were what? Barely eighteen?"

Aly pulled the rubber band from her hair, making the dark brown waves cascade over her shoulders. She combed her fingers through the strands a few times before nodding. "I planned to visit a nearby college. I got a full ride. Before I left, I realized I was expecting. I didn't want to burden my brother and having the father be part of his life was out of question, so I still went and pretended everything was all right. I couldn't go back. After all, how would I explain a child? I didn't want to do that to my brother. In the end, he had just gotten free of me to enjoy his own life. No one deserves to be burdened with a child they didn't ask for," she explained, being careful to pick her words.

She closed her eyes for a moment, taking a few deep breaths to enforce the lie. She had practiced it for so long; it felt like her true life-story. Now, after so much time, it was easy to imagine, too. She barely felt like she was deceiving anyone anymore.

As it was, Greg had supported her from day one. Each week, she'd get money from him, two hundred dollars every time, and even though she had no idea where he got it from, she put it aside to get him out of trouble should the need arise. Had she wanted to ask him where he got the money? More times than she could count. Yet she knew Greg would not have told her anyway.

"Lesso's father—"

"He was my brother's best friend. I think I was his last choice, but he always had been the one for me." God, how much she wished those words weren't true any longer, yet she could feel them resonate deep within her.

The elderly woman stayed silent for so long, it made Aly wonder if she had checked out on her, when she spoke again.

"I'm guessing your brother was what? Twenty-one when you left? So Alessandro's father is about the same age."

"He was just about to turn twenty-one, yes," Aly agreed. They all had been so young and too many things had been left unsaid.

"Alessandro's father was just a boy really. They don't turn into men until later, do they?" Dorly questioned, and Aly wasn't sure if she needed to answer.

"I think certain things will make us grow up much faster than others," was the comment she opted for, and Dorly reached out to brush her thumb over Aly's cheek.

"Mom, why are you crying?" Lesso asked, joining them. Only then did Alessia realize her cheeks were wet.

"Mommy's just so happy she has you," Aly explained, trying without luck to stop her tears from falling. Her son watched her for a long moment, appearing much older than his ten years.

"Tom is coming over tonight. Do you remember?" he asked, and she nodded, checking her watch. She had no more than thirty minutes left, but luckily, she didn't need to prepare anything. She always had frozen pizza and popcorn in the house. It was obviously the only thing feeding two ten-year-olds.

"How about you go inside and get ready, and as soon as Tommy gets here, I'll send him up to your room?" she asked, and Alessandro planted a wet kiss on her cheek after grinning in agreement. He left the two women alone again, and Aly tried to remember where her boy had interrupted their talk.

"Aly, did you ever wonder if the boy you knew turned into the man you though he could be?" Caught off-guard by the question, Alessia pushed herself off the stairs and wrapped her arms around herself.

"After I left, I never allowed myself to think about him. It just hurt too much," she eventually answered, watching how Dorly's glance settled on something behind her.

"Ten years can turn a boy into a breathtaking young man, Aly. Ten years can make all the difference in the world," the old lady remarked, and Aly took a deep breath.

"You don't know anything about the world I left behind," she insisted, and her neighbor actually smiled.

"I know enough about you to know the guy you left behind wasn't a bad guy. In fact, I'd guess he was anything but. Besides, the way I see it, the last choice might actually be the only one. Did you ever think about that? Maybe he wanted to give you time to be whatever you wanted to be in the world before getting serious with you?"

Aly swallowed as the air around her seemed to vanish. She felt like lashing out because this was getting way too personal. What-ifs didn't belong in her world any longer.

"Maybe he actually was a crazy stalker and I ran. Did you ever consider that?" she snapped, and the older woman got up, still focused on the ocean behind her shoulder.

"You don't look scared, child. You were never one constantly looking over your shoulder. You have friends around here. I don't think you'd have stayed this long in one place if you were afraid of someone. You're lonely, though, and I've seen guys walk up to your door, but you don't want to keep them. In fact, I'm not even sure you give them a chance." Dorly walked closer, reaching a trembling hand out to touch Aly's ice-cold fingers. "You know, sometimes opportunity is too scared to walk up to the door and knock, so maybe you should give it a chance by walking toward it."

Aly took a deep breath and forced a smile. "Thank you. I guess." She had no idea what to make out of that statement, but Dorly nodded, and Alessia started walking up her porch to the backdoor.

Behind her, she could hear Dorly talking to someone, but it took until the person answered to pull the ground from under-neath Aly's feet.

≈

"*Y*ou look better, boy," the old woman mumbled, walking toward him with shaky steps. Jamison Loane took a deep breath and gave her a smile without really looking at her.

"First good sleep I've had in months," he answered and then saw how Aly stiffened with a gasp. She still recognized his voice, even after all these years. He couldn't look his fill, no matter how long he stared at her back. Waiting with a bated breath for her reaction, he couldn't help his aching heart when she just continued, following the path she had started, and vanished inside the house.

Jamison had spent months on the road, and no matter how often he turned this over, there just was no right way to step in front of Aly without scaring her. Ten years he had lived a shallow life—getting up, working hard, and making sure Greg paid all the money to Aly and the kid. He never tried to contact her because he feared someone would connect the dots, and that was the last thing he wanted. He had been young and stupid back when he had asked Aly to take his son. Now, he'd do it all different.

Not that Aly hadn't been the perfect choice, but she would be locked up for a very long time if this ever was discovered. She shouldn't be suffering for something he had forced on her.

"Jamison?" He shook his head, realizing he had totally checked out on the little woman in front of him.

"Miss Rome, I'm so sorry," he apologized, scratching the back of his neck in embarrassment. "I wondered so much how this moment would go, the first time seeing her again, but I didn't think it would be like that."

"Why don't you come with me? You look like a capable young man, and I need someone to fix a drawer in my kitchen. I'd offer dinner in return," she said, and Jamison was more than glad for the suggestion. He had nowhere to go since each and any guesthouse was too far away from Aly and his son.

"You know, seeing you now and her earlier, I wonder how the two of you looked when you both were carefree. Both of you seem much older than your years, and it just hurts my heart. People like the two of you should be dancing and singing, laughing and enjoying life, not look at the world as if nothing good ever came from it," she mused. Jamison took a deep breath.

There was no doubt Aly had to grow up faster than the average girl, but then, a lot of teenagers had a hard time. Only none was ever burdened with the child of the guy they loved—and hadn't brought into the world themselves.

"I could use a good dinner," he eventually answered, his eyes going back to the house into which Alessia had vanished. To his utter surprise, she was back on the porch, watching him.

Dorly turned, following his glance and then patted his chest. "You know, the drawer doesn't need fixing that bad. I'll start on dinner and you go and say hi, okay? I think it's something you both need," she announced gently, and he barely registered her touch, nodding only the slightest bit.

She left and Jamison took an enforcing breath. His legs felt oddly stiff as he made them move toward Alessia. She no longer was a girl; that much was obvious. She had grown into a stunning woman, and it made his throat go dry. Aly had filled out in all the right places, looking lean in her blue jeans and white tank under a knitted sweater. Her ebony hair fell in thick waves over her shoulder and down her back, making Jam wish he could drown his hands in it. It looked like silk, shining whenever she moved. Her cheeks were sun-kissed, and he guessed he'd see tiny freckles covering her nose if he were close enough.

Jam couldn't imagine himself falling for the same woman over and over, but standing where he did now, he knew it had taken one look to fall right back in love with her. Not that she ever would believe those words if he were to say them.

Alessia didn't move toward him, but then he hadn't expected her to. She stood on the porch and he stayed in front of it, not going up the two stairs. He wanted to give her the feeling she was in control of this, and it was true. Only when he dared to meet her eyes did he realize she was crying again. It made his heart skip a beat.

"Are you gonna take him away from me?" Aly asked, her voice breaking. It made him speechless that she thought him capable of such cruelty.

"What?" His voice was rough, full of disbelief.

"Why else would you be here?" she inquired, and he buried his hands in his pockets because it was all that kept him from reaching out and drawing her into his arms.

It was crazy, and no one would ever be able to understand, but he had never kissed Aly or even held her the way a guy would hold the girl he loved since he was a little boy.

That moment he wanted nothing more than to pull her into his arms and hold her for as long as it would take until he was ready to let her go again. Only he couldn't. He never had been the boy for her, and now, he was even less man enough to deserve her.

"I needed to see that you and he were safe. I just... I wanted to see both of you. Ten years is a long time, Aly." She shivered visibly at the use of her nickname, even though she probably had heard it coming from his lips a thousand times before.

"We've been safe ever since I left. No one ever contacted me or came to ask me about him," she whispered, obviously calming down at least a little.

"What did you tell people?" He needed to know so he wouldn't blow her cover. And because he wanted to hear her voice; the only thing he allowed himself to take comfort in. It had gotten slightly deeper, softer around the edges, almost sultry. He was sure it could drive a man crazy.

"I told them I had planned to go to college and just realized I was pregnant weeks before I left."

"You changed his birthday?" He didn't know why that worried him, but Alessia instantly shook her head.

"No, I didn't. I couldn't. I always say I hid out in some tiny town, gave birth, and then figured I needed to change my plans. While, in truth, I came here right away, I always add some months between leaving and arriving. I pretend I wanted to work before college started. Oh well, no one really questioned me much about him. They did ask about his father, though," she explained, wiping a leftover tear from her cheek while looking up to the sky. He could tell she was trying hard to stop crying, but it didn't work very well.

Jam bit his lip for a moment, wondering which of the things on his mind he should mention next. "What did you tell Greg?" he finally asked, and she took a deep breath, brushing some stray strands of hair from her face. Jamison couldn't stop admiring how beautiful she was.

Of course, he knew what story Greg had been fed since he'd been informed from the beginning, but somehow, he didn't think she'd take the news well that her very own brother had been in on this whole scam.

"It was a lonely night, and I wasn't ready to make an unborn suffer for my mistake. He took it surprisingly well."

Jam almost coughed out a laugh. Of course, he had taken it like a pro. After all, Greg knew his sister didn't do lonely nights… and hadn't been pregnant when she left. "The lies came almost too easy, and people believed them like that, too. I should be insulted."

Jam wanted to say something, but then the screen door moved and his eyes fell on his son. He wasn't sure anyone could imagine how it would feel to a father after not having seen his kid for so long to then face him. In fact, he had doubts the guy even knew who he was. It was another thing he needed to ask Alessia. What had she told his son?

Ten years was a long time for a man to regret his decisions, no matter how well meant they had been, but upon seeing that boy, Jamison knew one thing for sure—making Aly his son's mom was the only thing he wouldn't ever regret in all the years to come.

$\approx$

*A*lessia felt her son touch her leg and then, ever so carefully, look around her body at the man who was his father. Words seem to evade Jam as his emerald eyes focused on the little boy. She wasn't even sure he noticed, but tears came to his eyes while his lips parted in wordless wonder.

Even while Tommy had arrived only seconds after Aly had vanished inside her house, Lesso clearly took more interest in the second guest they had now.

"Mom?" Alessandro asked, wrapping his arms around her hips while he never once stopped looking at Jam.

"Lesso?" she inquired, combing her fingers through his blond curls with a smile. He was the perfect height to cuddle, and now that the utter shock of knowing Jamison was there was over, she could actually take pride in how well his son had turned out.

"Why's he crying?" the boy wanted to know, and Jamison seemed to come out of his stupor, rubbing at the wetness on his cheeks.

"I'm not crying. I'm just not used to the windy beaches and the sand grains," Jamison explained. He took a few deep breaths to calm himself, and then he knelt on the lower porch step. Aly pushed her son forward slightly and noticed that now the two were about the same height.

"Hi, I'm..." Jamison started, breaking off as he tried to find the right words.

"I know who you are. You're Jamison Loane," Lesso announced. "I'm already ten, and my mom tells me everything," he then went on, pride clear in his voice. Jamison gave her a brief glance, and Aly hid a smile. Jam was in for a huge surprise.

"Yes, I can tell. You're the man of the house, aren't you?"

Alessia almost laughed as Jamison's eyes flickered to hers before settling on his son again.

"Yeah. Why are you here? Did they finally let you go from where you have all that hard work?" Alessandro asked, and Jam seemed startled.

"I told him that you were working hard to make a lot of money so Lesso and I could have an amazing life," she injected.

"'Cause that's what daddies do," Alessandro agreed. "My friend Tom's dad sells things to people so when a wave breaks their house, they get money. He works very much, too, and Tom never sees him, either."

When Jamison looked at her this time, she mouthed the word 'divorced,' even though she knew his questioning gaze wasn't about that.

"Baby, don't you have a guest? Where are your manners?" Aly scolded, and Alessandro looked up at her before surprising them all by hugging Jam tightly. His father's hand looked huge on the little boy's back as he pressed him just that little bit closer before releasing him.

"Will you let dad come for pancakes tomorrow morning? Mom makes those pancakes with faces and... I'm a big boy, I don't need smiling faces, but Tom never got them, and he always wants them," Alessandro explained, quickly toning down his excitement to look more grown-up. It made Aly laugh and Jam smile, but then Aly got serious.

"Your father might be busy, Lesso. You know how hard he works," she reminded her son, not even sure why, but she didn't want him to be disappointed if Jam wasn't staying. They had settled that he wouldn't take Alessandro away from her, but still, she had no idea about his motives for showing up in Sunrow.

"If your mom lets me enter the house, I'd be happy to come," Jam promised, and Alessandro looked from his father back to her before putting on a serious expression.

"If you treat a woman nicely and bring flowers, she might just allow you to set foot in her house," he recited something he had obviously heard a lot. Aly lowered her eyes, hiding her grin.

"That's right," she agreed and then brushed a hand over his hair again before gently pushing him toward the back door. "I'll be right in. Tell Tom to get ready for pizza," she ordered, and Lesso nodded, starting to hum while he vanished inside the house again.

Aly focused back on the man who still kneeled on her porch step, looking more broken than ever. "Here you thought you'd surprise us, and instead, we surprised you."

She smiled, moving to her knees in front of him. He didn't look at her or talk to her, so she reached out and brushed her hand over the five o'clock shadow on his chin. He was trembling, and for the first time since she knew him, she wondered what he was thinking. Due to her brother and those two constantly hanging out, she had become a pro at reading him. Or so she thought. Now, there was no telling what went on behind those soul-deep green eyes.

"Aly," was all he had said before she found herself in his arms for the first time ever. He smelled all male and clean, a hint of his favorite cologne still on his clothes. It was crazy how much his scent reminded her of her childhood and teenage years. He always had been a part of that—strong, independent, and handsome. Nothing had changed about the last two, but she couldn't help but think she was the strong one this time.

~

*J*amison stared at the table and wondered how he deserved a son like that or a woman who had treated him the way Aly had even while he hadn't been there.

A bottle appeared in front of him, and he looked up in surprise. "You look like you need this," Miss Rome commented and then poured him about two fingers of the amber liquid. Jam wasn't a drinker, but maybe that would calm him down enough to actually get some sleep. Right now, he couldn't imagine closing his eyes since his thoughts were going a hundred miles an hour.

"What did Aly ever tell you about me?" he asked, and the older woman shrugged her shoulder.

"I don't think she mentioned you that often. I might be old, but I can still tell when not to force a story. Aly isn't exactly forthcoming when it comes to her relationships," she explained, and Jam almost cursed himself.

"She has a new boyfriend?" he asked, and the woman took a deep breath.

"That, boy, is something I don't know. One guy comes by more often than others, but I don't think anyone has ever really taken her out. I offered to keep Lesso with me, but she wouldn't have it. If there's a guy in her life, it's her son. Besides, when mentioning you earlier, she almost instantly had tears in her eyes. I think there's something unresolved between the two of you, and no one can move on if the past isn't in the past, right?"

Jam couldn't agree more, but his past would probably never let him go. It was best that way, and he knew it. Until Greg called him, though, he would at least stay around.

"I sense another story untold," the woman went on, touching his arm to regain his attention.

"Aly deserves a guy who stands up for himself and her. She deserves someone who has no past and no baggage to carry," Jam mumbled, and the old woman started to laugh.

"Everyone has a burden to carry, and I'm no exception. It's how you handle it that defines whom you're worthy of. And the way I see it, you haven't figured that out yet. Be the man you think she deserves, and you'll be who she wants."

It was a good suggestion, but Jam wasn't sure he could actually follow it.

*A*ly hadn't slept all night, so she was more than exhausted when her son jumped into the room with a happy scream at barely six in the morning.

"Mom, come on, didn't you want to make breakfast? What if my dad comes and he doesn't get anything to eat?"

Aly groaned. "What if he comes at ten and won't get anything because you and Tom ate it all?" She knew she wouldn't get any more sleep if she thought about the fact that Jam had promised to drop by, but getting up at that hour wasn't exactly her favorite thing to do, either.

Her son settled down on the mattress next to her, looking thoughtful. "Cold pancakes are sure good, too." She had to chuckle. It was true; Lesso loved pancakes even if they were not freshly made.

"But is that what you want your father to remember about us? We promised him breakfast and then had it without him?" she probed, and her son shook his head.

"No. I want him to love having breakfast with us. I know he works hard to make this great, but don't you like our life? I don't think there's need for him to work any longer, mom. Maybe you could try and make him stay?" The hope in Alessandro's eyes almost made her heart crack. She couldn't promise to hold Jam there. She never had been able to capture his attention, so there was no chance for her to get him to stay. Besides, she needed to find out why he had come in the first place before she'd promise her son anything at all.

"Our life is perfect just the way it is," she agreed. "How about we take this slow, Alessandro? Breakfast is a start, and then we'll see where things go from there, okay? Why don't you and Tom watch some cartoons while I prepare some coffee?" she suggested.

Instantly, her son's eyes lit up. "You're allowing us to watch cartoons?" Usually, she hated placing the kids in front of the TV, especially when Tom was over, but that morning she just didn't have the nerve to keep them busy. She'd get up, start her coffee, and then enjoy a few minutes on the porch. Gazing at the water always calmed her, and that was what she needed most.

"Go ahead, but only until breakfast is over. Then you'll go and play outside."

"Aww, Mom!" Lesso planted a sloppy kiss on her cheek and hurried from the bedroom, already calling for his friend. Aly got up and slipped into her favorite sweatpants, pulling her hair into a messy bun before putting on one of her brother's hoodies. She hadn't kept much from the stuff at home, but those were the most comfortable clothes she could imagine, and comfortable was what made her feel safe.

She skipped the shoes, burying her feet in the cold sand while walking close to the water's edge. Aly closed her eyes as the waves washed around her feet. The coolness cleared some of the webs from her head, making her smile.

"You have an early day," she heard, looking up to find a jogger coming closer. She recognized that grin easily.

"Spence, hey." She smiled, waiting until he was close enough. "Lesso has Tom over again, and they kinda thought it was okay to get up at six on a Sunday morning. I needed some air and decided to come out here." Spencer was a guy she had occasionally been seeing. Even though he was nice and quite good-looking with sandy hair and blue eyes, he had nothing on the guy she saw every time she looked at her son.

"It's been a while since I've seen you out this early. I was wondering if you had moved away. After all, your phone doesn't seem to be working, either." He cocked a brow, and Aly rubbed her neck in embarrassment. She had seen his calls and always wanted to call back, but she had to admit it usually slipped her mind.

"I promise I wanted to call you, but then something always

came up, and then something else… and I forgot," she confessed. The truth was she worried he'd get touchy. Every time they had been out, he had been nothing but respectful, but a guy wouldn't wait forever, right?

"Why don't you and me—"

"Mom! Come on! I'm hungry! Please?" her son called as the screen door banged behind him. She turned away from Spence and looked at the boy.

"I thought we agreed to wait?" she called back, and Lesso shook his head.

"We don't have to. He's here," he answered and then looked expectantly at her while she pressed her lips together.

"You're having someone over for breakfast?" She could hear the crack in Spencer's voice, and it made her feel guilty. Not that she had any reason to, since they weren't an item, but she still knew the etiquette. Spence now surely thought she had gone behind his back to find someone else while keeping him on the back burner, just in case.

"Little man, why don't you and I go inside and start preparing? You know how to make pancakes, right?" Aly's heart stopped as Jam, too, stepped out on the porch through her screen door, looking like a man who didn't shy away from hard work. He had never been small, but over the last decade, he had clearly filled out well from manual labor. He didn't look at her for long, just forced out a smile and a curt nod toward Spence, then he picked up his son and walked back inside. They looked so good together it made her wish she could take a picture.

"Spencer, this is not what it looks like, I promise. How about I deal with the mess inside and then I'll call you? There's that movie we wanted to watch together. I'll get Dorly to watch Alessandro and then you can pick me up and—"

"That movie hasn't been showing in weeks, Alessia. Don't think I didn't see that look in your eyes when you saw him," Spencer said quietly, and she reached out to touch his arm, only to pull back at the last second. "We've been going out for weeks, and I have never once set foot in that house, yet he… who is he even?"

"Mom, you can't let dad do all the work! We invited him for breakfast!" Alessandro called from behind the screen door and then vanished again.

"Oh, wow, that explains a lot," Spence grumbled.

"No, it doesn't. Spencer, I really wish I could explain this whole thing to you, but I can't. Let me call you and we'll have dinner. I'll cook and…" She trailed off. Even if they sat down, she couldn't tell him all about this complicated situation. He'd forever assume she had slept with Jamison, and she couldn't ever correct him.

"It's okay, Alessia. There was always something standing between us. Get this over with, solve the issue with him, and then, whenever you're truly free, come and see me," Spencer pleaded, framing her face to kiss her forehead.

Aly closed her eyes, wondering if this 'issue' could ever be fully resolved.

~

*J*amison had wanted to call out to Aly, but just then, the guy leaned in and kissed her forehead. Jealousy burned through Jam hot and bright, making him grind his teeth.

"That's Spencer. He wants to be mom's friend, but she doesn't like to play with him, so she never lets him into the house. And when she's on the phone with him, she always says she has to work." Alessandro stood next to him, also watching the two outside.

"Don't you want your mom to be happy?" Jam asked and then watched his son's reaction.

"Mom's happy when she can have a coffee with that syrup thing she likes. It's in the cupboard. And she's happy when she can make pancakes for Tom and me." He said this with a nod and then turned back around while Jam realized Aly was returning to the house.

"Next time you feel like spying on me, try to remember that windows work both ways," she snapped defensively as she passed him, making him grin. Somewhere in that womanly shell, she hid the girl he once knew.

"I'm sorry. I brought flowers," he pointed out, nodding toward the bouquet that lay on the counter. She turned to him, cocking her head while pushing her hip out.

"And that makes everything better, huh?" she asked, a smile playing over her lips.

"It got me inside just like Alessandro said it would." He grinned sheepishly, and she shook her head.

"You wanna hear what I think? It was the chocolate that gained you entry," Aly accused, and he wasn't the slightest bit surprised she had caught on so quickly. "Are you supposed to have chocolate before breakfast?" she then asked her son who'd just returned to her side, and Jam watched as Alessandro looked at Aly with a trembling lip.

"I just took one piece, Mom, I swear," he mumbled, and she knelt down, wiping the obvious evidence from the corner of his mouth.

"Technically, seeing as it's Jam's fault you're breaking my rules, I guess he should take the punishment for it, huh?" she asked with a twinkle in her eye. As much as Jam wanted to protest, the serious expression with which his son turned to him made him laugh out loud.

"I'm sorry, Dad, but she's right."

Jam sobered, biting back his grin, and looked at his son. "What's the punishment for eating chocolate before you have breakfast?"

"You're the last one to get a pancake. And you need to help her prepare and wash up afterward with her. You can't play until Mom's ready," Alessandro announced as if it was the end of the world.

"No, really? I hate cleaning up," Jam fussed. Lesso leaned in as if he was going to share a secret, so Jamison bent down.

"I hate it, too. Usually, if I'm really nice and tell her I love her, then I get out of it," he explained conspiratorially.

"Good suggestion," Jam replied with a grin.

"Stop whispering," Aly scolded, placing her hands on her hips. She looked serious, but Jamison knew her well enough to recognize the signs of amusement on her face. "Jamison, you have been a bad boy, so you need to help me prepare. Up," she went on, pointing at him with a threatening finger. As much as he loved being around his son, he couldn't deny that he wanted a few moments alone with the woman who had saved the little boy all those years ago.

He joined her in the kitchen where he and Alessandro had already taken out everything they would need to prepare the batter. "He calls me dad as if it's the most normal thing in the world," he whispered, and she nodded, breaking the eggs while licking her lips.

"For him, it is," she finally admitted, and he leaned back against the wall, watching her in silence for a moment as he waited for her to continue. "When I left, I wondered what I should tell him, but I figured I should stay as close to the truth as possible. As soon as he was old enough, I started to tell him about you. Greg always sent pictures of you and him doing things together, and I would point you out. Eventually, it simply became a tradition. He was sure you'd come by one day. He knows everything about you that I know." She wasn't looking at him, but he could tell her mind wasn't on the task at hand. She spilled nothing, though, apparently having prepared breakfast like this more than once.

"In the beginning, I thought you'd show and try to take him back. Or that they would figure it all out. No matter what I feared, though, I wanted Alessandro to be an open, happy child. I taught him always to be friendly to people yet never go with anyone. His teachers think he's the most polite kid out there. I don't know what you'd want your son to learn, but I figured respecting women and being a sweet kid was all a dad could ask for." Her voice was quivering. He reached for her, but she avoided his touch.

"You did everything just the way I hoped you would." His throat felt thick as she looked up.

"He has so much of you, you wouldn't believe it. He's a hit with the ladies, especially the ones he wants something from. During summer, there's an ice-cream stand down the road. I allow him ice cream two days a week. Sadly, he knows how to talk to that lady, so he always gets one for free. He has your strong mind and happy demeanor. Sometimes, when I see him…" She trailed off as if she had been close to saying something that wasn't intended for his ears. As it was, he had heard enough anyway.

She had no idea about what was hidden beneath the face she had known for so long. A happy demeanor was something he no longer possessed. And if he would have the strong mind Aly obviously had admired back then, they'd never be where they were right then.

"Stop talking about me as if I'm someone amazing," Jam barked, and Alessia's head snapped up, total surprise on her face.

She meanwhile had taken out a pan and was flipping the food like a professional cook. He loved watching her, yet he wanted to leave. He shouldn't be with her, and still he was unable to help but be proud of what his son had become.

"You and I may never have been close, as in best friends or lovers, but I've seen you. I've heard you. I've spent so much time watching you and listening to you that I know exactly what's inside that handsome skin!" Her protest was lost on him. She knew nothing, but he wasn't ready to comment on that any further.

"How did you come up with his name?" He could tell he'd startled her with the topic change. He also realized he had taken on a rather aggressive stance, so he put a smile back on and took a deep breath. She shook her head, confused, and he couldn't blame her.

"I wanted him to have something from me. You and I know he's not my child, but at least now he has a part of my name in him."

Before Jam could comment on that, though, she had called the boys into the kitchen, making the serious talk instantly vanish. As it was, Jam couldn't wait to just sit at a table and watch his son in action.

~

*B*reakfast had been draining, and Aly was glad when Tom's mom, Shelley, had picked up her son and taken Lesso along. The boys weren't ready to part yet, and it suited Aly just fine. The moment silence spread in her house, she was incredibly aware of the fact Jamison was there. The living room suddenly seemed too small, and with his intoxicating scent filling her house, she couldn't think. There were things they needed to talk about, though, so she decided to change and get outside.

"I'll be right back, okay?" She didn't think she needed to remind him to stay, so she just looked at him for a second before hurrying upstairs to put on some jeans and a different sweater. Passing the mirror, she suddenly stopped. She knew she was being ridiculous, but she decided to put on some mascara and lip-gloss. It had been a while since she had gotten pretty for a guy, and she missed it. Besides, Jam wasn't just *any* guy. Her heart hadn't once stopped reminding her of that very fact. She felt as if she had been running a marathon because her heart rate hadn't gone down ever since Jam appeared on her porch the night before.

Her cheeks were flushed, and she realized she missed this kind of anticipation. None of the guys she dated had ever caused this in her. With Jam, though, all she needed was one look and she wanted to tear his clothes off.

Not that she'd ever do that.

Not that he'd ever allow it.

She used her favorite perfume, the one too expensive for her taste but that she had treated herself to some years back. She missed getting it from Greg for Christmas.

Taking a breath, she went back down, seeing him stare at the pictures of his son and then, at the pictures of himself.

"You weren't lying," Jam whispered in awe as she came to stand next to him. She knew every photo by heart and even had a few favorites.

"Take a walk with me," she implored in a low voice, worrying he'd turn her down.

"Happily. Your scent will drive me crazy if we stay in here. And don't think I haven't noticed that you make sure not to touch me anymore. I couldn't guarantee I would stay away if we stayed in closed-off rooms." She wanted to protest, but he had always been rather observant. She heard the hurt in his voice, though.

"Don't take it personally," she pleaded.

"Explain it then," he requested, but Aly couldn't. Touching him again would ignite a fire in her she had worked long and hard to quell. She still felt the stubble against her palm even though that had been almost twelve hours prior. The way he'd held her seemed to have molded her body, and she had no doubt she would fit just as perfectly in his arms again. No, she couldn't do that, nor could she guarantee anything, either.

"If someone has to explain something, it's you, I think," she told him, leading him out of the house and locking the door behind her. Small towns were safe, no doubt, but she still liked knowing all her possessions were out of easy reach.

"You're right," Jam admitted, burying his hands in his pockets again. It was something he did a lot, she noticed.

"Talk. I have all day now." She didn't mention she planned to spend it with him of sorts. She wanted to sit on the sofa, stare at his pictures, and eat ice cream. Buckets of it.

"Collene's gone and no one knows why she vanished."

Alessia almost stumbled at those words. "And your first impulse was to come here? What if she was following you?" She knew she wasn't as quiet as she thought, but she couldn't help it. "Ten years and everything was fine. She never once guessed I had anything to do with it, and now that she's gone, you get in a car and come here? What's wrong with you?"

Aly stopped, wishing she lived somewhere out in a forest. No one would hear them for miles, and she could cry out in frustration. Instead, she needed to calm down and focus.

"You don't seriously think I came here right away! I changed cars twice and took a plane in-between. I was on the road for four days before coming, and I paid in cash. This was never supposed to be my life, but because I worried about you, I took that upon me. Greg wanted to come, but I told him to stay. Someone needs to keep me updated on what's happening with the Karmison-family. This was my chance, Aly. You have no idea what I've been through. You have no idea who I *am* any longer. I changed. In fact, I was already changing when you took my son. I'm not who you want me to be. I probably never was. No matter what, though, I needed to see him again. I was curious." Aly saw him shake with suppressed anger, and she read something in his eyes that she never before had seen in him: self-hatred.

"I always wondered how a father couldn't think about his only child," she admitted, and Jam shook his head, looking everywhere but at her.

"You have no idea about Collene, Aly. The things that went on after you left were beyond crazy. I… I cannot tell you about it. I'm not proud of some things I've done. I've been part of Collene's life for too long and…"

He stopped there, not giving her any more information, and that was something she wouldn't take.

~

*J*am saw the way Aly's forehead furrowed in stubbornness. He didn't want to tell her; he was too ashamed.

"Alessia, you were always such an amazing girl, and now, look at you. You studied, and you love your home here. You managed to do something with your life. I'm going to stay only long enough to make sure no one figured it out. Collene never wanted that child, but once he was gone, she went insane. She accused everyone of taking the baby. The police questioned everyone and their mother. I never had a reason to call you, but I had every reason to believe Collene's father had my phone tapped. I could've gotten another one, but I didn't want to stir up your life. You needed to settle in and find your routine. If I had called you, you probably would have thought I was trying to control you, and no woman, no person, should ever feel as if someone else is trying to run their life for them." He combed his finger through his hair and watched her reaction. Her lower lip was trembling, and she settled down on the sand. He did the same, moving close enough he was almost touching her.

"I never went to college after I left. There was no way for me to do that with the baby. Your money, you know the one hidden in the carry-on, helped me find a nice little house, and then I looked for work where I could take him. There was a restaurant in town owned by a woman. She had her boy there and the little ones were together from that day on. Alessandro was an easy child. I guessed it was because of... Collene. After all, that's what she taught him early on. Don't make a sound when you need something. I waited five months to bring him to a doctor and have him thoroughly checked. Luckily, he didn't have any lasting damage."

She stared straight ahead, lost in thoughts, and Jam wanted to pull her close and hold her. Hell, he'd be satisfied if she'd only rest her head against his shoulder. Any contact would suit him just fine because Aly was everything Collene was not. As emotional as it made him feel, he wanted to be with a woman like Aly.

"I always thought you went through with it. College, I mean. Seems Greg didn't tell me everything. And he didn't tell you everything, either, Aly. Don't hate him... but he knew. From the very first day, he knew your child wasn't really your child." The pain crossing her features at his words made him correct them. "He wasn't your child by blood. The money he gave you each month... that was mine. I couldn't live with the thought of making you pay for my mistakes." Every penny he had earned went straight to her and his son.

"I didn't spend it. I worried Greg had stolen it because it was so much," Aly told him and then chuckled. "I thought I'd need to bail him out one day and figured the money was better off in a bank account."

"It was for you." Jam was almost insulted she hadn't spent it.

"My charm got me everything pretty cheap here." She winked at him and then stared at her hands. "Dorly sold me her shop in town, and I turned it into a café. It makes money, enough so we can live well off it. The house... she always thought she'd have children or grandchildren, but I guess sometimes life doesn't work out the way we plan it." She sounded defeated, and it made him wonder if she thought she'd never have her own child.

"You're not even thirty, Aly. You'll have children of your blood one day, too," Jam assured her. The need to touch her was overwhelming, and he fisted his hands at his side, making sure she didn't see it.

"Jamison, did you ever take a step back to think about why I took that child when you held him out to me? I mean besides wanting to save him from an abusive mother?"

He had wondered about that more than once, but each time, Greg's words from that day came back to him—*Alessia has loved you for as long as I can think*—and made him wish things were different. No matter how much he doubted what Greg had said was the truth, he needed to stop her from saying words they both would regret.

"Collene was gunning for you when I started to date her. In fact, I started dating her *because* of that. You were nice. And pretty. I don't know if you ever realized it, but she had a thing for Greg, too. She thought maybe if she'd start terrorizing you, she could bully him into being her lapdog. Besides, someone had mentioned to her that you would one day be the most beautiful girl to ever leave our high school." Jamison knew that he'd forever feel guilty for that comment, but he hadn't known Collene back then the way he knew her now.

"Stop being ridiculous. She was beautiful and—"

"We both know that sometimes a pretty face is not enough. I knew the stories. You knew them. I should have known what a monster she was back then." Jam watched as she closed her eyes.

"No one could have guessed how rotten she was to the core," Aly said, and Jam couldn't agree more. Only, she had no idea how bad it really was.

~

*A*lessia couldn't say what it was, but Jam was no longer the guy she had once known. No one could rival his beauty with his unruly blond curls and green eyes, but his smile now seemed to have a shadow. Looking back at him, she realized that just watching him made her willing to take a leap of faith. She wanted to kiss him and be in his arms. He'd be going away again anyway, so where was the harm? She was lonely, and he seemed to need healing touches.

"Jam," she whispered, startling him out of his thoughts. She had her knees pulled up and her cheek rested on them, watching his expression. He instantly shook his head, not even meeting her eyes.

"Don't, Aly. Trust me, you won't want to open up that can of worms," he pleaded, and she was taken aback. Did he mean them as a couple? Or had he tried to guess what she'd ask? Either way, she couldn't help but feel hurt.

"You don't even know what I wanted," she protested, and he reached out, hesitating before brushing the pad of his thumb over her lips.

"Why have been you been with her for so long? Why haven't you ever seen me? What happened to you in the last years? What's wrong? None of these questions has an easy answer, Aly, and I don't want to ruin the image you have of me, no matter how wrong it is. I like the way you're looking at me," he explained, surprising her with being spot-on about her questions. There was just too much she wanted to know. Too much that… she stopped that thought as something he said finally triggered. "You knew I was in love with you."

Embarrassment colored her cheeks, and she lowered her eyes. He inhaled sharply at her words as if it was still news to him after all.

"I didn't dare to hope," was all he said, and she gaped at him. It almost sounded as if that was something he would have liked.

"Jamison," Aly started, not sure where she wanted to go with that sentence, but he made that irrelevant anyway since he leaned in, catching her off-guard.

She had been kissed before, and she knew she'd be kissed after this, but for Aly, Jam's kiss was the only one she'd always remember. It was tentative, hesitant, yet the sweetest thing ever. She'd never forget the way his stubble scratched her skin, or the way he tasted like Heaven to her, unique in a way no one else had before.

Neither had moved much, so she still had her arms wrapped around her legs and he still had his hands buried in his pockets, but she swore she felt him all around her. His scent wrapped around her, making her head swim and her heart soar until he pulled back. It was as if she was tumbling from a cloud or reaching the surface after a deep dive. Aly was confused because one kiss seemed to have transformed her whole world. One kiss made her realize what she was truly missing in her life—a partner to share cold nights and happy moments with. She needed romance, and she hadn't even realized it.

≈

"We should head back, Alessia," Jam told her even though it was the last thing he wanted. Their kiss had put him in a kind of bubble where no past existed and no future loomed over the happy horizon. In that bubble, there was only the present; the only time he'd ever allow himself to admit he still wanted her. Maybe even more after seeing her with his son and hearing about the life she had created.

"Alessia," she repeated, her own name dripping with venom as if she hated nothing more. He ignored it, getting up. As much as he wanted to help her up, he didn't trust himself enough not to pull her into his arms right away and hold onto her as if she'd be able to make his world right again.

They made their whole way in silence, and as much as he was itching to apologize, he didn't. Aly wouldn't understand why he was apologizing. The kiss was something he'd never regret in a million years, yet she would think that way. The only thing he was sorry for was never having done that when she was still all doe-eyed about him. When their feelings had been innocent and untamed.

There was nothing doe-eyed about Alessia Rhyme now.

"Where are you staying while you're here?" she finally asked as they reached her house. Jam looked at her, but she didn't meet his eyes any longer. Her voice was cold and distant.

"Miss Rome has a spare bedroom, and she told me I could use it. I hadn't planned on anything else. I didn't think I'd be staying that long, so my car it was. I can't exactly pay rent, so she told me I could fix things in her house in exchange for food and a bed." He shrugged, actually looking forward to some manual labor. He wanted to exhaust his body so he would have a dreamless night. He needed to get Aly out of his system, even if it seemed a futile intention.

"I need to talk to Dorly. She can't just take strangers in. What if you'd been a killer? I happen to like that woman." Aly tried to joke, but the humor got lost since she couldn't even bring herself to smile.

"Jamison, why don't you come over? I need something from the top shelf," the object of their talk called from the porch next door, waving.

Aly laughed quietly, shaking her head. Jam loved seeing her like that. "Come over tonight and hang out with Alessandro. I'm sure he'd love that," she offered, softening her words with a wink.

"I sure can come back here, but remember it will be just you and me then. Do you want that?" He turned to her, looking at her face. She wanted it. The realization slammed into him like a baseball bat. The longing in her eyes was obvious even from where he stood.

"No, wouldn't want to have you and me sitting in silence because you refuse to talk to me about anything that's important. Tell Dorly hey." With that, she went inside, and Jam suppressed the impulse to call after her. Instead, he went over to the old lady.

"Watching you two is like seeing a romance play out on two different sides of a wall," Miss Rome commented, and Jam looked at her.

"I'm caught in a nightmare, and she's a daydream. We are two sides of a coin, and I don't think we'll ever get a chance to be on the same side," he explained, and the old lady arched her brow.

"You aren't one of those people who thinks love conquers all?" She wanted to know, and Jam choked out a laugh.

"Miss, I'm standing in a black hell. Are you sure you want me to pull Aly and Alessandro down, too?" God, Jam had never hated himself more than he did at that moment.

"Tell me, what did you do? What's that big secret between you and her? What are you two not telling me? What are you not telling her?"

Jam gave her a grin, shaking his head. "You're not nearly as subtle as you think you are," he teased.

"Subtle? I asked outright. And I swear I'll find out. You'll tell me your secret, boy, trust me," she insisted, and he sighed, deciding to change the topic.

"So what's it you need of me now?" he asked instead, and she smiled sheepishly.

"You needed to get away or she would have probably torn down your walls right there and then," Miss Rome admitted. "You didn't look ready to have that happen just yet. But while you ask, I still have that drawer that needs fixing, and I was thinking my porch needs a new coat of paint. What a coincidence that I have the paint, too."

"Yes, what a lucky turn." He laughed. He wasn't ready to paint outside, but he was sure there was more than enough to do inside the house.

chapter Three

*N*ight had settled, and Jam noticed with pleasure that his muscles felt thoroughly used. Besides the drawer, he had fixed some broken boards on the front porch and a missing piece of the railing outside. Not only did the porch need a new coat of paint, but so did the whole house. He figured he'd see how long he was going to stay and then maybe get to the remainder. Cleaning his hands in the kitchen sink, his eyes rose to the house next door. There was a single light on, illuminating the porch, and a woman standing there, staring out at the dark waves.

"I always thought I'd see the day when Alessia was standing there, her expression thoughtful, until a guy walked out and embraced her from behind. He'd kiss her neck, and she'd turn around, shining brighter than the Northern Star. The years passed by, and it never happened. She's still there almost every night," his host mumbled next to him. Jam squinted, but no matter how much he tried, he couldn't read the expression on her face.

"Miss Rome…"

"Would you call me Dorly, please? I feel so damn old otherwise," she fussed, and he grinned, pointing at her white hair wordlessly. "Tactful, Mister Loane, pointing out the age of a woman." She then huffed, and he sobered, bowing.

"I sincerely apologize for pointing out the obvious," he teased, and she playfully slapped him. Jam liked her a lot and figured his own grandmother would be like that if he hadn't lost her when he was young.

"You should laugh more often. It makes you seem so much younger," Dorly commented thoughtfully, and Jam turned away from her again to watch Alessia.

"What I wanted to say was that I can't see her face clearly from here. How do you know she looks serious? Maybe she's smiling because she remembers something."

"Jamison, I know her. Trust me. She's a woman at twenty-eight, and she has a silent night because her son is gone. I don't remember when that last happened since Tom usually stays over and not the other way around. All she's thinking about is how life would have been different if someone, let's say you, for the sake of the argument, would have led her down the altar before creating a family with her. Seeing you again probably makes her lonelier than ever. Ten years of no kisses and stolen moments will do that to a woman. I always thought that maybe there just wasn't the right guy yet, but she didn't even invite them in to find out if they were the wrong ones. Who does that?" It was a rhetorical question, so Jam stayed quiet. "A woman in love, that's who."

"You sure you should be telling me all that? I don't exactly think this is your business."

Dorly waved him off with a noise that sounded a lot like a balloon slowly losing air. "Please, I'm an old woman. I butt into everyone's business. After all, nothing's better than love stories and conspiracies, right?" She winked, her eyes sparkling with mischief.

As much as he wished he could be living in her world of glitter and romance, it just wasn't in the cards for him. Staring at Aly motionless on her porch, though, he wanted to be that man for her —the one she deserved, the one who would carry her over all obstacles.

"Go over, son. You never know what healing properties a night can have."

"What if instead it utterly destroys us? Besides, she wants answers I cannot give her. If I walk over there and do what my hearts tells me to do, she'll be even more curious. She never knew what she meant to me." It was weird saying those words out loud, but they were so true. He had been in love with her since he could remember. He and Greg had been friends early on, so when Greg's little sister was born, it was almost like fate for Jam. Over the years, he had fallen for her, first as a friend and then, once he had gotten a little older, as more than that. It had taken him years to gather the courage to tell her when one careless slip ruined it all. Collene had entered the picture, and Jam had done everything to make his wrong right. Not that Aly knew any of this.

"Why?" Dorly asked, and Jam took a deep breath, thinking the answer over.

"Because it would have meant being an object of hate and torture in high school."

Dorly laughed. "Everyone feels like that in high school, Jamison. It's why everyone is so glad to get out of there." She had no idea. High school was hell for the people living in one town with the Karmison-family.

They both watched Aly for a moment longer, hanging onto their own thoughts, and then Dorly turned to him again. "You're far away from school now. As it is, I'm guessing you are far away from home, too. What are you afraid of, Jamison?"

'Everything' probably wasn't the answer she wanted to hear, so Jam stayed quiet. Could he dare to take one night out of his life? He just had to try. For all he knew, she'd turn him away anyway.

Nodding at nothing in particular, he walked out of the house. The wind blowing in from the water instantly caught in his shirt and cooled down his overheated body during the few steps it took him to stand in front of Aly, just like the day before.

She wore a long knitted jacket that evening, holding it together over her stomach while carrying a glass of white wine in the other hand.

"Let's pretend you just turned sixteen. Nothing has been lost yet. We still have all the possibilities in the world, and I haven't been stupid yet. Just for tonight, let's have what we should have had all those years back," he pleaded, opening his arms to show they had all the possibilities in the world for the night.

"What?" She looked at him as if he had grown another head. Maybe not exactly another head, but definitely another personality.

"For today, let me be the guy you always thought I was." Jam could see it. She was turning him down, and he couldn't even be mad at her.

"You want to be the guy I thought you were at sixteen," she mumbled in disbelief, and he was ready to leave but still nodded. "Sorry to tell you, but I don't have my virginity any longer." She winked, and it took a moment until he caught her meaning, but then he couldn't help but grin.

"That's who you thought I'd be for you?" Jam inquired, and Aly carelessly pulled up her shoulder, a secret smile playing over her lips. He didn't plan to sleep with her. In fact, he didn't even plan to let her touch skin except for where it was showing, but the thought still sent tingles of heat through his body.

He took a step toward her, and she lowered her wine glass to the porch railing. "Jam, this night is not back then. This night is today, in all the mess that's you showing up here."

"I didn't say it had to be that night. I just want us to be like that," he explained, and she threw up her arms.

"I was hopelessly in love with you back then and had nowhere to go with those feelings." That was all he needed to finally move close to her.

"Well, now you do," he whispered against her lips before walking them back until she hit the door and the full length of his body touched hers. This was nothing like the kiss they had shared earlier and everything like the kiss he had planned to give her back then. Aly was surprised, that much was obvious, but then her arms wrapped around him and he breathed a sigh of relief. The desperate kissing quickly turned into something less frantic but equally intense.

"Let's go inside," she whispered, and he put her down on her own feet again, not even having realized he had picked her up. "You want some wine?"

He slowly nodded even though he wasn't the guy for wine. It was too exquisite for his taste, and he was usually a simple man.

Aly poured him a glass and Jam watched her, glad he no longer needed an excuse. "I don't have beer here or I would have offered you some," she admitted, appearing flustered. Was she getting nervous because he was in the house with her? He liked that thought much more than he cared to admit.

"It's good. Means your man's still too little to have some and no one else is here often enough for you to be prepared," he explained, gently swirling the glass between his fingers.

"Jam, whatever happens tonight, you need to remember I'm not letting you get away that easy. I want you to tell me what was going on back then. I want to know what's going on with you now. If you didn't think Collene would show up, why didn't you just walk up to my door, meet Lesso, and then leave again? Why—"

He hushed her with his finger on her lips, invading her personal space on purpose again. "One night, Aly. Give us that. Please. No heavy topics. I think you need some little lovin', lady." He smiled, and she watched him for a moment.

"Why me? Why now?" she asked, and Jam nuzzled her neck right below her ear, feeling her shiver in response.

"It was always you. And now because, for one night, I'm trying to pretend I'm free of my past," he explained, hoping she'd finally shut up and let him hold her. He almost grinned as she pressed her lips together in an obvious attempt to keep herself from speaking.

Reaching around him, she pulled open a drawer and handed him a pack of matches. "Candles, now," she instructed, her voice softened with a smile. Never in the last ten years had he imagined he'd be taking orders from a woman again, but with Aly, it was different. Alessia never would treat him as Collene had treated him.

"On my way, Ma'am." He grinned and then left the kitchen.

~

*A*ly released the breath she hadn't been aware she held. What he was offering tempted her and even if she now tried to pretend to think about the pros and cons, she knew it was futile. Her heart jumped at the opportunity he presented, and she wanted nothing more than to cuddle in his arms. Would she be able to go back?

Most likely not.

This was like a dream coming true, and who in hell was able to ever forget that? She knew, though, as much as she was obviously still feeling for him, this couldn't be more until he stopped making cryptic remarks and started spilling the truth. She shouldn't believe one word of it always having been her for him, but no matter how often she said that to herself, her foolish heart instantly had taken the words in as universal truth. And how could it not with the way his green eyes had begged her to trust him?

"Ugh, Jamison Loane, you will be the death of me," she mumbled before deciding there was no reason two consenting adults needed to be lonely.

She grabbed his glass of wine and found him in front of her personal gallery. He actually reached out to touch a picture of her, one Alessandro had insisted on, and it made her heart crack just a little. Eventually, he moved over to the sofa, looking almost unreal in the soft candlelight.

"You're such a damn handsome man," she commented, walking over to him. She placed the glasses on the coffee table, wanting to sit down next to him, but he pulled her on his lap, cuddling her close.

"Tell me about your café," Jam pleaded quietly, his breath washing over her neck in a way that made her want to purr.

"It's just a café. Small reading corners, a couple of tables, couches, armchairs... everything people didn't want any more found a home in my little shop." She smiled, thinking fondly of the green monster that stood in the back where not everyone could see it right away. A girl from town, Summer, had turned it into her little corner of Heaven and had actually started the decorating in the shop. Every now and then, she'd bring in new quotes and tape them to the wall, naming the book and the author in case one of these quotes caught another patron's attention. Others had followed the example and now it was just something people mentioned when talking about her shop. "Besides Alessandro, it's my life. You should come and see it, Jam," she whispered, turning enough so she could look at him.

"Your eyes are shining when you talk about it. What's it called?" He almost made it impossible for her to think. His fingertips had started out circling the spot behind her ear before caressing her neck. Now, they were dipping below her neckline, giving her goose bumps.

"A's Salvation." Jam's finger stopped, and she met his gaze. It was obvious that he knew and understood what the 'A' stood for.

"No one knows what it stands for, do they?" he eventually asked and resumed his caressing. Aly moved so she could place her legs over his, resting her head against his shoulder while she snuck her hand around his hip, ever so slightly lifting his shirt so she could feel his skin under hers. She felt him stiffen, but since he didn't comment on it or stop her, she just kept going.

"They always assume it stands for Alessia, and I never bother to correct them. Why should I? No one needs to know it's your son's name in there. That little side shop allows me to keep him here and happy. It made it possible for me to buy this house, even though it was a steal. Sometimes, it feels as if Alessandro is the grandchild Dorly never got," she explained, not letting her hand wander off his abs and chest. Both were firm, just as she had guessed they'd be. Out of impulse, she kissed his cheek and then nuzzled his neck for a few seconds. This was nice, and she had no trouble seeing herself and in a position like this with him more often.

"Jam?" she eventually whispered and then moved again so she was sitting right in front of him.

"Aly?" His voice was nothing more than a rough whisper while he looked at her expectantly. She framed his face, taking every little thing in. There were the dimples she knew so well, no matter if they were hidden underneath a day-old scruff. There was a tiny scar right next to his upper lip, and she could still remember how swollen it had been. The split had barely healed when Jam had opened it again with one careless action or the other. Her thumb brushed over it, and his eyes clouded with pain.

"Does it still hurt?" she wondered, and Jam ground his teeth. She could see it in the way his jaw was working, and she knew it by the way his fingertips were digging into her hips.

"Just the memory of it does," he answered cryptically.

"Wasn't it a football injury? Or was it something else?" Aly could remember the cut, but had no recollection of how he had gotten it. His expression darkened, and she was sure he mumbled 'or something else' under his breath, but when she asked him to repeat, he just shook his head, raising his own hand to bring it to her face.

"I'm no longer the pretty boy you used to know, am I?"

"No," she agreed, cupping his cheek as Jam's eyes left her face. "You're no longer a boy. As I said earlier, you're a damn handsome man."

"That's just because you can't see my scars," he told her and then leaned in to kiss her forehead ever so gently. People said a forehead kiss expressed longing, and after this touch of his lips to her skin, she knew it was true. He was holding himself back, and she had no idea why.

For a moment, she thought about asking him to show her what he meant, but they had agreed to skip all the questions. Something about him appeared almost self-conscious.

"Tell me your biggest regret," she pleaded, and for a moment, it seemed as if Jam would protest, but then he bit his cheek.

"I regret most not having gotten you pregnant back then," he replied, and Aly laughed.

"You're such a romantic," she fussed, and he grinned even more.

"What can I say? I was meant to be Casanova, but then the role was already taken." She nodded, still laughing.

"You just regret not being my first," she then accused, and he sobered considerably.

"I regret not being your anything."

She knew she was staring at him open-mouthed, and the

humor came back to his eyes as he playfully touched the tip of her nose. "What's yours?"

Only half an hour ago, she would have said it was leaving Greg behind, or not forcing Jam to see Alessandro earlier, but now her answer was a different one.

"Not getting pregnant by you back then," she answered because it was the truth. She had taken Alessandro with her because she had wanted Jam's kid so bad and never saw a chance for it. Nothing had changed about the fact she wanted his children. It was crazy. Who in hell fell in love with 'the one' before ever reaching puberty? No one—that was who.

Jam pulled her close, kissing her softly. He handled her as if she was the most delicate thing ever. "Thanks for being here," Aly whispered as she leaned into him, listening to his heartbeat. The quick rhythm mirrored her own.

"Thanks for having me," he replied, kissing the top of her head.

~

*J*am knew Aly had fallen asleep, and as much as he wanted to stay, he couldn't risk her waking up before him. "Hey," he said, shifting her so he could watch her face. She just snuggled closer, though, making him smile.

"Not yet," she mumbled her voice thick with sleep.

"Where's your bedroom?" he wanted to know, and she didn't even bother to open her eyes.

"Upstairs. Not the one with the rockets," she explained, and he lifted her off the couch and carried her upstairs. He opened the first door and found it chaotic and covered in rockets. Even the bed was painted with them.

"Not rockets," she said another time, and he realized she was watching him now. He chuckled, kissing her cheek before moving out of the room again and on to the next door. "Nope," Aly mumbled, cuddling into his arms again. So it was the last one on the right that belonged to her, and once he opened it, he realized why. It was the smallest room and her bed barely fit, yet there was a balcony. She most likely wanted to give Alessandro the biggest room.

"It's been forever since any man slept in a bed with me," she whispered as he placed her on the pillows. As much as it pained him that he wouldn't be with her during the night, he still needed to go.

"I'll be right back," he lied as she cuddled deeper into the blanket and then smiled.

"Okay." It was barely a breath, but he could still hear the satisfaction in the word. Only once he was sure she was fast asleep, Jam left the house. Once outside, he pulled his cell out since he had promised Greg to contact him.

"Tell me she is fine," Greg pleaded the moment he had answered the phone.

"You never told me that you sent her pictures of us," Jam instantly shot back, and Greg groaned.

"I didn't think you'd get that close to her that fast. I never told her that you gave me the money, and you never knew she had your pictures. I hoped she'd teach Alessandro about you. Did she?"

"He looked at me and called me dad. It's as if I was just gone for a week or two. I know nothing about him besides that he loves rockets. I was so scared someone would overhear us and... why did you allow me to stay away from him for so long?" Jam knew it wasn't Greg's fault, but he still couldn't help but lash out. He regretted all the time he had missed not only with his son but also with the woman who raised him.

"Honestly? I have a few reasons, dude. I know I never wanted that boy to stay with his real mother, and I supported the decision of handing him over to my sister, but that doesn't mean I was going to allow her to get locked up for it. Plus, Jamison Loane, you have a dark secret. Until you spill those beans, you will *not* get the okay from me to have anything with my sister. It suited me just right that you never thought about going to see her."

Jam actually had to sit down. "What?"

"I'm a guy. And you're a guy. We don't do that emotional talk, but you've been living with me since you left Collene. That makes ten years. I ain't gay or anything, and I sure as hell don't need you running around naked, but honestly, you're always wearing a shirt. You dress in the bathroom. What guy does that? We sling a towel around our hips and then we walk to our rooms. Besides that, you lost your Jamison-ness. You used to be cocky and smiley and all flirty. Then Collene happened and you changed forever." Jam stared at the phone and then knocked it against his leg.

"Who the hell are you?"

"Funny, Jam," Greg growled, and Jam rolled his eyes.

"I gave away my only son, who was abused by his mother when he wasn't even a year old. Of course, I changed," he snapped and then wondered why it had taken him to leave for Greg to say what he had on his mind.

"You were different even before that, Jam."

"She wanted to hurt Aly."

Greg stayed silent for a moment. "Who?" It was obvious he already knew.

"Aly had just turned sixteen. I knew I was falling head over heels for her. There was this party, remember? The one at the mayor's home? I stood next to Collene and her mother. Aly came in and I just mentioned that one day she'd be the most beautiful thing Tarance High had ever known. You should have seen the look on Collene's face, Greg." Jam closed his eyes as anger surged through him. "It didn't take long, and I saw Collene gunning for Alessia. Right there at the party. She kept bumping into Aly until I could see your sister's face contorting with pain. Elbows, kicks, pushing her into tables... I couldn't take it, especially after Aly left and cried her eyes out in the mayor's garden. I watched her for a few minutes until I heard Collene and her friends coming. She talked about blue eyes and how well they'd look on Aly. I stepped in her way and told her no one was as pretty as she was and that I'd been in love with her forever."

"Collene always was after you. You were missing in her little collection. It was almost like an obsession. I don't think you ever showed any interest in her until that night," Greg mumbled.

"Nope."

"Because you wanted Aly." It was a recap rather than a question.

"I knew exactly what I was going to say to you. I swear I had an awesome case to plead." Greg laughed shortly, just as Jam had hoped. "That night changed it all. I kissed Collene then and there, and Aly was forgotten. She never really returned to being cruel to anyone else, either, so I thought what was my happiness against everyone else's?" It was weird. He had never said that out loud, and it was scarily liberating.

"Yeah, that would have probably changed me, too," Greg finally said. "So what's the plan now? Collene hasn't reappeared, and no one knows where she is. Her mother seems relieved, and her father is furious." Jam remembered her mother well. She was a timid little woman and probably the only one who ever had been remotely nice in their house.

"Collene isn't here, either. Aly's still safe and so is Alessandro. I should probably come back and—"

"Maybe you should stay and win Aly over. This can be your second chance, Jam. Especially if you spent the last decade being unhappy because Collene's a fucking bitch. How did you ever get yourself to sleep with her?" Jam could almost hear the shuddering over the phone.

"She was a beautiful girl, no matter how she treated others." The lie slid off his tongue easily.

"Damn, Jam." Greg sighed, and Jam pinched the bridge of his nose. He hated the lies, but by now, they were almost as much part of him as his left hand or right foot. "Anyway, how about staying there?"

"Never, Greg. She deserves someone better. You should want someone better for her," he whispered, looking up at the star-covered sky.

"You two had secret feelings for each other for ten fucking years. You stayed away from her to protect her. Now, she doesn't need to be protected from anything any longer, and you can leave it all behind."

His best friend had no idea. Jamison couldn't ever leave the past behind, especially not when he was wearing the evidence all over his body.

"I'm gonna go now. The lady who's letting me stay in her house is demanding. Half of her house needs fixing and I have to get up early. I just came from Aly's place and needed someone to talk to."

Greg stayed silent on the other end, and Jam figured he had finally overdone it on the emotional front. "Uh, yeah, anyway, I ..." He checked his watch, realizing with utter shock that it was three in the morning. "Damn, why are you even awake?"

Finally, Greg laughed. "I used the time your ass was out of the house and had a lady friend over. She was a disaster, so I ended up playing computer games. You got lucky."

"This time, at least," Jam commented, getting up again and turning. To the right was the house he wished he could return to, and to the left was the house he'd most likely lie awake in now until the sun came up. He shook his head and then went to Dorly's home.

"Later, dude," he said and ended the call. He felt drained. Only after hanging up did he think about the fact Greg would most likely mention his little story to Aly. It was the last thing Jam wanted, but it was too late now. He wouldn't call his best friend back to accuse him of gossiping. Besides, maybe, just maybe, he'd tell Alessia about this part himself. After all, it was possible just to retell part of his story. It had worked well with her brother. With that thought in mind, Jam went to bed, almost smiling.

chapter
Four

The morning was slow, and Aly walked along the walls of her café. She had read those quotes times and times again, yet she loved each and every one of them. It didn't matter if they were from Airicka Phoenix, an indie author sadly not enough people knew, or Shakespeare, who everyone knew. She loved them all and, by now, could recite each one to perfection.

"I didn't even think about the fact that today is Monday. How can you let Lesso stay over at someone else's place on a school night?"

Aly turned, disappointment and anger churning in her stomach. "Good morning to you, too, Jamison Loane! How dare you come in like that after last night?" she asked, outrage evident in her voice. "It obviously was nice enough to cuddle me and promise me a night when you never intended to give me that full night. Then again, in the morning everything looks different. Oh, you didn't even *wait* until morning!" She was hurt, very much so, and didn't care he suddenly tried to act like a father, even though that should bother her far more.

"Aly, you don't understand—"

"Of course, I don't because you won't tell me. No serious talk, remember? No asking questions. No nothing, Aly. You get to save my son and go to prison if they ever realize it, but you don't get to have answers or a single night with me. So no, I don't understand. And just FYI, your son has off today. The school has some teacher education thing, and he's going to be..." The door jingled and Alessandro came in, beaming at her, totally ignoring his father. "...here in no time," she finished, kneeling to catch Lesso and hug him tight.

"Mom, Tom has this new book he really likes and his mom read it to us and we wrote down lines we liked most. Can I tape it to your wall? Please?"

"Of course, baby!" She laughed, wondering if he had even seen his father.

"I want to place it on the top. Dad, can you pick me up?" He looked at him with big eyes, making his cute face. Aly crossed her arms, knowing very well how calculated the move was on his part. That face almost always got to her.

"I'm gonna make you your cacao, okay?" she called, moving behind the counter and away from the two guys.

"Dad?" his son asked in a hushed voice, as Jam picked him up to set him down on his shoulder. Lesso never had been very good at whispering, though.

"Alessandro?" Jam gave back.

"Can you stop making Mom sad? I could hear it in her voice when I was outside. She never screams, and I don't like my mom sad," Alessandro explained while pulling off some tape. Aly closed her eyes, regretting that she had fussed at Jam there. She should have anticipated her son's arrival.

"I didn't mean to make her sad," Jam said quietly.

"Why did you then?" Jam lowered him back to the ground and Aly watched how he then knelt to be on his son's eye level.

"Because I'm scared."

Alessandro actually blinked and then started to laugh carefree and heart-warming like only little boys could.

"You are scared of *her*?" her son asked, and she saw from the corner of her eye how he pointed a thumb over his shoulder at her.

"I have secrets, and I worry your mom will find out about them. Then she won't like me anymore," Jam gave back so quietly, Aly wasn't sure she had heard right.

Alessandro leaned in. "She's very good at that. I once tried to keep a fish Tom and I caught. I wanted to make sure she doesn't realize I have him and she found out. She was really mad at me. But she still loves me."

"He forgot that fish needed to eat... and that you don't keep them in the fridge."

She knew Alessandro made a face at Jam, most likely rolling his eyes. "Are you supposed to do that, young man?"

"Sorry, Mom," he called over his shoulder and then shrugged. "I broke a window once with her favorite bottle perfume. She still loves me," he went on explaining, and Jam's eyes got wide. Aly wasn't pretending to be busy any longer. She was just curious.

"All those things are not as bad as my secrets. Imagine how it would be if you were the reason your mom lost everything. You wouldn't have a home anymore, and she wouldn't have the café any longer. That's how bad my secret is."

"Mom would still love me. We once started from scratch, so we can do it again." Alessandro shrugged.

Oh God, Aly loved her son.

∽

*J*am wanted to cry. Alessia had made sure her son knew she'd never give up on him and that she never, in her entire life, would stop loving him. It was all a child could ask for and everything a father could hope.

"Hey, Dad?" Alessandro leaned in even closer, and Jam could smell the jellybeans on his breath. Oh, Aly wouldn't like that at all.

"Yes?"

"Mom always liked you. She never stopped. Even when you didn't come to see us. I sometimes see her holding a picture of you. She's having white grape juice, and she keeps staring at it. I really think she'd be less mad if you'd just come out with your secrets. It works best for me. She's always telling me that honesty wins you more points. Promise." His son gave him a beaming smile and then nodded toward Aly. She was watching them now, and Jam knew she'd get behind his secrets, too, if he stayed, so he made a decision then and there.

"Okay, I'll be honest. I have to go back home tomorrow. I can't stay any longer, but I see you and your mom have a great life. You can always call me," he explained and then looked up at Alessia. "I'm sorry for making you mad."

She just nodded, her expression hard. "So am I."

"But, Dad, you barely spent any time with me," Alessandro fussed, a stubborn pout making an appearance.

"I know, buddy, but—"

"I understand. Work's more important. Everything's more important. Do you have another son down there? That's it, right? Another family. You have a new woman and son. That's why you don't stay with us!" The accusation was so unexpected; Jam couldn't do anything but gape at Aly.

"Alessandro? What's up? Where did you get that crazy idea?" Aly asked, coming around to take his son from him. It nearly killed Jam to see doubt on her face. She was buying into that theory even though she should know better.

"Tom's mom watched this show, and they took a guy in because he had two families." Lesso sobbed now, and Alessia pulled him into her arms, giving Jam a look to clearly solve the situation. Only Jam had no idea how.

"That's not true, son. I only have you," he said softly, but the little boy just buried his face deeper intoAlessia's stomach.

"That's what he said, too. It doesn't matter. We didn't need you these last years, so Mom and I don't need you now!"

"Baby, you've been so excited to meet your dad. Why are you being mean to him now?" Aly asked, desperation obvious in her voice and clear on her face.

Alessandro pulled back enough to look at his mother and Jam wished there was something he could do or say.

"Because he upset you and because he doesn't want us. He's leaving again. Tomorrow. Mom, can you call Spence so he takes us to the movies again? Please?"

Jam got up, his heart aching. He knew his son was hurt, yet he couldn't help but realize another guy had done everything to win Aly, including dates with her and her son. He wanted to say something, put a claim on her, but he had no right to whatsoever.

"You don't like Spencer, baby. You've been fighting him every time he came over," Aly reminded her son, squeezing her eyes shut.

"I thought Dad would come one day and do those things. I thought Dad loved us even if he had to work a lot. I thought..."

Jam didn't even wait to hear how that sentence ended. He couldn't listen to another word, so he stumbled out of the café. He heard Aly call out for him, but she never followed and he was glad about that. Numb, he returned to Dorly's house. He would give her porch that layer of paint he had promised, and then he'd tell the nice little lady he was leaving.

His heart was racing in his ribcage, hurting with every unsteady beat, but Jam couldn't help it. He wasn't the father Alessandro needed, and he sure as hell wasn't the man Aly should want.

~

*E*very muscle in Jam's body hurt. He was used to being outdoors, but the crouched-over position he had been in to paint was something else entirely. It had taken all day, but at least, now the porch looked fresh and inviting. It was something Dorly deserved, and he had to admit, he liked the spring-green color she had picked.

The hot water poured down his body, not releasing the tension at all. He knew that had nothing to do with the work and every-thing to do with the fact he had not only disappointed Alessandro but had also hurt Aly, too. He couldn't believe she'd start doubting his intentions, or that she'd believe he had another family down there. After all, Greg would have told her something like that. No, Jam could no longer see himself with any other girl. Aly was his one and only; only he wouldn't allow himself to be with her the way she longed for.

Turning the water off, he got out of the shower and dried

himself off. Reaching for his boxers and his sweatpants, he realized he had forgotten to bring a shirt. Listening for a moment, he heard Dorly mumble downstairs. The old woman had a tendency to talk to herself, and he had to grin. The first time he heard it, he had been confused until he realized she wasn't talking to him. Now, he shook his head, opening the bathroom door and walking over to his assigned room.

Stopping in front of the full-length mirror, he took a moment before raising his eyes. He usually avoided mirrors until he was dressed, but it had been so long since he had looked at his damaged body. Tattoos covered a lot of his skin, but they still couldn't hide the evidence he knew by heart. There was a knock on the door and then the person came in without even waiting for his answer.

"Jam, you and I..." Aly trailed off, catching his glance through the mirror. "I didn't think giving you the chance to say 'no' was necessary, so I came right in, but... Jamison, what in the world...?" Her eyes focused on his back again, and she came closer while he reached for a shirt or a sweater—anything to cover his skin.

Grinding his teeth, he pulled a black hoodie over his head, mad at her for barging in and angry with himself for not having dressed as he usually did. She stopped the material halfway down his back.

"Alessia," he growled, a clear warning in his tone that she ignored, pushing the hoodie back until it was barely covering his shoulders.

"Do they hurt?" she asked as if she hadn't even heard him.

"No, they're just ugly," he forced out, closing his eyes as her soft hands touched skin no one had touched in ten years.

He felt stupid half dressed, so he threw the sweater to the side again, resigned to the fact that he couldn't make her forget what she had seen. And as much as he wished it wasn't true, he had longed for her to see him. All of him. She was gentle as she touched each and every scar. He watched her in the mirror, drinking in her beautiful features. He couldn't read her face, and it unnerved him.

Eventually, she leaned in and pressed a kiss right between his shoulder blades, making him shiver. "We need to talk," she whispered and then came around, touching his chest the same way she had his back.

"Aly, please, just let me pull on a shirt," Jam pleaded, feeling self-conscious. She barely shook her head, but Jam saw it.

"That's just because you can't see my scars," she repeated his words, making him swallow. She recalled his exact wording. Finally, she met his eyes. "Now, I can, and I can just repeat it. You're damn handsome," she whispered, gently poking her finger into his chest to make him walk back until his knees hit the bed and he sat down. He almost smiled as she settled down on the floor, reaching for his hand. She'd picked up that habit long ago. Whenever she and Greg had talked about something serious, she sat down on the floor looking up.

He wasn't ready to talk, though, so he cupped her cheek and brushed his thumb over her lips. "You don't want to hear that," he whispered, mainly because he didn't want to talk about it.

"Jam, I came here because I want to know what you're hiding. Because, as much as I hate to say it, you're running. Seeing you like this now makes it pretty obvious it's from something big. I might not be the woman you want or love, but I sure can be the friend you need."

"I don't need a friend, Aly. I need you to do what you've been doing the last ten years. Take care of my son and move on," he whispered, still feeling the need to cover himself. She obviously saw him eyeing his shirt and grabbed his chin so he'd look at her.

"Since when have you ever been ashamed around me? When you were like twelve, you and Greg ran around butt naked," she reminded him, her eyes sparkling with humor, but he couldn't even get himself to smile.

"Stop, Aly," he pleaded and disappointment shadowed her eyes. She got to her feet, and he followed her example, wanting to say something when she pressed her hands flat against his chest and then rested her lips against his cheek for a few seconds in a soft kiss.

"Fine, I understand. You don't wanna tell me, and it's fine. But you know what has healing properties? A child. Your child. Come and spend the evening with him. Watch his routines, cuddle in bed with him, and read him a story. It eases the tortured soul," she promised, and Jam saw the plea in her eyes. She wanted him to make it up to his son.

She stepped away from him, waiting, but he didn't say anything. Finally, he pulled a t-shirt and a hoodie on, thinking that only then could he think freely again. "Let's go," he whispered, and she breathed a sigh of relief.

Coming down the stairs, Alessandro didn't look impressed. He checked his mom's face, looking for whatever, but Aly just gave him a wide smile.

"Guess who's reading a story to you tonight?" she asked, and Alessandro gave Jam a look that came as close to his mother's icy stare as possible.

"Why? He's leaving."

"Tomorrow, not tonight. I can still tuck you in if you want to," Jam offered, holding his breath even as he saw excitement flare in his son's eyes. Alessandro covered it well, though, by carelessly shrugging.

"Whatever," he said and then leaned in to hug Dorly tightly. "Bye, Auntie Dorly. We have to go fishing again soon. Tom told me he caught a huge fish with his uncle the other day, and I wanna catch a bigger one." With that, the little guy walked out the door and Aly leaned in to kiss the older woman's papery cheek.

"Talk to you soon. Bye and thank you." Dorly just nodded as Jam gave her a sheepish smile.

"She goes fishing with him?" Jam asked in a hushed voice once they were outside.

"In case you didn't notice, I don't exactly have a father figure in the house. I hate fishing and Dorly loves to sit with him on the bank. She prepares a picnic, and he tells her everything about his day and school. I don't think he's ever brought anything back, though. He can't get himself to kill the fish. He hates blood." She smiled while watching her son. Alessandro held the door open for her.

"Lady?" he said, and she giggled, stepping inside. Jam wanted to follow, but his son picked up a brow. "Are you a lady?" Jam couldn't help but laugh, nuzzling his son's head before letting him enter first.

Aly told him to get ready for bed and then vanished in the kitchen. Jam felt a little lost, not sure what he was expected to do, so he followed Alessia and stood in the doorway to watch her. She had turned on the radio, humming along to some pop station. She took a cucumber out of the fridge and cut it into little slices. She placed it on a plate then she prepared a sandwich with wheat bread, swaying her hips slightly. Jam wanted to go over and kiss her neck before he'd walk up the stairs to take care of his son.

"Stop staring at her," his son fussed the next second when he appeared next to him. Aly looked up in surprise, embarrassment coloring her cheeks. They settled down at the table while Alessia took some milk out of the fridge.

"Hot or cold, babe?" she asked, and Alessandro shrugged.

"How does Dad drink his chocolate milk?"

Aly met his eyes, and Jam saw the chance to get into his son's good graces. "Double chocolate, marshmallows on top, and just exactly drinkable."He grinned, seeing how Aly gave him a dark look while his son started beaming.

"Good choice. I'll take the same."He grinned and then high-fived Jam.

"Just tonight because your dad's here," she fussed, giving them a serious look before turning away.

"I never get marshmallows before going to bed," Alessandro whispered.

"Thought so." Jam grinned back.

"Stop whispering, you two, or you'll get only milk," Aly called from the counter, her back toward them. Alessandro rolled his eyes at Jam with a smile. "And stop rolling your eyes at me. It's impolite," Aly went on, making Alessandro giggle. Jam couldn't help but bite his cheeks, rolling his eyes as well. Alessandro giggled even more. "Jamison Loane, stop encouraging your son!" She hadn't turned yet seemed to be able to see it all. Alessandro held his hand in front of his mouth so he wouldn't burst out laughing, but Jam couldn't help it and they started chuckling like crazy.

Aly came over and smirked as she placed the steaming mugs in front of them. Jam caught a whiff of cinnamon and spice and gave her a questioning look.

"Chai cacao, Mommy's specialty," Alessandro announced before drinking his whole cup without a pause and then smacking his lips in utter satisfaction. "Try it," he encouraged Jam, and Jam lifted the cup. As ordered, the chocolate was exactly the right temperature and tasted unlike anything he ever had tried. It was good and actually reminded him of Aly. It was crazy how much he liked it.

"Wow," he remarked with pride in his voice. She gave him a smile, obviously pretty smug.

"There's a lady from Atlanta who comes to Mom's café just because of this," Alessandro told him while almost literally inhaling his food.

"That's true. How about you go and brush your teeth and pick a story. I'll tell your dad about the lady, and when I'm done, I'll send him up?"

Alessandro was gone before she had even finished her sentence, and Aly got up, carrying his plate and cup to the kitchen sink. Jam took his own and followed her. He settled against the counter while she cleaned the dishes.

"Her aunt lives two towns over and is pretty sick. She comes over maybe four times a year, and each time she's here, she'll drop by to get a cup for her and her aunt. She loves her cocoa," she explained.

"I'm in bed, Dad! Mom, you can tell him the story later," Alessandro called from upstairs, and Aly sighed.

"Smell his breath and then send him to brush his teeth again, okay?" she pleaded, and Jam couldn't resist. He reached out, brushing his thumb over her lip.

"Will do, Mom," he teased, and she threw the towel at him, shaking her head. He could still hear her laughing as he made his way upstairs.

"Let me smell your breath," Jam said to his son, and instantly, Alessandro's face fell.

"My tooth paste smells like chocolate," Lesso insisted, crossing his arms in front of his body.

"Go and brush your teeth while I check out all your rockets, okay?" Jam suggested, already walking around the bed to show he meant it. Alessandro hesitated for a moment, and then he bolted out of the room. Jam couldn't help but smile. He was all child, contrary to what Jam was used to seeing from TV shows. Sometimes, he was sure childhood ended at five. He was glad it wasn't the same for his son.

"I'm gonna go and read in my room. Come and say good-bye before you leave," Aly said from the door, carrying Alessandro's dirty laundry. She looked every little bit the amazing mother he knew she was.

"I will," he promised, watching as she turned away. "And Aly?" She looked over her shoulder at him. "Thank you for..." Jam shrugged, not exactly sure where he should start. He could be thanking her for so much, yet only one thing stood out at that moment. "Thank you for loving Alessandro like your own."

"He is mine," she just replied as a way of explanation and then left. Jam cursed under his breath because each and every time she softened toward him, he managed to make her mad again.

He could hear how she and Alessandro exchanged quiet words in the hall, ending with a quiet 'love you' and then Lesso came back in.

"So how do we do this story-thing?" Jam wanted to know, holding out his arms to show he was clueless.

Alessandro picked a book from the shelf and then looked at

Jam. "You sit on my bed like this," he explained, pulling Jam over and positioning him until he had stretched out his legs on the bed and leaned his back against the headboard. "And I'm going to sit like this. You put your arm around me and hold the book." Throwing his own legs over Jam's, he cuddled into his arms until Lesso's head rested right under Jam's chin. The little boy was warm and soft, smelling of strawberry toothpaste and children's shampoo. "And now you read," Alessandro ordered, and Jam did as he was told.

He opened the book, noticing the bigger letters. It was obviously a book for beginners. He started to read, but Lesso stopped him after less than a page.

"Is that how you talk?" he asked, looking at him with wide eyes. Jam couldn't hide a smirk.

"That's what your mom tells you when you read, right?" he asked.

Alessandro nodded. "You need to give life to a story. No one would read books if they were all like recipes. Your voice needs to go up and down, and then, before you know it, your voice creates a whole world around you," he explained.

"How long have you been reading with your mom?" Jam questioned, and Alessandro grinned.

"She read to me before I could, and now, we do it together since I learned to read in school. She makes me read a lot, but you know what the best nights are? When she's reading. I'm in the rocket when she does. She's the best," his son announced with so much love it made Jam want to squeeze him.

"Then let's create a world." He grinned, starting again; this time he made sure he used his voice to his best abilities.

~

*I*t was close to midnight when Jam finally left his son's room. Even though the boy had fallen asleep before Jam had even reached the middle of the book, he hadn't been ready to let go. Just for the fun of it, and if he were honest with himself because he was curious, he finished reading the story and then had simply held his son. Aly had been more than right—holding your child was healing.

Eventually, he moved his son carefully, covering him with blankets until he was sure he wouldn't freeze, then he kissed his hair, promising himself to make it up to his son one day. Alessandro deserved more time with him. Besides, Jam wanted to see him, read to him, and show him the world. For that, though, things needed to change, and so far, Jam wasn't ready. After one last look at his boy, he turned off the light and closed the door.

The house was dark by now, and there was only a sliver of light falling through the partly open door of Aly's bedroom. Jam knocked softly, but once he pushed open the door a bit, he saw she had fallen asleep, her cheek resting on the pages of her paperback.

Jam smiled to himself, moving over to cover her with a blanket and take the book away before leaving, when he had a different thought. Pulling off his socks and jeans, he slipped into bed next to her, placing the comforter around them before kissing her neck.

"Jam," she whispered, sleepy.

"Healing properties, Aly," he just gave back, and she moved, freeing herself from her top.

"Take off that shirt then," she demanded, and he hesitated before he did. He had left his hoodie downstairs, and now, he'd do something he hadn't done in more than a decade. He'd sleep skin to skin with a woman.

"Better," she decided, cuddling into him again. It didn't take long, and her regular breathing let him know that she was back asleep.

Jam knew he wouldn't find any sleep that night, but he did know it would still be the best night in a very long time.

*A*ly stretched as her alarm clock screamed for her to get up. She smiled until her hand touched something cold. To be exact, she touched the side where Jam had been laying. Instantly, Alessia was wide-awake, pushing herself off the pillow. On her nightstand, she found a single rose and a note.

Aly,

You were right about the healing properties, but it's not only my son, but you, girl. I've never had a night of sleep this amazing. How can it be that simple contact eases your worries until your mind is nicely blank?

I've loved you since I was young. You deserve to have someone who is the owner of his life, and I want to be that exact person for you. You and Alessandro are the most amazing things out there.

I know you've waited for me until now because your son told me so. Please, wait just a little longer.

I want to be yours. And I want Lesso to be ours.

Jam

*S*he read the words over and over until she looked at her clock and realized she needed to get Alessandro ready for school. She reached for her dressing gown, pulling it over her while rushing out of the room.

"Dad!"She heard her son just a second later followed by deep laughter. Relieved, she hurried down the stairs and found Jam in her kitchen. Alessandro was on the kitchen counter next to him and chatted excitedly about some dream from the night before.

As much as she appreciated the romantic gesture with note and flower, she was even happier he was still there. She wanted him to stay for just a few more days. Nothing rushed him home and she intended to show him exactly how amazing he was.

"Breakfast, son, then school," Jam finally said, getting the boy down from the counter.

To her utter surprise, Alessandro didn't protest. Instead, he grabbed a plate and carried it over to the table, humming softly while eating.

"I hadn't realized you two were getting up so early. I wanted to at least leave breakfast for the two of you and..."Jam shrugged as his cheeks heated. He absolutely didn't like that he had been caught, and it made Aly grin. She wanted to cuddle into his arms.

"You sneaking out is a habit we need to break," she decided and then walked over. He was still busy with the pan in front of him, flipping bacon while stirring the scrambled eggs. She embraced him from behind and then leaned her head against his back. His heart was racing, and it made her smile.

"Stay just a few more days, Jamison. I'm begging you," she whispered, and he placed his hands left and right of the stove, hanging his head.

"Aly," he started, but she absolutely didn't like his tone.

"I'm not asking for promises, Jam. I'm asking for a glimpse of the life you want us to have. Let me show you this can work. Let me be there for you. Let me enjoy waking up next to you for once, please," she pleaded, pressing herself closer to his body.

Jam took her hands in his, kissing them before turning in her arms. Indecision colored his beautiful features before he finally shook his head.

"I don't know how to do this family stuff. I've never had a relationship that... I've never had a relationship, and I've certainly never had a family. I don't know how to be a dad, and I know even less about how to be a good guy."

"Let's take it one step at a time. You do great being a dad. And about the rest, I'm not sure what to say about the relationship thing, but we're adults. We don't have to turn this into something serious to enjoy each other's company. How about I cook for us tonight and you come over for dinner and a movie? Alessandro will love it. Please, you won't even have to cuddle with me. Just be there for your son,'" Aly pleaded.

Just then Alessandro came in. "Dad, are you gonna drive me to school?" he asked, and Jam looked from her to her son.

"Of course, I will. How else will I know where to pick you up this afternoon?" Jam replied, and Alessia released the breath she had been holding. "Go and get your shoes. I need to have a quick word with your mother before we leave," he then added, and Alessandro beamed, leaving with a happy shout.

"Alessia Rhyme, you don't seriously think I could sit on a sofa next to you without touching you?"

"You did for years," she remarked. She could not believe this was true; that he really stood in her kitchen. It was almost unreal. Regret crossed his face.

"Aly, if I stay, you need to promise me something," he said, cupping her cheek. She instantly knew where he was going with that and shook her head.

"I can't promise you that. Seeing your scars certainly didn't make me less curious. I *will* find out who did that to you and why, Jam, so if you aren't ready to do that grown-up thing with honesty, that's your thing, but I won't stop asking for the truth. I have a feeling you need to talk about it, handsome," Aly told him, kissing his palm. He groaned.

"Woman, you'll be the death of me," he fussed gently, making her smile. It wasn't a 'no,' and that was really all she could ask for.

He leaned in and kissed her forehead, ready to leave before turning back to her. "And I'm gonna cook. You'll be at work, right?" he then asked, and she cocked a brow.

"Breaking and entering is a crime, even if it's for a good cause," she teased, and Jam laughed.

"I think Dorly has a spare key, so there's no need for that," he remarked. Aly grinned with a nod, and then was surprised as Alessandro came back to give her a kiss.

"Bye, Mom. Have fun at the café. I'll bring Dad by later on," he promised and then took Jam's hand to pull him along.

"See you later." Jam smiled and then winked at her as he left. It was weird how silent the house seemed to be. Aly took a moment to enjoy the quiet before a horn blared outside. She pulled open the front door, staring at her friend, Phil, who jumped out of the car.

"You aren't dressed yet! Or do you want to go and cater to the women's social group like that?"

"Shit," Aly cursed, hurrying inside. She had totally forgotten the annual meeting at her café today. This special event paid Aly's bills for two months straight and only because she went beyond expectations. She closed the café for the day and even offered alcohol, which the women paid for triple the cost. It would be a whole day on her feet, but it was so worth it. Philomena thankfully agreed to help each year just for the gossip. Aly offered her money each time, but since Philomena was a stay-at-home mom, she was bored out of her mind and loved doing shifts at the café. It was payment enough, she always said.

It didn't take long and Aly had thrown on her favorite dress, brushed her curls out, and then grabbed her handbag. The mess Jam had made would have to wait until tonight.

Getting in the car with her friend, she exhaled. "You're my hero today. I would have totally forgotten that meeting until the women were standing in my café. My last days have been a little hectic," Aly explained, and Phil arched a brow.

"Can it be that guy I saw driving your son around?" Phil inquired, and Aly told herself to not blush or look excited.

"He came out of the blue, and it's been a whirlwind since then," she admitted. Two days. That was how long it had taken Jam to turn her world upside down. Again. Last time, he hadn't even needed that much time. Aly touched her hand to her forehead, her thoughts swirling.

"Al, wasn't that the elusive Jamison?" For the first time ever, Alessia regretted having told Philomena about him. She was her closest friend and usually a safe bet, but now, Phil looked rather worried.

"He just came to check on us," she whispered, feeling like a teenager who needed to justify her new boyfriend.

"In ten years, he hasn't come to check on you. Why now?" There was no way Phil would understand, not without Aly needing to tell her secret. Something she wouldn't risk.

"Because he finally could."

"Because his girlfriend finally let him go? Or his wife? What is it, huh?" Aly felt as if cold water doused her. Her day had been a rollercoaster so far, and it didn't seem to stop.

"It's not like that. He came for Lesso," she protested, being glad as they reached the café. Luckily, most of the day would be too busy for them to talk.

She unlocked the door, turning on all machines before she started to wipe down the counters again. Phil moved some tables so the women sat the way they preferred. They knew by now which women shouldn't be sitting together, and they arranged it accordingly.

"Aly, he might have come for your son but look at you. You never stopped loving him. A guy who never once saw you for you. He was your brother's best friend and nothing else. What's wrong with you? If you play house with him—"

"I don't play house with him," Aly protested even though it was exactly what she had asked of him this morning.

"Oh, sweetie! You aren't one of those stupid mistresses, hoping he'll change his ways for you! What happened to you? He came in, gave you a dimpled smile, and you were all gone?" Aly simply refused an answer until Phil came around the counter, taking her hands to get her to focus on her friend.

"That's not—"

"Ladies!" Aly had never been more glad the women's committee was always early. From then on, they didn't have any time to talk, and in the blink of an eye, it was already half past three.

The little bell over the door jingled and instant silence spread through the café as first Alessandro and then Jam came in. All eyes were on him as he froze in the door.

"Mom, Dad let me show him all of my pictures in school, and the award I got for spelling bee last year. He says we have to go grocery shopping like real men. Can I have a cacao? Dad wants one, too. We were so excited about it," Alessandro chatted away, not even noticing the weird mood in the shop.

Aly couldn't imagine how Jam felt with thirty women above the age of fifty staring at him as if they wanted to eat him alive. And he looked good. Obviously, he had changed after dropping Alessandro off at school. Now, he wore low-riding jeans and a blue and white lumberjack shirt with rolled-up sleeves, showing off his muscled-covered arms.

"Weren't we, Dad?" Alessandro asked into the silence, nodding his father over. Finally, Jam moved, coming to stop in front of her.

"That's right, buddy," he said with a strained smile. He looked at her, and his features softened. "Hey, Aly," he added, and she cleared her throat, not saying anything though.

She threw together their chocolate in no time at all, putting them in carry-out cups. "The real guys take it on the road, Jam, don't they?" she asked meaningful.

Jam nodded. "Only men do, I think," he said, looking thoughtful. "What do you think, little man?"

Alessandro puffed out his chest. "Let's take it for the road, Dad," he agreed, and Aly handed over the cups.

"Just the way you like them, sirs. Not too hot with marshmallows on top. Thank you for being our customers today." She grinned, feeling her heart skip a beat as Jam's skin brushed hers.

"Thank you." She only nodded as she watched the two leave. The moment the door fell closed behind them, noise exploded in the little room.

"Twenty years younger, Rose, twenty years younger," one lady said to the woman next to her.

"Uh, now I know why women turn cougar," another announced.

"Now, that's a DILF if I've ever seen one," a third one decided. That exclamation actually caused a few cries of outrage.

"Isobel, watch your filthy mouth!" The women laughed, and Aly closed her eyes for a second. Her whole body was thrumming just from the simple touch and the look Jam had given her. She knew he had wanted to lean in and kiss her cheek. Even though she was somewhat disappointed, she knew that would have caused even more talk.

"I don't think you ladies are what he's preying on, so show some respect. No objectifying any men in here unless it's me doing the objectifying," Philomena announced, moving around the tables to pour some coffee. Thankfully, the topic shifted from there to men the ladies also found objectify-worthy, and Aly bit her cheeks to keep a stupid grin from appearing.

"Wow, Aly," Phil hissed as she finally stood next to her again. "I tell you, woman, I would've tumbled into bed with him after a smile like that, too. No wonder you let him right back in."

Aly just shook her head. "It's for Alessandro, not for me," she insisted.

"Who are you trying to convince? Did you see the way he looked at you? Aly, that man wanted to own you in the best way possible. I swear he's just as doe-eyed about you as you are about him! I know I totally changed my tune about him, but then I hadn't seen the way he looked at you yet. This was..." She fanned herself. "Still, a word of caution. You know how it is with flames. They burn bright and hot before quickly extinguishing. Be careful, okay?" Alessia just looked at her friend and gave a tentative nod. After all, when did a heart ever care about caution?

$\sim$

"Look, and that's what Mom sometimes buys. And then she buys that, too. And over there, she buys that, too." Jam highly doubted that, since all of the things were more or less sweets.

He decided to divert Alessandro's attention from them to something far more important. "Okay, I wanna impress your mom. What does she like to eat?"

"Noodles," Alessandro decided, and Jam rolled his eyes. He sure wasn't going to impress Aly with noodles.

"And what else?"

"Beef and rosemary potatoes, peas or mushrooms on the side. I think that's something she likes. Jam it is, right? I'm Spencer," a voice behind him stated, and Jam turned around. It was the beach guy Aly had talked to the other day.

"Jamison," Jam corrected, shaking Spencer's hand.

"Oh, you," Alessandro said next to him, and Jam placed a hand on his son's shoulder.

"Alessandro," he scolded with a warning in his voice. Lesso instantly rolled his eyes.

"I'm sorry. Hey, Spence," he then corrected, meeting Jam's eyes. "Can I go look at the comics?" He pointed at a stand in Jam's view, and Jam nodded. The boy left, and he focused back on Spencer.

"Aly always has to do that, too. The scolding, I mean," the other man mumbled, and Jam just nodded. He wanted to tell Spencer to stop calling her Aly, simply because it sounded as if Spencer had real feelings for Alessia.

"Thank you for the tip with the beef. I'm gonna try that, I guess," Jam replied, hoping to change the topic.

"It's nearly impossible to impress Aly. Taking her to a movie and then dinner doesn't work, just dinner doesn't work, huge bouquets of roses don't do the trick... I never tried cooking for her, though."

Jam felt smug. "Aly hated the movies. She always had. The dark room, and the fact you don't have much privacy never suited her. She used to say that dates belong in an atmosphere where you can exchange deep, meaningful looks and secrets smiles. Taking her to dinner will work if it's a cozy restaurant. She hates show-off restaurants where you can't pronounce the meals and have a plate as big as the table without anything on it really. She's the fries-and-burger kind. And of course, you couldn't get her with the roses... she likes them meaningful, and it must be a single rose or no roses at all. She loves colorful flowers. She..." Jam actually stopped himself as he noticed how Spencer was looking at him.

"Why did you ever leave her?"

Jam laughed. "I never left her."

"Oh," Spencer commented, paling. Just then, Jam realized how that sounded.

"No, I mean that she and I never really were an item."

"You have a child together." *Shit, true.* He hadn't even thought about that.

"It was one night. She... I... this didn't exactly work out the way we wanted it, and she moved away anyway, so... you know."

Spencer's jaw dropped, and Jam made fists in his pocket. "You're a real jerk. I guess that's what Aly needs to get off, huh? No wonder a nice guy like me couldn't get her in bed," Spencer taunted, and Jam wanted to punch him right there.

"Watch your mouth, buddy. Alessia is an amazing woman. The thing between us is complicated, and I'm not going to try to explain it to you. I never planned for her to stay alone after she left. In fact, I was sure she had found someone by now, but it seems you just weren't the one for her. I bet you always asked her if it would be okay to kiss her, too." The way Spencer's eyes glittered with anger told Jam he had been spot on. "Dude, you don't ask a woman you want if you can kiss her. You frame her face, draw her in, and then kiss her until she's gasping for air. Women want to be owned in certain aspects of life. Sweeping her off her feet won't happen with polite questions," Jam explained, wishing he could do exactly that to Aly now. He wanted to possess her and make her knees weak.

"Yeah, or you give her a child and always tie her to you. What-ever you did, you certainly made her addicted to you. But you wanna know something? You aren't here to stay, so I guess there'll be a time when she'll need a shoulder to cry on, and I'll be there to come in—the hero on his white horse. She's amazing, you're right about that, and one day, she'll see I'm her safest bet," Spencer snapped, and Jam just wanted to reach out when a papery hand closed around his fist.

"Young man, come and help me get those beans down the shelf, will you?" Jam looked at Dorly and then up at his son, who was still flipping through the magazines. When he focused back, Spencer was gone, and it was probably better that way, too.

"Alessandro, come on," he called, and instantly, Lesso complied.

"Hey, Dorly! You should have told us you needed something. We would have brought it," his son exclaimed, giving the elderly woman a hug.

"I had no idea you two handsome men would be buying groceries today. Besides, I'm glad I'm here." She gave Jam a sharp look, and Jam pulled his shoulders up until they almost covered his ears, looking sheepish. "You better if you stop antagonizing Alessia's friends," she went on, and Jam nodded.

"I didn't mean to. He just made me so mad."

Dorly just shrugged. "Because you worry he's right. You wanted to leave today, remember?" Jam knew that, no doubt, but he planned to come back.

"You should've heard how he talked about Aly," Jam defended himself, and Dorly patted his arm while Alessandro kept putting stuff in her shopping cart.

"Two of those, darling," the old lady told Alessandro and then looked back at him. "He's hurt, Jamison. He worked hard to get Alessia where he wanted and then you come in and she doesn't remember his name. Besides, I heard the way *you* talked about her, and I think that was enough to make anyone jealous," Dorly explained.

"It doesn't matter. I should find him and apologize." And didn't it suck to be grown up?

"Nah, boy, no reason. He certainly needs to know that Alessia needs passion, not polite. Especially if you plan to leave her to him." She snuck a sidelong glance at him, but he didn't care. He didn't plan on anything besides getting home and cooking for her so he knew she was with him and no one else.

~

*A*ly was beat. She had been on her feet all day, and as much as she had looked forward to spending the evening with Jam and Alessandro, she now wanted to crawl onto the sofa and read.

She went around the back, wanting to feel the water around her feet and enjoy the calm for a few minutes before finally going inside. Laughter and music instantly greeted her, as well as a mouth-watering scent. Walking quietly to the kitchen, she watched how Jam and Alessandro danced through the kitchen. It was rap music, which made her want to cry out in protest until she realized that kids were in the song, too, and it was about astronauts and heroes. She had never heard it before, but the boys seemed to have the lyrics down already.

Jam spotted her and held up his hand. "Everybody freeze!" Instantly, Lesso stopped, his hip cocked to the side. "Don't turn around, but we're being monitored," he then explained, whispering to his son.

"A woman?" Jam looked over Alessandro's shoulder and then nodded. "Is she hot?"

Jam looked at her again. "Pretty much," he agreed.

Lesso waved him off. "It's just my mom. She won't tell anyone we're dancing," her son decided and then turned to her, smiling. He wore an apron, just like Jamison, and she wanted to take a picture.

Jam's features softened as she picked up her son and placed him on the counter. "You look exhausted," he commented and reached out, but she avoided his touch, bending down to tug at her son's clothes. Philomena's words stuck with her, and this was insane. Then again, this was Jam, the only guy she had ever wanted. And she was lonely. Very lonely. Who could blame her for wanting a little time in paradise? She could, and she knew she would regret it once Jam went back, but maybe, just maybe it was worth it. After all, wasn't that saying 'better loved and lost than never loved at all'?

"I'm..." She trailed off because she wasn't sure if she was mentally or physically exhausted anymore.

"Champ, turn around," Jam called, coming over to her.

"You got it," her son called, turning his back toward them. It took a second until Aly realized what Jam was aiming at, but by then he had already reached around her, bent her back a little, and grinned with mischief in his eyes.

He was kissing her as if he hadn't seen her in forever, tasting of rosemary and something sweet, then he stood, straightening her. "Hey," he beamed, obviously feeling pretty proud of himself.

"Oh, Jam," she whispered. She wouldn't be able to resist him. Ever.

"Can I look again?" Lesso called, seemingly getting bored.

"Sure thing. Rosemary. I want it," she commented, catching her breath while biting her lip. Jam's eyes got dark, and she wished they were back in high school. She wanted to be brave and talk to him. She didn't want to give him any chance to turn her down. God, how she wished she had avoided Jam getting anyone else's kid. She wanted him to be the father of *her* kids.

"Champ, tell your mom what we cooked while I prepare the table," Jam ordered and Alessandro nodded, taking her hand to lead her over to the stove after hopping down from the counter. He could barely look into the pots, but he still pointed at them all.

"We wanted you to have something you don't get every night, so we cooked some steaks, made potatoes that we then... what was it called?" He scrunched up his face in thought. Eventually, he shook his head. "We threw them in butter and some green stuff that smells like Dorly's candles. And we made black salsifies. They look like asparagus, but they taste a lot better." Alessia did a double take.

"You tried them?" she asked in utter disbelief, and Lesso nodded.

"And he liked them," Jam interrupted, coming back in. "Wash up, we can eat."

Aly cleaned her hands alongside her son, making sure they were dry before they went to the table. There was a candle burning. Jam had foregone the tablecloth, and she was thankful for that. Alessandro had a tendency to pull on the material and make everything tumble over.

The food was incredible. The beef was soft on her tongue, just the right kind of cooked with only a little rosy color left. She hated blood and couldn't eat anything that was still spilling onto her plate. The potatoes were well done and bite-sized. The mixture of herbs came off well, and she couldn't get enough of it. Alessandro didn't have any of the potatoes, which didn't surprise her. He only ate them if they were fried and cut into wedges. She didn't trust her eyes, though, as he had two helpings of the vegetables; the salsifies vanished quicker than she'd ever expected.

She stayed silent while Lesso told her about his day at school and the way he and Tom had teased some younger girls.

"I told him that was no way to treat a girl and asked him if he'd ever treat you that way. He promised he'd apologize to the girls tomorrow," Jam assured her before she could say anything at all.

"We weren't really mean. We just *pretended* spiders were on their clothes," Lesso pouted, but Jam just gave him a stern look. It was exactly what she would have done, and she liked that a lot. "I will apologize," the boy promised then, and she sighed, pushing her plate away.

"So about that movie." She changed the topic, and the boys grinned at each other.

"We picked," Lesso started, looking expectantly at his father.

"*The Chronicles of Narnia*," Jam finished, and Aly's jaw dropped.

"Fairytales?" She made sure she had heard right.

"Mom, it's a story with heroes and sword fights. Do you even know Narnia? There's war in Narnia! Kids need to save the world."

She knew for a fact Alessandro didn't know Narnia, so she guessed Jam had influenced him.

"I'm gonna change into comfy clothes," she announced, pointing at Jam to follow her.

"Can you prepare everything? I need to wash my hands. I'll clean the dishes once you two are in bed," Jam said to his son, and Alessandro marched away while Jam followed Aly upstairs. In her bedroom, she moved to her closet.

"Thank you. I don't know what you did with my son, but I could've never convinced him to watch this. We'd discuss him wanting to see the *Die Hard* movies because all his friends have, and I'd get mad until he ended up walking straight to his room. And usually he just eats green beans and a little meat. I... thank you."

She reached for the hem of her shirt, waiting, but he just lifted a brow. "Turn around, I want to change," she prompted, and he started to laugh. It made him look boyish and young, especially as he combed through his blond hair, giving him that ultra-sexy, just-out-of-bed look.

"I've seen you in a bikini when you were still so young you didn't need a top," he commented, making her blush.

"Turn. Around." This time, it wasn't a plea. He cocked his head before finally turning. Aly did the same, just to make sure he wouldn't have anything to see if he did decide to peek. Her heart was racing in her throat, so she decided she would talk some while changing. Opening her dress behind her back, she lowered her head.

"I'm sorry for the disaster in the café today," she whispered, being strangely aware of the fact that she was left standing in nothing but her underwear while her absolute dream guy stood across the room, staring at the door.

≈

$\mathcal{H}$e couldn't remember what she talked about. In fact, Jam couldn't even remember his own name as he looked over his shoulder at how Aly wiggled out of her dress, pulling some sweatpants on. She pushed first her left, then her right leg into the material, giving him the perfect view of her ass.

"I had totally forgotten about that meeting until my friend, Phil, picked me up this morning." That actually got his attention; no matter how hot she looked bending even farther to put on some socks. Was Phil another one of her admirers?

"She luckily kept a clear head all day." *She.* Phil was a girl. Perfect, it meant he could go back to staring at her perfect curves without needing to worry. Aly just pulled her hair up into a messy bun, which seemed to be her favorite home look. She stared out the window while doing so, stretching with only her bra and sweatpants.

"Those women were terrible. I mean I already thought it more than impolite that they couldn't stop staring at you, but that they even stayed quiet the whole time? Please, who does that? Anyway, the moment you left, all hell broke loose. They…"

She was babbling. The realization hit him right in the gut, and he had to take a deep breath. "Aly," he interrupted, noticing that his voice sounded rough while his body seemed to move toward her of his own accord.

"Yes?" she squeaked.

"You're rambling," he told her and then saw how she drew in rapid, little breaths.

"Well, you make me damn nervous. I haven't been naked around a guy in forever, so excuse me if I'm worried that maybe I'm not attractive. Not that you'd know since you're a gentleman who didn't turn around to watch me change," she snapped defensively.

She had a top in her hand that she pulled over her head, but before it fully covered her upper body, Jam had placed his hand left and right on her ribcage, right below her bra. He stood behind her, and she drew in a sharp breath while he moved in so close that their bodies were touching. He lowered his head until his lips brushed the outer shell of her ear.

"Every bit of you is perfect, Aly." She bent her neck slightly, giving him access to her it, and he let his lips wander down the side of her head. "Your legs are perfect. Your ass is perfect. Your shoulders are perfect. Your neck is perfect. Hell, even your anger is beautiful. You, Aly, are a dream. Besides, gentlemen are boring." He nipped on her shoulder, feeling her tremble. He wanted her to a degree that scared him, especially as he had thought Collene had killed off every need to ever get naked with a woman again. Aly didn't even need to try, and he was on the edge. "Gentlemen would've let this moment slip by unused when tasting your skin like that is—"

"Mom, are you ever coming down again?" Aly jumped out of his arms, a flush working its way over her shoulders and up her neck.

"Sure, baby, we're coming. I'll be there in a minute." She was flustered, and Jam laughed silently. It was too much fun to watch her like this. Finally pulling that top down, she turned to him, heat in her eyes.

"If he weren't downstairs, Jamison Loane, you wouldn't be wearing those jeans much longer, boy. Now, move your pretty ass downstairs, so this girl here can take a minute to calm down," she fussed, pushing him toward the door.

Jam walked downstairs, finding himself stomach to face with a ten-year-old who glared at him. "If you made her cry again, Dad, I'm not going to be happy," Alessandro promised, but before Jam could say anything, Aly came down the stairs.

"I'm fine, baby," she promised, passing Jam on the stairs and walking into the living room with her son. The movie was set on pause.

"Can I sit betweenDad and you?" Alessandro asked Alessia, and Jam almost groaned as Aly nodded.

"Of course," she told him, and he sat down, patting the spots to the left and right of him. Jam wanted to cuddle with both, not only his son, but he dutifully moved to Alessandro's side, smiling as Lesso instantly pushed himself closer to his body.

Aly pulled up one leg as she sat down. They started the movie, and Jam could hardly believe how perfect this felt. Lesso commented on almost everything in the movie; a habit he seemed to possess ever since being small if you could believe Aly.

Jamison found it hard to focus on the screen. If any of the teenage girl he once knew remained in Aly, she surely loved this movie. He watched her from the side, wishing he hadn't missed ten years with her, yet being glad she had been safe over the last decade.

Reaching over the back of the sofa, he gently let his finger go up the side of her neck, seeing how she smiled and then moved a little closer so he could go through her hair. Without even looking at him, she pulled the rubber band from her bun and shook out her waves. He finally returned his attention back to the movie, but he didn't stop caressing Aly. At one point, she kissed his palm, stealing a look at him.

This was why men strived to have a family. This was a perfect moment of peace.

~

*A*ly returned from tucking Alessandro in. He had fallen asleep between them, and she had carried him to bed because she hadn't seen enough of him that day. As much as she loved that Jam took the time for him, it was weird sharing her son with someone else, even if that person was his father.

Jam was watching the final scenes of the movie, and Aly walked around the room, lighting some candles before she turned off the TV.

"Hey, I need to know how it ends!" Jam protested, and she cocked her head, shaking it slightly.

"You can finish that some other time," she explained, settling down next to him again, facing him. Besides all the secrets he seemed to have, she didn't know much about him any longer. She guessed some stuff from the pictures Greg had sent her, but still, she wanted to know *more*. Plus, they needed to talk about what was between them because, as sure as she was that she was still in love with him, she had doubts about what he felt for her.

"I know you said you came here because you needed to see that we're safe, but you could've left after seeing that. There was no need to talk to us," she started, not sure how else to approach the topic.

"I said as well that I needed to see you and him up close," Jam reminded her, his voice cautious.

"And you did that, too. I know you wanted to leave, and I begged you to stay, but Jamison, why did you really come? You've always been strong-minded. If you hadn't wanted to stay, I couldn't have convinced you. I know why I wanted to keep you here, but I can't figure out your motives."

Jam lowered his gaze, taking a breath. "My affection for you is not as sudden as you think," he commented, and she sighed in exasperation.

"So you pointed out in your note. And even before that." He cringed at the mentioning of it, making her realize he had seriously intended to leave but had been caught because he didn't know their routine. Hell, he didn't even know their lives really.

"I know you think I don't know you any longer, but Alessia, I do. I've watched you for as long as I had the chance. I still know when you don't believe me. I know that the first time I've ever held you was two nights ago. Trust me, I couldn't be more aware of that. I *do* realize, too, that it took twenty-eight years for our first kiss even though we've known each other since you were born. I know all those things and nothing I can say will prove my intentions or let you know I didn't lie in those few lines. If everything had been the way I planned, neither you nor Alessandro would've ever known I was here. I walked past your house, and Dorly was outside. I should've been surprised then that she recognized me, but I wasn't. She stopped me and asked me if I was here to see you." He closed his eyes, rubbing them. "I told her I wasn't, but damn, Aly, I wanted to. I just wanted to see you smile. I have no idea if she saw something on my face that day or not, but she commented on my exhausted appearance. I told her I hadn't slept in a bed in awhile, and she offered me her spare bedroom. I was tired, so tired, and a bed sounded heavenly. I didn't even think about why she trusted me. I was little better than a stalker."

"Dorly needs someone to kick her ass. That woman's gonna get her herself killed with her kindness," Aly mumbled, angry that Dorly was that trusting yet thankful she had given Jam a reason to stay.

"I knew your street, but not exactly where your house was. I would have walked up and down the beach until meeting you. That was the plan at least. After I had woken up, I found a note saying that my darling savior had gone to her neighbor and that I was to come and say bye at least. Of course, I wanted to do that. I owed her, after all. I saw her sitting on the porch and a woman was facing her. It took only a moment for me to realize it was you. I knew I needed to talk to you then. Just once. Seriously, I just wanted to say hi and tell you about Collene. It was the first time in ten years I didn't have to worry about anyone guessing my feelings for you." He looked sincere, and Aly wondered if he had sacrificed his happiness for something she didn't yet know.

"Okay, even if you liked me back then—"

"Aly, I never stopped." She stared at him, wishing so much that he'd be serious. "The only reason I stayed here was because I finally had the chance to live the life I've always wanted. You've been so sure about me needing to stay this morning, and suddenly, you look at me as if I'm breaking every rule there is," he added while watching her face.

She shook her head; trying to arrange the things her head told her and the things her heart wanted so badly. Were there even rules? Their only restriction was the horizon they allowed them-selves to have.

"My friend, Phil, basically told me to kick your ass to the curb. After all, if you didn't want me ten years ago, what makes me believe you do now?" she admitted, searching his eyes for a reaction that would tell her which way to go.

~

*J*am could prove that to her. Seeing her features in the soft glow of the candles made her appear so much more vulnerable than during the harsh daylight. Then again, maybe it was the way she was looking at him—hope making her eyes shine while fear paled her cheeks.

"Oh, Aly," he groaned, cupping the back of her neck to draw her in. He pulled her in his lap, tugging her as close as he could while his lips tasted hers. She was trembling again, just as she had done earlier, and he wanted more, hoping nothing would interrupt them this time.

In a quick movement, he had buried his hands under the material of her shirt, finding her skin warm to his touch. She was kissing him back now, a fierce dance of tongues and lips. Years of longing and passion poured into the kiss so strongly, it was almost bruising.

"We can't. We're in the middle of the living room, and I know Alessandro's asleep, but if he wakes up, he'd be... we can't," she breathed against his mouth, and Jam grinned. He saw in her eyes how much she wanted it. Besides, it gave him the perfect excuse to stay fully dressed while making her feel good.

"There'll be nothing he can see, Aly, trust me," he coaxed; being more than glad for the wide sweater she had pulled over. In contrast to her other ones, this wasn't knitted, and therefore, not see-through. It was perfect.

"Jam," she started to protest her, but he hushed her with a finger on her lips.

"Trust me," he pleaded, and she finally nodded, kissing his fingertip. He went right back to her lips, making sure she had placed one leg on each side of his lap before going back under her clothes, finding the clasp of her bra and unhooking it. He almost smiled as he realized his heart was racing in his throat as he carefully moved his hands to cup her breasts. They fit into his palms perfectly, and she gasped as his thumbs caressed her sensitive peaks. He leaned in and nipped at her throat, biting softly as she cocked her head back to give him more room. She tasted faintly sweet; probably remnants of her lotion, and she tasted uniquely female. Jamison wished his lips could explore more than her neck, but he was giving her passion in an unexpected moment. There'd be time for other things later.

Or so he hoped.

Rolling her nipples between his fingers drew a low moan from Aly, and he loved that sound. She was biting her lip, and he enjoyed watching her reaction so closely. Her hair was tumbling down her back, looking almost on fire as the candles reflected the red in her brown curls. It wasn't obvious during the day, but now, she seemed to glow of her own accord.

Jam moved his hands away, just to caress her skin and give her a short reprieve, but she didn't exactly play along, rolling her hips against the erection straining his pants. Instantly, he stilled her movements, making her pout in protest.

Chuckling low, he leaned in and nibbled at the lip she so seductively presented. She drowned her hands in his hair, leaning in to get another deep kiss. It was addicting, no doubt about that. She tried to pull his shirt up, but he stopped her hands.

"Stop. I won't tie you up to keep you from touching me because... well, I just won't." He bit his tongue at his slip and then gave her a smile. "I won't, but please, let me be nice to you, Aly. Let me treat you to what I wish I could have treated you to years ago," he then went on, and she sighed in resignation.

"I want to touch you," she whispered, resting her forehead against his.

"Well, hold on then," he replied, letting his left hand slip beneath the waistband of her sweats, finding her sweet spot over her underwear.

"Shit, Jamison," she gasped, and he felt her breath wash over his lips. She had closed her eyes again, pleasure playing over her features, making her appear much younger than her almost thirty. It was as if the years just melted away between them. He slipped a finger into her panties; meeting heated skin that made him, too, draw in a sharp breath.

"God, Aly, you're so wet, and it's for me," he whispered, feeling how she nodded softly. She was breathing hard, and he circled her sensitive nub before rubbing over it ever so lightly. She instantly arched, making him feel like the best lover in the world.

"More," she begged, and he heightened the pressure just a bit more while finding her nipple with his free hand. Her nails were digging into his shoulders, but in contrast to what he was used to, this felt incredible.

He knew he'd get her to the edge quicker if he used other parts of his body, or if he got her fully naked, but that wasn't his intention. He liked that this was more than private because no one could really tell what he was doing. It was intimate, too; simply because they were so close to each other he felt her breath whenever she exhaled. Therefore, Jam decided that this was the best sex he ever had. And he wasn't even naked.

Increasing his intensity, his rubbing finally brought her over the edge, making her shiver in his arms and then collapse against him. Grinning to himself, he cupped the back of her neck and lazily went through her hair.

"I think I might have scratched you," she eventually whispered, her voice still a little shaky. It made Jam feel even better. She pushed up his t-shirt sleeve enough to see the half-moon marks she had left on his shoulders. "I'm sorry," she added, and he could hear the sadness in her words.

"They'll go away and no one will ever see them again," he promised, trying to get her to look at him, but she focused on his shoulder and, he guessed, the scar he had there.

"I should be more careful with you. You're marked enough," she mused, rubbing her thumb over her indentions. Jam had to admit that the marks she left on him would probably be more sexy than any of his other marks were, but he didn't say that. Instead, he took her chin between his fingers and made her look at him. She seemed ready to cry; not exactly the reaction he had been aiming for.

"Alessia, please, don't worry," he whispered, and Aly cuddled into him, caressing his chest over his shirt.

"How can I not when you came here scarred like that?" she asked, and he sighed. Jam couldn't say why, but he had hoped she had simply forgotten. It was the naïve side in him.

"Maybe… because I just made you come?" he replied, and she playfully slapped him. He could almost instantly feel her getting tense, though, and he knew her next words wouldn't be much fun.

"You have a lot of scars. Which hurt the most?" She was clever; he had to give her that. Aly had avoided asking who had done it, and she gave him a choice as to how much to tell her, yet she tried to satisfy her curiosity. Jam decided to give her at least something, even though there wasn't one scar he remembered hurting more than another did. Most of them had been terribly painful.

"I can't tell you which hurt the most, but I remember the first one I ever got. I mean besides the normal ones like scratched knees or chicken pox. It's on the left side of my ribcage. I needed three stitches because it wouldn't stop bleeding. A glass bottle hit me. There was so much blood. It was crazy. Once the scar healed, I got my first tattoo, too, just to cover it up," he explained, and Aly moved slightly.

"Can I see it?" she asked, and he got up, showing her the side of his body. She reached out, touching cold fingertips to his skin. "My defending warrior," she read, and Jam watched her face for any signs of recognition. Luckily, there were none. The font his tattoo artists had used was small and elegant, making the words hard to read. To most, they looked like a few simple lines. He wasn't surprised that Aly could read them, though; her handwriting always had looked similar.

Her questioning eyes met his, and Jam pulled her to her feet. "One day, you'll figure out the meaning," he promised, kissing her forehead while she caressed his tattoo.

"Will I one day also figure out who did this to you?" she inquired, pulling back enough to look at him. Jam tried to avoid her eyes, but she just moved with him.

"I hope you won't," he admitted and then drew her in until his cheek rested against the side of her head. "I hope that once I fix my issues back home, I'll come here to the light and never have to face the dark again," he whispered, kissing her shoulder without letting her go.

"So that means if I'd let you go now, you'd come back quicker?" she asked. It was such an obvious attempt to lighten the mood, and Jam wanted to press his lips against hers again. And he did, before nodding.

"That could be, but I have to be honest here. I'm not yet ready to leave. Not like I was yesterday." He grinned and then noticed how she breathed a sigh of relief.

"So I should get going. You and Lesso have an early day tomorrow," he finally suggested, and she pulled back, staring at him as if he had grown another head. "It's the right thing to do, Aly. Respect your virtue and…"

Aly lifted a brow and looked back at the sofa they had been doing less virtuous things on not too long ago.

"Okay, that maybe was a moot point, but you know the rules," he reminded her.

"We're breaking them all anyway," Aly insisted, and Jam took a deep breath before walking around the room to blow out the candles. It took a moment for his eyes to adjust to the sudden darkness, and then he found Aly, nudging her until she jumped up into his arms. With ease, he carried her upstairs, finding his way only because the hallway light was burning, which she turned off in their passing. She helped him out of his shirt in the dark of her bedroom, making him feel a lot more secure than the last times she had seen him shirtless. He still needed to take care of something before slipping into bed with her.

"I'll be right back," he whispered, and she sighed but then nodded. He had to grin, but then excused himself, marching into her bathroom. Inside, he rested his hands left and right on the sink, breathing hard. It had been years since his body had reacted so strongly to a woman. Even though he was male and naked breasts usually stirred something in him, it never had been such a burning need like the one he felt after having taken care of Aly. He wanted to make love to her, sweet and fast, strong and slow, but it wouldn't exactly look good if he did, then soon left again. He couldn't say what it was, but it just felt wrong. Still, his erection didn't think there was anything wrong with him just going for it. Instead, though, he opened his jeans and swallowed strongly. It had been a while since he had done himself any favors, so it almost made his knees buckle with relief when he palmed himself. Gritting his teeth against the onslaught of long missed feelings, it didn't take more than five strokes and the image of Aly coming to make Jam create a mess in Aly's sink. With a blush on his cheeks, he cleaned up, not daring to look at his reflection in the mirror. He flushed the toilet for good measure and then went back into the bedroom, crawling into bed next to Aly. He pulled her close, kissing her neck.

"I could've taken care of that, you know?" she mumbled and again he felt heat creep up on his face.

"I don't know what you mean," he mumbled. "Try to get some sleep."

He felt how she shook her head and then cuddled closer. Jam felt himself relax.

Holding her until she fell asleep was something Jam would never tire of. He even planned to let her wake up with him this time.

chapter
Six

*I*t had been more than a week since Jam came into their lives and seamlessly integrated himself into their routines. It was too easy building her day around evenings with him and Alessandro together. Except for the night she had heard about his first scar, she hadn't gotten any more information out of him and it annoyed her. She wanted to know more. In fact, she needed to know it all.

Alessandro was spending the night with Dorly, and Aly had thought about preparing food, but then she figured that if Jam were mad at her, they wouldn't get to it anyway. She wanted him to stay with them. He didn't need to go back for anything; Aly was sure about that by now. She had talked to Greg and actually hoped she could convince him to just uproot himself and come up to join them in Sunrow. She'd have her whole family there then, and she wouldn't ever have to return to Townsend, especially now that Jamison was here with them.

He had gone into town and was expecting a game night with Aly and Alessandro, but now she was waiting for his return, staring out at the ocean. It was angry, the usual blue waves carrying a steel color. A sense of foreboding filled her, and it gave her the chills. She hugged herself, a knitted coat playing around her legs as the wind teased her body.

"This doesn't look good. And if I combine the empty house with your thoughtful posture, I'm guessing I'm not gonna like where this is going to head." As much as she wished it were different, Aly almost melted as Jam's deep voice carried over to her. He embraced her from behind, kissing her cheek before looking out at the water with her.

"I need to know more about your scars, Jam. This thing between us has taken a very serious turn in no time at all, and I won't have it if you keep things from me. Especially when I know they are such a big part of you."

She turned in his arms, glad he hadn't yet run. His expression, though, told her clearly that it was just a matter of seconds. She framed his face, probably holding on a little tighter than necessary, but she needed him to stay. "You belong with us, and I know you know that, but… you are still about to walk out on us every damn second. Don't think I didn't notice how you couldn't look at yourself in the mirror. You're beautiful, Jamison Loane, more than anyone else, but you just don't believe that. And I want to know why. Tell me about *all* scars. Please."

Jam looked as if she had asked him to walk through fire and then peel his skin off all by himself. "Aly, I'm not going to tell you…"

"Who did it? I guessed as much." And she didn't need him to say a name. She'd figure that out; she just needed to hear about enough scars to maybe find a pattern.

He stared at her for a long moment and then ran a hand through his hair, staring over her head at the waves crashing onto the shore.

"Fine," Jam finally agreed, and she took his hand, kissing it softly. He gave her a shaky smile. "You can do better than that, can't you?" he asked, wiggling his eyebrows. She laughed breathlessly, relief making her almost dizzy as she pushed herself onto her tiptoes to kiss him deeply before leading him inside.

He was getting more nervous with every step as they approached the house, and once they stood in the living room, he spread his arms wide. "How do you wanna do this, huh?" he questioned and his tone proved how much he was on edge.

"Take off your shirt," she whispered, suddenly unsure if she should push him toward this or not.

"I always imagined you saying those words to me, but not like this." He laughed humorlessly, and then pulled his hoodie and his shirt off, staring at her. Aly swallowed, walking around him, wondering where to start. She found a spot on his back, touching it.

"A chair. It bruised my ribs and got taped but didn't exactly heal the way it should because it was reopened again and again," he said through clenched teeth. Aly leaned in and kissed the scar before touching the next one.

"I hit a table corner. It hurt for weeks, especially because that spot was hit again and again," he reported, his voice having gone flat. Aly kissed that, too, then moved on. He had so many marks on his body she wanted to cry. In fact, silent tears were running down her cheeks. Thirty minutes later, she knew she had a victim of abuse in front of her, but her mind couldn't figure out when this happened. Jam sometimes told longer stories and sometimes just gave one-word answers.

Finally, she walked around to him, touching his lips. "This?" she asked, and he looked away from her.

"I was repeatedly punched. I stayed inside the house for weeks, refusing to see anyone until most of the swelling had gone away. The cut on my lip opened again and again because I was slapped a few more times." Finally, she had a hint of when this had happened, and it made her gasp. She remembered those weeks. Greg had been more than pissed for not seeing his best friend, and even afterward, Jam had basically said nothing about where he'd been.

At that time, he had lived with his mother after his father had left them and never returned, but his mother wasn't a violent person. In fact, she had been as close to the walking dead as one could get. Besides, Jam hadn't been so small that pushing him around had been easy. He let all those things happen to him, and for the life of her she couldn't figure out why.

"Why, Jam? Why did you let someone do that to you? You've been tall for as long as I can remember. You were a quarterback in high school, for God's sake! Why?" She stepped back, thinking about all the things she had ever heard about domestic violence. There was no denying that men, too, could be on the receiving end of violence, especially if they tried to protect their kids or… it hit her then. The small, bruised body he had given her for safekeeping. All the stories she had heard.

Her knees gave out as the thought settled in her body, growing and throwing shadows until she could almost tell him his own story. Only how had they created a child together if she had repeatedly beaten him? Why had he never reached out?

"Collene. Oh God, Jam, it was Collene."

Agony crossed his features, and he reached for the plain white tee, pulling it over his head before walking over to her door, resting his hands on either side of the doorframe.

"People wouldn't have believed me. You know her. You knew her back then, too. She was small, a blonde doll, and everybody's darling."

"People were scared of her and her influence, so of course she was everyone's darling. You feared retaliation if you said something against her," Aly whispered, her voice breaking with choked sobs. "You need to press charges, Jamison."

"I don't. She's gone, and this whole nightmare's been over for close to ten years. As soon as I realized that no one knew where my son was, I left. She no longer had any leverage over me."

Aly jumped up, her outrage causing her almost scream. She wanted to hurt Collene for all she had done to Jam. "She was the reason you and I weren't together. You preferred *all this* to *me?*" she asked, disbelief coloring her voice.

He spun around so suddenly that Aly took a step back, hating herself for being afraid. "I didn't *prefer* anything, Alessia. You have no fucking idea what I've been through in those years. Don't you dare put a guilt trip on me now just because you didn't get exactly what you wanted, okay? *I* never got what I wanted," he spat, and she hugged herself.

"Why did you stay with her? You could have walked away the first time you realized what she was like! Why stay with her, Jamison? Tell me! Why fuck a woman who punches you? Slaps you? Makes sure your wounds don't heal properly?"

He shook his head angrily. "You don't have any idea, Aly, and I sure as hell won't enlighten you. I did it because I had my reasons, and as much as I wish I had seen a different way, I didn't. Don't judge me, Alissa. Not for this. Judge me for having been so selfish as to believe we could get over this without me ever telling you my deep, dark secrets. Judge me for wanting a life with you and my son now. Judge me for having hopes, but don't you dare judging me for those years." He was shaking with anger, and Aly couldn't see past her breaking heart. He had tears in his eyes, and she knew she should be comforting him instead of challenging him, but she just couldn't believe that she had hurt all those years because he had wanted *Collene*.

"If you don't tell anyone, you'll never get over it. You'll never be free for a future if the past is your constant companion. Press charges, Jamison, no matter how long ago it was. I can't and won't believe that our great country will let her get away with that!"

He laughed a bitter laugh, making her skin crawl. "Right, Aly," he said, stalking toward her until he was almost nose-to-nose with her. It took every ounce of will not to shy away from him. "I'm just gonna walk into the police station in Townsend and tell them the mayor's daughter had belittled, threatened, and beaten me for years. Me—a guy who's about three heads taller and twice her size. A once pretty successful quarterback, as you pointed out. I've been lifting weights since I was sixteen, Alessia." Her name sounded cruel coming from his lips like that. She couldn't stop herself from crying.

"So? What was it she had on you?" She could see in his eyes that he wanted to tell her but then decided against it, a vicious smile playing over his beautiful mouth.

"Why? Weren't you the one insinuating I preferred her to you? What else would she need on me? I couldn't walk away, and I didn't want to. We created a child together, remember?" He started walking again, and she finally moved back until her back hit the door and she couldn't go anywhere else. "You know how babies come to be, right? A boy and a girl get naked together. They spend a few hot hours together. Boy, Collene is into some crazy shit in the bedroom."

"Yeah, beating up people," she breathed, her words barely hearable.

"Oh, handcuffs and leather, wax and other stuff. Things someone like you would never understand or approve of. After all, look how easily it was for me to get you off on that sofa a few nights back."

The tears finally dried on her cheeks, as she felt nothing but numb. That night had been one of the most intense and sweet experiences of her entire life, and he cheapened it by making it sound as if it had meant nothing to him.

She couldn't think of one word to reply.

"Collene and I had a relationship that no one ever will understand, so don't even try."

"You're damaged," she finally stated, meaning he needed help. Deep down, she knew he was lashing out since she had cornered him. He showed all the signs: He was shaking, but it was clear that it wasn't anger. He was pale, and as much as he tried to appear scary, the look in his eyes was nothing but haunted.

"I'm dark and twisted, Alessia. There's a difference."

"Take back your life, Jam. Go and see a psychologist. It's not your fault you've been abused, Jam. Talk it over with someone. Find a lawyer. Find a way, Jamison," she pleaded.

"Stop saying my name, Alessia. I'm in full control of my life."

She wasn't sure he was even aware of the tear that slipped down his cheek as he pushed back, looking at her as if it was the last time he'd ever see her.

"It wasn't your fault," she tried again, her voice breaking. Finally, he shook his head, and she thought she had reached him.

"No," he admitted. "It was yours."

Aly had never known pain like this.

"Out!" she screamed, and he looked at her with something akin to satisfaction. She should have known then that this was exactly what he had aimed for, but his words had cut her too deep.

"As you wish," he said with a fake bow, leaving afterward. The moment he was gone, Aly sank down the wall, crossing her arms in front of her chest in a desperate attempt to keep herself together. It was useless, though; she was shattered into a million pieces and didn't think anyone would ever be able to put her back together.

∾

$\mathcal{T}$he first time Aly moved from the floor was when the doorbell rang. She knew Alessandro would come in through the back, so she guessed it wasn't him. She prayed to whoever was listening that it was Jam. She hadn't forgotten any of the words he had said, but she wanted to work through the issues with him if it was what he needed. She couldn't possibly get herself to forgive him, but maybe, over time, they'd be able to work through that, too.

She didn't bother to change, but she checked her face in the mirror just to make sure she wouldn't scare away an unsuspecting mailman.

Her heart plummeted though the moment she saw who stood on her doorstep. This couldn't possibly be happening. Not there, not now, where she was ripped open and raw anyways.

"Alessia. Hey, love. Can I come in?" The woman passed her without even waiting for an invitation, walking over to her living room without any suggestion from Aly at all.

"I'm going to make this quick. I'd be very pleased if you could run upstairs and pack a bag for Zack. I'm going to take my grandson home, and we both know you have no say in it. In fact, you have no chance to keep him, so why not make this as quick and painless as possible? I know he's not here right now, but he'll be back in no time."

Zack must have been the name Collene had given her baby boy. "Mrs. Karmison, what the hell are you doing here?" she asked, gripping her own elbows tighter to avoid doing something stupid

—like hitting the unwanted visitor. The woman across from her, who had settled down on Aly's sofa without any prompting, clasped her hands together in her lap.

"Okay, you want the long version. I've known where my grandson was for almost all his life. I hate to admit that I considered you, a stranger, safer for him than my own daughter."

"You know the monster she is," Aly accused, and Mrs. Karmison had the decency to look embarrassed.

"Of course I know. I've lived with her father for almost as long as I can remember. Collene had two choices. Either she was going to turn into her own mother or her own father. In her case, it was the father. The first time he ever hit her, she was four. At six, I think, I saw the cruelty in her eyes for the first time. I won't lie. I started hating my daughter then. She treated me like her father treated me, but once he started focusing his anger on her, I was off the hook. It was a reprieve, no matter how short-lived."

"You should've taken your daughter and run," Alessia snapped, and Mrs. Karmison nodded.

"I should have, but I was never brave enough or had the means to do so. Disappearing costs a lot of money, Alessia…"

"Since you're not exactly here as a friend, I'd prefer it if you could call me Miss Rhyme. I'm no longer a little girl," Aly demanded. Unspoken anger replaced her numbness. It was one thing letting Jam destroy her life like that, but she would not allow a stranger to tear apart what she considered her family.

"I can tell, Miss Rhyme."

To Aly's utter disbelief, the features on the other woman's face softened. "You've raised a great little boy. His grades are outstanding. He's a friendly little guy."

The color drained from her face. "You can't possibly know that," Aly whispered, leaning against the wall to find at least some support. She wouldn't sit in front of this woman because as long as she looked down at Collene's mother, Aly had the feeling she was at least slightly in control.

"Oh, I don't have any money, Miss Rhyme, but my husband

does, and as long as I do whatever he asks of me, I can use it. And I have paid the best private investigators I could find. I probably have more pictures of you and your son than you can imagine." For the second time in as many days, Aly wanted to collapse and never get up again. Her eyes flickered across the room, searching every corner for a camera she hadn't noticed so far.

"Please, I have some integrity," her intruder explained, and Aly focused back on the woman. "I do think, though, you've talked to some of the PIs. Like a few weeks ago, there was this guy in your café and he ordered a black coffee with a spoon of cinnamon sugar."

Aly felt her stomach turn. She wanted to throw up at the mere thought of being spied on. "He was so young. He actually tried to flirt with me," she mumbled and then felt herself shaking. She absolutely didn't like where this was going.

Mrs. Karmison nodded carefully. "He liked you a little too much, which is why I planned on taking someone else the next time." *The next time...*

Aly shook her head. "How many times have there been?" she inquired, and the woman finally stood up, shrugging her shoulder carelessly.

"Every three months ever since you left, so you do the math," Mrs. Karmison explained, and Aly touched her throat as a strangled cry wanted to make its way out of her mouth. "And please, stop questioning everything. They only ever took pictures of you two in town. I respect your privacy to some degree. This was the safe haven you provided my grandson, and I'm more than thankful for that."

"If you knew all this time, then why haven't you sent the police after me? Or worse, Collene?"

Mrs. Karmison laughed a cold laugh. "It's interesting that you consider my daughter worse than the police, who could lock you up for twenty years and more."

Aly swallowed. "Collene's the devil. She would beat Alessandro.

That knowledge alone would be worse than spending my entire life in prison."

"Zack. His name is Zack."

Aly simply ignored her protest. "Why did you never tell anyone?" She had other questions, but that one mattered the most at that moment.

"Just like you, I didn't want him to be treated the way his mother intended to treat him. Besides that, I couldn't watch what she did to that boy any longer. He sacrificed his happiness before, and I knew if we'd ever get Zack back, he'd do it again. He was Collene's perfect victim because he knew how to act when others were around."

Aly didn't need to ask who 'that boy' was. "You knew what she was doing to Jam, and you never figured you should step in?"

"Step in and take the punishment for it? He was much stronger than I ever was! If I had interfered, my husband would have probably killed me." It chilled Aly to the bone how emotionless that woman managed to talk about her own possible death.

"Between you and Jam, you could have gone to the police. You know that. He had the wounds to prove it," Aly protested, and Mrs. Karmison shook her head.

"Who believes that a girl can beat up a guy? What guy lets himself be beaten up? None. Besides, my husband bought half of the police. They would never dare to go against him unless there was no other way. But we're wasting time. My daughter is gone, and no one has heard from her in more than two weeks. I'm positive she won't be back. If you would now please pack my grandson's clothes so he and I can leave?"

Aly stared at her. "What makes you think I'm handing over my boy to you now?"

The older woman suddenly stood right in front of her, almost poking Aly's eye out with a skinny finger. "He's not your boy! He's my grandson, and you kidnapped him. You will hand him over because it's either that or I call the police. If you let him go nicely and never show your beautiful face in Townsend ever again, you will one day have the chance to have your own family with a son who truly belongs to you. If not, you'll rot in prison. Don't get me wrong. I don't think you deserve this fate, but I will not hesitate."

Aly forced herself to stay calm and try to see a way out. She knew one thing for sure, though. She needed to stay out of prison if she ever wanted a chance to see Alessandro again. "I will not pack a bag for him, though," she insisted, and the other woman rolled her eyes.

"Fine, I'm gonna buy him new stuff. He needs to look more like a Karmison anyway."

Just then, the back door flew open and her son came in, his face tear-stained and angry. "He left! It was your fault! Why did you make my dad leave? We finally had him here! I hate you! I hate you so much!" Alessandro walked over to her, beating his little fists against her stomach.

"Lesso—"

"Zack, it's good to see you. You don't need to see your mom anymore anyway. I can take you to your dad."

Aly was sure she couldn't take anymore. She knew she had it coming for years since she had hung her heart on two guys who didn't belong to her, but hell, it had been fine for such a long time. How could she possibly have guessed this day would still be coming?

"Who are you?" Alessandro was now moving behind her, and Aly breathed a little easier.

"I'm your grandma," Mrs. Karmison explained, and it disgusted Aly how she suddenly looked all nice and teary. "I live where your dad lives and your mother allowed me to take you back with me so you can spend the summer with us. How does that sound? She figured you would like to hang out with your dad more now," the woman lied, and Aly had to stay quiet.

It was for the best.

For now.

"But I still have a week of school left," Alessandro said carefully. Aly could tell how much he liked the idea of spending more time with Jam. After all, he didn't know he wouldn't ever return to her. It broke her heart.

"That's okay. You're such a good boy that they're fine with you leaving early. Don't you want to see Jam?"

"Can Mom come?" Her heart went out to him, but still she stayed quiet.

"No, your mom has the café, remember? She can't leave, but the summer isn't that long."

"I won't see Mom?"

Mrs. Karmison shook her head but then gave him a bright smile."But you'll be able to spend time with your father and your grandma. Don't you want that, boy?"

He did.

God, Aly could tell, and she was sure his grandmother could too. At least that way he would go without a protest and it was the perfect excuse.

"I do," he said, and instantly, his grandmother reached for him.

"We have to leave right now, or we'll miss our flight. I have your clothes in my car," she explained, and Alessandro looked back at Aly.

"I'm mad at you, Mom, but I'll still miss you. Maybe I'll call you when Dad tells me he isn't angry with you anymore," he promised and then was out of the house. She couldn't believe it was that easy for him to trust a virtual stranger.

"He seriously wants his dad," Mrs. Karmison commented and then pointed at a bag she had left on the sofa. "Two more things before I leave. First, this," she said, "is for all the expenses you had through the years for Zack. And second, you didn't ask the most important question of all." She obviously waited for Aly to say something, but Aly knew if she opened her mouth, she'd break down. She didn't want to do that in front of the woman who just had fully destroyed her life. "You didn't ask how I knew you had my grandson."

This time, it was obvious Aly wouldn't find out unless she inquired the answer. "How?" she croaked out.

"You were the only woman Jamison ever loved. I was there the night my daughter decided that you were her next project. By project, I mean victim. Jamison said something about you, and Collene stared at you. I realized it, he realized it; we all did. I saw how she bumped you into tables. And then, from one second to the next, she stopped, and Jamison was with her. I think she forgot you the moment he decided to be with her. When my grandson was gone, I remembered. Who could be a better choice than the woman you could never have?"

With that, Mrs. Karmison left, taking Aly's whole life away. Her hope about Jam returning to talk to her was down the drain, too. Alessandro had made it pretty obvious that Jam was gone. Aly hated herself then and there. If she had waited just one more night to confront Jam, he'd still be by her side.

As it was, she had no idea what to think or do. Eventually, she reached for her phone and called the only person who came to mind.

Faintly, she heard the back door open and close, but she was too numb to react. She sank down to the floor while she waited for someone to pick up.

"Aly?"

"Greg, they took my son, and I can do absolutely nothing about it," she sobbed, choking on the pieces of her broken heart.

∼

*J*am had driven all night. The moment he had walked away from Aly, he had gotten into the car and left. He had a hole where his heart used to be, and eventually, he needed to stop the car in the middle of nowhere. His hands were shaking so hard he no longer trusted himself to drive. Stumbling out of the car, he fell to his knees and allowed himself to sob. They were dry and choked and even though Jam had known a lot of pain in his life, nothing came close to what he was feeling there at that moment.

"God, Aly, I'm so sorry," he mumbled, knowing she couldn't hear him. His phone started blaring, and he cursed. Not many people had his number, and it was exactly right that way, but that usually meant whoever was calling wanted something important.

"Loane?" he croaked, clearing his throat.

"You sound like my sister does, Loane." Jam wasn't sure he'd be able to sit through a sermon now.

"Greg—"

"I don't care what went down between you two. Okay, that's a lie because she's crying, but we have bigger problems. Much bigger problems."

Jam didn't think there could be anything worse than this.

"Thea Karmison took your son back home to Townsend. She threatened Aly. At least that's what I gathered between her gut-wrenching sobs. She told Aly never to show her face in Townsend again, so I guess you need to move your ass back here, and… I don't know. I can't believe she knew all this time. She waited until she knew Collene was gone and then went to get him back. Aly's a mess, Jam. Maybe you should call her up and ask what exactly that woman said. I…"

"I will not call your sister, Greg." He couldn't because hearing her voice would push him over the edge.

"You will, Jamison Loane, because you need to know everything that hateful woman said! *Then* you move your ass back here and solve this problem. I can't walk in there and take Alessandro back. Please?"

Jam knew he was right because, even though he was sure Aly was screwed either way, he needed to know what he was up against.

"What if she refuses to talk to me?" That was probably what scared him more than hearing her cry. He had walked out on her while she'd been crying, so maybe he could make it through that.

"Someone took her son, and excuse me for being harsh, but that puts everything else in perspective. I don't think she cares about anything you said to her right now." It *was* harsh, but Jam had to agree that most likely Greg was absolutely spot-on.

"See you in three hours. I'm almost home," Jam promised then he hung up, thinking for a moment. Aly needed someone by her side, and even though he couldn't reach Philomena, that friend Aly had talked about, he'd be able to call Dorly.

It had taken a few rings before the old woman picked up, sounding out of breath. "Rome?"

"It's me," he said, wanting to add more, but she already interrupted him.

"Jamison. You should be here. I've never seen the girl like that. It's terrible. You—"

"Dorly, I can't be with her and get back her son at the same time. I know she most likely won't be able to make you understand how someone could just take her son, but—"

"She told me."

It almost tore the ground from under Jam's feet. The more people they told, the higher the risk would be that Aly might end up in prison. "I saw that old hag taking her boy away and went over. I don't think there's much Aly cares about right now. I called Phil, too. Boy, how are you?"

"I wasn't there when the woman came. You knew that. I'm okay."

"How can you be?"

It dawned on Jam then that Aly had told her *really* everything.

"Please, Dorly, I don't have time to think about it now, and I'd prefer not to do it anyways. What I do worry about, though, is my son and Aly. Please, don't leave her alone and call me as soon as the police show and pick her up." He wanted to pull out his hair. This just couldn't be happening.

"I will stay with her. I just came to turn my heating off and get some of the chicken so I can make some chicken soup for that girl. She loves you, Jamison. You know that, right? Even if she maybe pushed you too far too soon; this girl always had her heart on her sleeve where it concerned you."

Jam didn't need to hear that after the way he had treated her. God, the way he had spoken to her…

He shook his head because he knew he couldn't change it now. They had to deal with more pressing matters.

"I have to call her, and then I need to get back to… I don't know. I don't know what to do, but I need to do something. I need to un-break Aly, and the only way to do that is to get Alessandro back to her."

Dorly sighed, sounding like a broke tire. "She needs both of you back. Call her now."

"What if I say something stupid? I'm not sure I can find the right words around her," he admitted, and then bit his lip.

"Follow your heart," she ordered. "Bye, Jam, and be careful."

He told her bye and then hung up before dialing. He worried that if he waited too long he wouldn't ever make the call.

For the first time ever, Jam had Aly's name on his screen. Her number had been in his phone since shortly after she had left back then, but he had never before called her.

"Rhyme?" Her voice was a shadow of what he was used to, and it hit him deep.

"I'll get him back," he whispered because he knew that was the only thing that really mattered to her. "Alessia, I'll get him back to you. I swear even if it's the last thing I do." And since he was up against a family like the Karmisons, it might even be true.

chapter
Seven

*A*ly felt another tear running down her cheek while Phil combed her fingers through her hair. "Can you please eat something?" she asked, and Aly shook her head, holding on tighter to the pillow she was hugging. The house was silent, although she knew she should hear many noises: Dorly was cooking, Phil was watching TV, and the voices were in the background, but Aly didn't hear those. They weren't the right noises.

She waited for her son to come running down the stairs; she waited for him to call out to her; she waited to hear a Matchbox car tumbling down the stairs. She waited for all those noises made by a child in the house and none came.

Worst of all, she wouldn't ever get him back.

"Alessia, it's been a week," Phil pleaded, and Aly wiped away another tear. It felt so much longer than that.

"Has she been eating anything at all?" she heard Dorly ask and then felt how Phil's body slightly moved. Aly had her head in her lap, and she still knew Phil had shaken her head.

"I ate," Aly croaked out. She remembered she had some steak some time ago. "I had steak."

"You didn't, Aly. You probably wanted to make them, but I threw them out a few days ago because they looked spoiled," Dorly explained gently.

"Oh." What else could Aly say to that?

"I made some spaghetti and Bolognese," Dorly continued, and Aly took a deep breath, sitting up.

"Sounds like heaven," she whispered, trying to smile.

"That's scary, Aly. Stop the smiling," Phil instantly said, trying her hardest to draw a real smile from Aly.

She just didn't think she had it in her.

She moved until she knelt on the floor next to the coffee table and tried her best to ignore the scrutinizing glances Dorly and Phil were throwing her way. Somewhere deep down, she still couldn't believe she had told those two she had kidnapped a child and now was mourning him as if he had died. And somehow, for her, he had. More surprising, though, was the fact they hadn't called the police. They even told her she had done the right thing.

"Kidnapping's a felony," she mumbled while twisting some noodles around the fork.

"Beating a kid to death is a felony. You saved that boy's life," Phil replied, her tone making it clear she should never ever meet Collene on the street. Aly had shown them the photos she had taken back then of Alessandro's bruised and battered body. If she hadn't taken him, he most likely wouldn't be alive anymore. Now, though, he was back, and if Jam's skin was any indicator, Aly wasn't sure if being dead would have served her boy better. Then she reminded herself that Collene wasn't there anymore and Thea Karmison would keep her son safe. Hopefully.

She raised the fork to her mouth but dropped it the moment her phone announced an incoming text message. It was a number she didn't know sending pictures.

Aly opened the first, and it was titled 'In case you thought there was anything left here for you,' being followed by six photos of Jam and a pretty redhead. He was smiling at her, and she touched his arm. One actually showed him hugging her; another one showed her reaching out to touch his lip in a gesture that made Aly want to throw up. She couldn't believe that her heart, in its shattered state, still had the capability to hurt more.

She brought her hand to her mouth, trying to keep the sobs from slipping out. Her son was in the hand of monsters; she shouldn't care about Jam meeting another woman. Especially not after everything they had shared for less than seven days. Obviously, it had been just a nice escape for him.

In fact, he shouldn't be caring about meeting other women if he loved his son.

"Alessia Rhyme, *do not*, for one second, believe what that number tries to make you believe. Philomena and I both have seen Jam around you. This is a lie. Maybe they're older. He's bound to have a history with women. He's a good-looking man," Dorly tried to soothe her.

"I don't care if he fucks her in the middle of the street but shouldn't he be worried about his son? After all, *he* knows best what this family can do." She shook her head and flung the phone across the room, unbidden anger making her wish she could get in a car and go down there herself. She wanted to take care of Alessandro if his father didn't even bother to help him.

She couldn't help all the terrible pictures that flooded her mind: Alessandro bleeding in a corner; him crying for her; him thinking she had stopped loving him.

With a new resolve, she got up.

"Alessia, what are you up to now?" Phil carefully asked.

"I'm gonna shower, then I'll eat, and then I'll go and find my son," she announced, running up. It was a surprise how refreshing the cascading water was for her body and soul. With new resolve, she dressed coming down the stairs where Phil waited, Aly's phone in hand.

"Greg called, Aly," she said quietly, and Aly pressed her lips together.

"What now?"

"He said that a friend at the station told him the Karmisons called in favors. If any officer sees you setting foot in Townsend, you'll be brought in for questioning."

Aly's jaw dropped. "What for? They hardly told them I kidnapped their grandson!"

"I asked the same. They want to bring you in and question you because of Jam's injuries. Greg said his friend put emphasis on questioning. Your brother is sure that you'll be locked up, and they'll find a reason if they need one. Don't return, Aly. You don't know what they'll do to you," Phil pleaded, and Aly sank down on the stairs, all resolve gone. If she were locked up, she wouldn't be doing anything to help Alessandro, so her only hope was the guy who now dated instead of saving his son's life.

The doorbell rang and Alessia shook her head. She was over unannounced visitors. "It's probably the police," she mumbled, not even bothering to get up.

"It's not, Aly," Phil whispered sheepishly. "It's Spencer, and before you say anything, listen. We need someone by your side while we are gone." Dorly joined them, and Aly lifted a brow. "You can't go there and see your son, but we can," Phil explained, and Aly sighed. She wanted to go.

"You make sure the café is okay, and Lesso has something to return to," Dorly interrupted. It was a plot to get Aly out of the house again, but she decided not to comment.

"What exactly did you tell Spencer?" she asked, and Phil shrugged a shoulder.

"I told him that you needed a friend. I know that he's head over heels in love with you, but trust me, Aly, the moment he sees you, he'll just be your support. I won't leave knowing you are staying here all the time. We'll get him back, but you need to be strong for him," Philomena insisted and Aly got up, opening the door. It surprised her, but she actually was glad to see Spencer. He hugged her, and even though it didn't feel anything like being in Jam's arms, it was nice to be able to almost hide from the world.

Especially since the guy who held her heart was with another girl.

≈

*J*am wrapped his hands around the hot cup standing on the small table while watching the redhead in front of him. She was young, no doubt about that, but everything he had heard from her so far had proved very well that she was amazing and devoted.

"Did I say thank you today yet?" he asked, giving her a smile. She actually looked serious, giving him a pointed look.

"Don't thank me, Jamison. We will need to touch up on tough topics today. I did some research on the Karmisons, and this is not gonna work. We need something to prove they are what you say they are," she explained, and instantly, his smile left his face. "I'll be honest. The scars on your body won't be enough. People have seen you play all kinds of sports. I found reports on you being in fights back when you were still in high school. I don't say I don't believe you, but I'm saying it'll be tough to prove she did it. Besides, it's quite a while back that all this happened and—"

"I don't want to talk about all that she did to me. I want my son away from that family. Is there any chance?" he inquired, and Shannon looked down at her papers. She was a year younger than he was, and he had found her through Greg. She was a lawyer, damn fresh, too, but that didn't matter. Greg swore she had the heart it would take to make this all right.

"That depends." He knew his face showed his disappointment at her announcement, but she reached out and touched his arm with an encouraging smile. "Don't lose hope. This is a unique situation. After all, your son was gone for ten years. Alessia Rhyme kidnapped him," Shannon reminded him, and Jam gritted his teeth,

"She didn't kidnap him. I gave him to her for safekeeping. He would be dead if she hadn't given in. Or I'd be on the run with a ten-year-old."

"Then *you* would've kidnapped your son." *Maybe involving Shannon wasn't such a good idea after all*, Jam thought.

"Okay, Shannon, thank you for having met with me again, but I don't think—"

She interrupted him by reaching out, her expression soft as she touched his lip. He knew that the scar was as big as Texas to him, when, in truth, it was nothing more than a faint line.

"This is one of the scars you carried away from the years you've been with her, isn't it?"

He took her hand, pushing it away because he was okay with Aly touching it, but he felt as if he should make this a privilege to for her and her only.

He nodded. "Yes, but what does that have to do with anything?"

"You're trying to avoid permanent marks on your son, Jamison. Please, try to remember that. All I'm saying are the things people in the courtroom will be saying. What we need is a plan to make it so you have a chance at taking him away from the Karmisons again."

That made him stare at her since he knew that tone. "You actually have a plan!" Finally this took a turn to his liking.

"I do. But first, I need to know what you plan to do with him once you have full custody of him," Shannon remarked, and Jam just shook his head in disbelief. With everything she knew, he hadn't thought that this was still a question.

"Aly gets him back." There was no doubt about that decision.

"Jamison, you can't do it like that," she said carefully, and he almost laughed. Why were they sitting there again?

"And why would that be?"

"We need to make this legit so no one ever can take your son away again."

He got up, not caring that they were in a public café. He had stopped caring what people thought about him long ago. "What are you saying?"

A mischievous grin came over her face, and she pointed for him to sit back down. "I'm saying I have a plan, and all we need is someone to back it up."

He sat again, and she took out a picture of him and Alessandro from a few days ago, as well as one from Aly and his son. "Alessia and my boy."

"There's nothing juries hate more than people who abuse children. We will go to court, but until then, you need to stay away from the Karmisons, and as much as I hate it, away from your son. We need to make this all official. We'll try to make it look as if you were only hiding your kid because you feared for his life. Alessia needs to support your story that you've been over there quite a few times. Seriously, as long as we plan it well and create a heartfelt story, our chances are good you'll get your son back and Alessia won't have to go to prison for long." He had liked the plan until she said her last words. Before he could say something, though, his cell chimed.

He checked it; his thoughts being on the things Shannon had said until his heart froze. It was an unknown number sending him one simple photo.

He should have known his words would lead her straight into the waiting arms of that Spencer-guy, especially because he had predicted it. Jam closed his eyes for a few moments and tried to regain control of his thoughts. Aly deserved to have a happy life without his scars hurting them both. There'd always be something between them because he wasn't ready to face any of this.

He'd never revisit his time with Collene again,

"Don't count on Aly. In fact, I'd prefer if we keep her out of this fully," he then whispered, throwing his phone on the table.

"You... don't... want Alessia to have your son again?" He had thrown Shannon off her game and felt sorry for it, but they needed to get it done without Alessia, too.

"She'll get him back. As soon as I have full custody and the Karmisons have no right to him whatsoever, that boy will be back with his mother."

Shannon thought for a moment and then collected her papers. "Okay, I need to rethink our strategy. I'm sorry, but this is not exactly the best way to solve this." She got up, and Jam stood.

"I sincerely apologize for causing trouble, but I owe her. She has to stay out of prison. Nothing else is acceptable."

"Jam, between you and me, as friends, I'm asking you to talk to her. Seriously, if she's anything as I remember, she'll understand why she needs to spend a few nights in prison. She saved a child. Illegally, but she still did. She'll be a hero in there. You and I know this. It won't be long. If we have the lawsuit in place, she'll be a savior. Just a few days. Try to talk to her," she pleaded, touching his chest.

"If we can manage this without her, let's do it."

"Okay, there's a way, but Jamison, don't you think there is one thing you'd like even less than having her in prison? Sadly that's the only other option we have."

There was nothing that… "No, Shannon, I can't."

"Either you share your story with the world or you bring Aly in for a few days. It's your choice. Just let me know which I need to prepare for. I'm leaving now, but call me as soon as you know. We don't have endless time," she insisted and then turned away.

"I need to see Alessandro."

She looked at him over her shoulder. "They call him Zack again. And if you go and ring their doorbell and they let you in, it's okay. If they turn you away at the door, *do not*, and I repeat, *do not force your entry*. The more you violate the rules, the less I can do for you."

"Duly noted," he commented and then was actually glad once she left. He needed time to think, and he was worried. As much as he was sure Thea wouldn't hit Alessandro, he didn't trust Collene's father.

The Karmison residence was a little outside of town, and he buried his hands in the pockets of his jeans, wishing for his favorite hoodie. There was something about your favorite pair of jeans or this exact sweater that made you feel a little more secure with who you were. His little piece of security was back at Aly's. What irony—since she already owned his heart and soul, she should also own what little else still mattered to him.

It took him nearly forty-five minutes to reach the mansion, and even then, he realized that as much as he wanted to see Alessandro, he never wanted to enter that house again.

It took a few moments for someone to open the door after he rang the doorbell. Jam had never seen the maid before, and he didn't care.

"I'm Jamison Loane, and I'm here to see my son. Tell Mrs. Karmison that, please."

"That's my dad. I heard my dad! That's my dad!"

He could hear Alessandro, and his heart sped up. At least he was okay so far.

"Zack…"

"That's not my name! Dad!" Jam forced himself to stay exactly where he was. It was hard to follow Shannon's advice, but if he wanted to reach anything without involving Aly, he needed to stay within the limits of the law.

There were noises of a struggle then he heard a hiss, and the next moment, children's feet were hurrying across the marble of the foyer. "Dad!" Jam knelt and then spread his arms to catch his son. The little body was shaking, but Jam was sure it was just from the exercise and nothing else.

"Are you okay?"

"No. I was mean to Mom, and now, I want to go back. I want to see Tom and the waves. I miss the water. I only went with this woman because she said I could see you, but she lied. And she calls me Zack. I'm not Zack. I don't understand why I'm here and not with you. Can I go back? This woman even said my mom isn't my mom."

Jam should have known the Karmisons would go with the truth, and it made him realize that after all this was over, his son would most likely need a psychologist, too.

"I'm so sorry," Jam whispered, and Alessandro hugged him tighter.

"Me, too." Even though he was sure that Lesso had no idea what he was apologizing for, Jam still patted his back.

"No one's mad at you, buddy, but you need to hold out a little longer. I'm gonna get you out, okay? I'm sure they gave you a lot of stuff."

"I don't want any of that. I want to go back home."

Jam only nodded.

"I know, but the best thing you can do is play Xbox or whatever you have there. Do what they tell you to do, okay? Promise me," he pleaded, grabbing his son's shoulders.

"But Dad!" he instantly protested.

"You need to promise me!"

"Why are you crying?" Alessandro asked, reaching out to brush a tear away. Jam took a deep breath, hoping to gain control of his emotions. He was too scared that they would hit his stubborn son eventually. It could lead to terrible injuries since Alessandro was small and the Karmisons didn't know their strength.

"Because I'm scared for you. Those people aren't nice. Just listen to them, okay? I'll be back soon."

He heard heels clicking on the floor, and he knew time was running out. Thea came into view, holding her thigh.

"You kicked me," she almost screamed, and Lesso pressed himself closer to his father. Jam picked him up just so he was towering over the woman who was responsible for his son at the moment.

"He wanted to see his dad. Hello, Thea. I just needed to see that he was fine."

"Took you long enough to come," she snapped, and Jam swallowed, telling himself not to let the woman provoke him. The truth was that for a day, he had dealt with Aly's more than pissed and worried brother, then he had taken a day to regroup, and after that, he had met Shannon. They had discussed how to make those meetings happening without the Karmisons realizing what he was doing, and they agreed that it would look best if he were dating her. So it was lunch, dinner, and unexpected visits until she had a rough idea of what was going on. And she had advised him to stay away at the moment, but since he had a feeling he had lost Aly for the second time in as many weeks, he needed something to hold on to. He needed a reminder of whom he was doing this for.

"I'll be back soon. Please, believe me, Lesso. I love you, okay? Be a good boy."

"Soon, Dad," Alessandro pleaded so quietly no one else could have heard. Jam nodded and then let go of his boy.

"I'm so sorry, Grandma. I was just too excited to see Dad." Alessandro looked at Jam and then got out his sweet boy smile. "Do you still have time to look at the birds with me?" he then asked Thea. Instantly, the older woman's face softened, and Jam breathed deeply.

"I'll be back soon to check on him," Jam said loudly.

"I can't wait, Dad. See you soon. Grandma and I will watch the doves now." His son was such a smart boy, reaching for Thea's hand.

"Until soon," Thea said coldly then she walked away and Jam left, hoping for a beer and a moment of peace.

～

*I*t was hell for Aly to walk through her routines without having to take care of Alessandro. She got dressed, opened the café, and then managed to talk to patrons who came in. She knew most of them were out for gossip since she looked like a ghost and Alessandro was gone.

"Where's that handsome boy of yours, darling?" an elderly lady asked, coming in. Aly recognized her from the Women's Committee, and she pulled up a shoulder.

"Meeting a redhead back in his hometown," she whispered, and the lady placed a hand over her heart, looking appalled.

"Now, I don't believe that. Miss Rhyme, he was head over heels in love with you. My Bernie, bless his soul, he would look at me like that. There wasn't a chance in Heaven or hell for him to notice any other woman. This boy would never leave you for anything in the world," the woman explained, and Aly noticed how the whole café had turned silent, all trying to catch the words.

"Since he wasn't really mine, I can't say anything concerning that. Alessandro's dad and I probably never were meant to be," she said quietly, and the woman took her coffee, sitting down at the table closest to the counter.

"Tell me about the first time you knew you were in love with him."

Aly wasn't sure if this would make things better or worse, but she figured it would at least keep her occupied and her patrons returning for more. People were suckers for a heartbreaking story.

She moved around the counter and then pushed herself up on it, collecting her thoughts.

"Jamison was older than I was by three years, and he was always such a handsome boy. I was fifteen, about to turn sixteen when one afternoon Greg, my brother, and Jamison got out of the car ..."

"*Honestly, do we need to take your little sister along?" Aly felt her little heartbreak. She was so happy about the new bikini she had gotten the day before and how she filled it out at least a little. She didn't have any of the boobs those girls from Jamison's class had, but she had some.*

As the boys passed her, Jam didn't even look at her, and Aly sighed. She had a crush on him and her best friend, Mary, always made fun of it, but seriously, how was a girl supposed to see other guys when Mr. Hottie himself was her brother's best friend?

"Yeah, we do. Hop in, Aly," Greg called out to her, and she took a deep breath, walking slowly toward the car. She was excited to go to the nearby lake with them, but Mary had ingrained in her that she needed to look cool and relaxed.

"Pigtails, really?" Jam snorted up front, and Aly touched her hair. She had heard him telling one of the cheerleaders the day before that her pigtails were sexy, so Alessia had instantly taken note of it. Now, she wanted to cry, especially since Jam still hadn't looked at her.

"Lighten up, man. You can still be nice to all the girls! Aly is probably gonna meet her own people there," Greg announced, getting back in the car with them after having gotten the picnic basket.

"Yeah, some will be there," she mumbled, ready to cry at the perspective of not spending the afternoon with Jam by her side. She'd be the coolest kid in school then. So much for that plan.

"Flake, too?" Greg asked, and Aly noticed how Jam's eyes flickered to meet hers in the mirror. There was something dark in them, and she couldn't help but feel challenged by it.

"Definitely. He's hot," she said casually, seeing from where she was

sitting how Jam's jaw ticked. It made her smile, but she pressed her lips together to keep it from escaping.

"He's a manwhore. He hangs out with the pretty girls and tells them all they are the one," Jam commented, his voice low with fury.

"I don't see how he's any different from you then," she gave back, almost gasping at her own boldness. She never talked to Jam like this. In fact, she never talked to Jam at all.

Greg burst out laughing, punching Jam's shoulder. "She got you there, man." He grinned and Jam turned to him, lifting an eyebrow with a smile.

"At least, I'm handsome. Flake is just skin and bones."

"Well, you clearly haven't checked out his ass yet," she snapped as Greg parked the car. Maybe she should reconsider crushing on Jam. He was a damn idiot. She opened her door, trying to grab all her clothes at once, but she still felt her towel hitting the concrete of the parking lot. Before she could bend down, Jam was there, picking it up and gently placing it on her shoulder, his fingertips brushing her bare skin. She held her breath, knowing she probably looked at him with parted lips, but she just couldn't get herself to shut her mouth. Her heart was doing crazy things in her chest, and she wanted to melt on the spot. The way he was looking down at her was what fantasies were made of.

Just then, the unthinkable happened and Jam reached out, touching one curly pigtail and letting it glide through his fingers. "No, I haven't, but I've heard enough about him. Be careful around him, Aly. He eats girls like you for breakfast," he warned, but there was nothing dangerous in his words. They were more like a silent plea. It was then that Aly knew she wasn't just crushing on Jam. She was in love with him.

"... *H*e turned around and then walked away. Not two steps from where I was standing, he slapped a cheerleader on her skinny ass while I stood there, arms full of my towel and a bag and whatever else I thought I needed to carry. Greg came around and patted my head, saying something about Jam being Jam. I think he knew back then what I was feeling."

Aly actually smiled to herself. She hadn't thought about that day in so long, and now, looking back, it suddenly seemed so different. Jam's expression was a lot softer, his words a lot less annoying, and his face so much more beautiful than before. It had been scar-free back then.

"I think that boy was in love with you back then already," a woman her own age commented. Aly hadn't seen her before, so she guessed that she, too, had been drawn in by the gossip.

"I don't know if it was anything that serious for him, but I guess he really did see me as something other than his best friend's little sister," she admitted, hopping down from the counter to get back to preparing coffee. Six or seven people had asked for a refill, and she happily provided that then she looked up as the door opened.

Just like with Jam when he had come in, people were staring at Spencer now. Her heart had skipped a beat before now plummeting in disappointment. As soon as people realized it was not Jamison walking in, they dismissed Spence as unimportant, starting up little whispered conversations. Aly heard Jam's name more than once, and she knew it wasn't fair to Spencer, but she couldn't help it, either. If she had a choice, she'd prefer to be talking about Jam, too. Only then did she notice his tense expression and she cocked her head.

"Someone's trying to put you in prison," Spencer announced without further ado, and her jaw dropped. "I know, Alessia. I got a letter telling me everything." He waved a paper, and she looked around her little escape, noticing that suddenly Spencer was a lot more interesting than before.

"And you tell me that here and right now why?" she asked, suppressed anger coloring her voice.

He leaned in closer; lowering his voice just enough so she knew he didn't mean to patronize her. "Because if I get information like that and don't do anything about it, they'll find another person until you're eventually reported and brought in," he fussed, and she shook her head in disbelief.

"No, I don't…" She reached for the paper, snagging it from him and then reading it. "They deliberately left out why I did it," she whispered, and he arched a brow, waiting. She crossed her arms, knowing she was challenging him. "You don't think there's a good reason, do you?"

He closed his eyes and then drowned his hands in his hair, looking as if he was ready to tear it out. "I'm here alone, aren't I? I was hoping it wasn't true," he admitted, and she looked at him, waiting. "Tell me. Right now, right here," he demanded, and she pressed her hands flat on the countertop.

"He was Jam's, and just like his father, he was being abused. Except he was only a baby. Jamison handed him over to me when he was no older than four months and asked me to take him away. I refused... until Jam unwrapped the blanket and a bruised body appeared. I didn't know there was more to the mother's beating until Jam returned and I saw his scars. So did I do something illegal? Yes. Do I regret it? No." She held Spencer's eyes, knowing though that everyone else in that room had heard her.

"How bad?"

"Jam feared for his life. He stayed away because he worried someone could figure it out," she explained.

"Well, girl, someone did. The woman who took away your son. How did she do it?" The elderly woman, who earlier had talked about her and her husband, got up and came over.

"How did she do what?" Aly wanted to know and another woman got up.

"How did she figure out that you had the child? Did Jam tell her?" she inquired, joining the little group forming in front of Aly's counter.

"She said she remembered from the one time he said I was beautiful. I kidnapped her grandchild, and she figured it out because of something he said," she whispered, surprised at how free it made her feel to talk about it with strangers who, very clearly, weren't judging her.

"It probably was the way he said it. It felt real to her. She saw on his face that he loved you. Have you ever been a couple?" another woman chimed in, and Alessia shook her head.

It was weird, but she suddenly didn't care if they locked her up. She still had the pictures the doctor had taken back then of the injuries on Alessandro's body. This way she could at least try to get a lawsuit and make sure Jam would get her son. Maybe she should return to Townsend. Someone needed to stop the Karmisons.

"No, never. I didn't think he ever had feelings for me, but it seems I was wrong all those years. He tried to protect Alessandro and me by staying away. No court of law would ever let me get away with what I did, no matter the reason. And everything was fine until this woman showed up because her abusive daughter is missing. I'm functioning, but that's about all."

"My son's a lawyer, girl. I can call him up. This is not fair. You're being bullied," one of her regulars, Mrs. Cleo, announced.

"I kidnapped a child," she reminded them, but the old woman just waved her off.

"You saved him. And by the way his father looked at you, I don't think he thinks you kidnapped his child, either," she explained, but Aly had a hard time seeing right as tears flooded her eyes.

"How do you know I'm telling you the story the way it is? How can you trust my word this easily?" she questioned out loud, realizing that the lady from the Women's Committee had joined her behind the counter and now hugged her tight.

"You're part of this community. We've known you since you arrived, missy. There's nothing we don't know, and your good heart is more than obvious to everyone here."

A few agreeing noises came from all corners of the room. "Besides, we ain't letting a stranger take away the woman who makes the best hot cocoa around here," Mrs. Cleo called out, and Aly felt the tears dripping down her cheeks. Getting up this morning, she had never expected the day to turn out like this, but now, she was actually glad she had opened the café after all.

~

*J*am threw open the door, feeling exhausted. He had been sanding shutters all day, the sun burning down on his back. A few times, he had been tempted to take off his shirt, but then he remembered why he never showed his skin anymore.

"Jamison?"

Great, Greg was pissed. It was exactly what Jam had *not* wanted when coming home. "I need a shower." It had been more than five days since he had seen Alessandro and almost two weeks since he had walked out of Aly's life. The unknown number, his personal demon, kept him updated on the fact that Spencer was a constant companion for Aly. There weren't any more hugging pictures, but it still cut deep.

"Your shower can wait. We have guests." Jam paused at the stairs, closing his eyes.

"Just a minute," he almost pleaded.

"Hey, Jamison."

He opened his eyes, staring at Aly's best friend.

"She can't be here. Philomena, I try everything to keep her out of this whole mess, and she just walks into that town?" He wanted to throw something.

"She's not here. I just needed to see you alone. I mean before you walk in there." Something in her eyes made Jam pause. She was looking like he felt—somewhat broken and a lot worried.

"What's up?" he finally asked, settling down on the stairs. He could think of better places to have an endless talk, but she didn't look as if she was moving.

"You don't look like a happy man," Philomena commented, and he sat up straighter. Anger surged through him. She had to be fucking kidding.

"I left your town after having a fight with the woman I try to protect at all costs. I walked out on her after thoroughly fucking with her mind and then receive a call because my son has been taken away from her, hurting her even more in the process. She's sad, heartbroken, and lonely. I'm not allowed to see my son unless his evil grandmother lets me into the house. I can't seem to find a solution that keeps Alessia out of prison yet finally solves all this. Besides that... I miss her like a parched man misses water. For thirteen years, I was okay with watching her, or not even that, but those seven days I actually held her changed everything. I know what I could have had if Collene wouldn't have been in my life. I'm lying awake at night, staring at the ceiling. How in the world am I supposed to be a happy man?" Maybe he could do the whole psychologist thing. He seemed to be quite articulate when it came to baring his soul. Then he shook his head. Telling Aly's best friend about the feelings he had concerning Alessia was something different from explaining to a stranger all the ways Collene had marked his body.

Phil fumbled with her phone, making him curious. "Someone is going to quite a length to make her believe otherwise. I know she's hurting a lot about Alessandro being gone, and she tells herself that this is all she should be worrying about, but I saw it on her face, Jam. She thought you were lying to her all the time you've been there," Phil reported and then showed him pictures of him and Shannon. It almost made him laugh out loud because now he could guess what Spence really was doing at Aly's place.

Getting out his phone, he showed her the photos he had gotten, his heart surprisingly light. He hadn't even realized how much the thought of having pushed Aly into Spencer's arms had bothered him.

"I called him when I realized Dorly and I would be leaving her alone," Philomena explained, almost outraged. "Jam, you should have seen her. She didn't eat, and she didn't sleep much. She just stared at the water and cried." So Dorly was the second guest waiting for him. He almost felt bad that the only mother figure Aly had was now gone from her side, too, even if it was only temporary.

"Why did you come?" Phil shrugged and hugged herself. It

reminded him of the way Alessia had tried to hold herself together the night they had fought.

"Someone needed to come and make sure that..." She shook her head, searching for words. It was then that Jam understood.

"You thought I was just hanging out with my girlfriend while her son was being tortured by his family," he concluded, and she pulled up her shoulders another time.

"All we had to go on was how you looked at Aly and the way that woman was allowed to touch you. You hugged her. We didn't know what to think. Aly didn't know what to think. And Jam, if what she told us about you is true, we wondered how you'd be able to stop worrying about your son to date." A pleading look was on her face. She wanted him to forgive her, forgive them, for having thought he'd just leave and betray Aly like that.

"So far she's my only hope to free Aly from the threat hanging over her head and she tried really everything, but I refuse to have Alessia here."

"Same," Phil agreed, not really surprising him. It still made him smile. "She was ready to come, Jam, and to be honest, I don't think all of that was for Alessandro," she admitted, and Jam shook his head. Man, he wanted to see Aly. He wished he could make her forget for just a little while.

The doorbell rang, and Jam cursed. He'd never get to have his shower. "I got it," he called out so Greg wouldn't even bother to get up. Phil stayed in the hallway with him, and he turned the knob. Before the door was even fully open, Shannon breezed in, already chatting away.

"Your girl obviously is much more amazing than we gave her credit for," she stated, and Jam picked up a brow. He doubted that because he knew exactly how great she was. "I got a call today from a very nice young man. His name is Lenard Cleo. Does that ring a bell?"

"That's probably the son of one of Alessia's regulars," Phil chimed in, and Shannon turned to her, beaming.

"Exactly. Hey, I'm Shannon. You must be Alessia Rhyme's best friend, Philomena."

Jam hid a smirk as Phil's jaw almost hit the floor.

"I'm a lawyer. I need to know my shit." Shannon grinned, and Jam shook his head.

"I told her about you," he clarified, and Phil nodded slowly while Shannon's expression softened.

"How is she? I've heard so much about her that I feel as if I know her personally," the lawyer whispered, and Jam was relieved as the shadow of a smile appeared on Phil's face.

"If you'd talk to her, I assume she wouldn't like you very much, but besides that, she is desperate and sad, I'd say," Philomena guessed, and Shannon gave Jam a questioning look, but he just waved it off.

"She's trying very hard to get herself taken into custody." The disapproval was clear in Shannon's voice, and Jam pushed away from the wall he was leaning against.

"What?" Greg and Dorly now joined them before Shannon could reply. Jam gave Greg and her a moment to say a proper hello then he waved a hand in front of her face.

"Care to elaborate?"He wanted to know, and Shannon nodded.

"I got a call today from Lenard Cleo because obviously half or more of Sunrow knows what Aly had done. That guy, her boyfriend—"

"He's not her damn boyfriend, for God's sake. I called him so Aly wouldn't be alone," Philomena protested, and Shannon raised her hands, trying to pacify Aly's friend.

"Well, seems there's more going on here. Someone's sending letters to her friends, telling them she kidnapped a child. We can be glad Spencer went to her first to ask for an explanation. She told everyone in the café her version of the truth, and they went wild. The support she's getting extends as far as her having a pro bono attorney. We need to fly out there and talk to him, Jam. Are you free in the next days? It won't be longer than three," she promised. "Lenard sounds really nice, and if we play our cards right, Alessia might not ever see a prison from the inside." That was all that mattered to Jam. Plus, he'd be able to see Aly.

The smile that almost appeared on his face vanished, though, the moment he realized he couldn't leave. "No, Shannon, I can't go with you. Alessandro is with the Karmisons still. I won't leave."

"Collene has not been seen, and I don't think anyone else will harm the boy. You need to go there, Jamison," Shannon insisted.

"Why?"

"Because someone needs to stop Aly from doing stupid things."

Since no one protested, Jam just lowered his head. "Can I at least shower before we talk more?" he asked, and Greg slapped his back.

"Definitely. You stink."*Thank God for best friends*, Jam thought with a grin. They always managed to make you smile no matter how terrible the situation was. And Greg definitely was a pro at that, making him irreplaceable in Jam's life.

*I*t was a foggy morning and the water looked almost as pale as the sky above it. Aly was drinking coffee and enjoying a time off. After the excitement the day before, she had decided to take a few quiet hours. She had even told Spencer to stay away. She knew he was only worried, but Aly needed to clear her head. It was scary knowing people were finally in on her big, bad secret, yet she felt liberated in many ways.

"I don't know what it is about mornings, but you're never more beautiful than in those early hours." Her mind was playing tricks on her. She was wishing for Jam so bad, she even heard him.

"Stop torturing me," she pleaded in a low voice, hoping her brain would follow suit and just stop its tempting whisper.

"I'm not here to hurt you more," the voice in her head promised, and she closed her eyes, hiding her face in her hands. She couldn't take any memory of Jam, especially not the way his voice caressed her skin. "Alessia, look at me," the voice pleaded and then warm hands engulfed her own, taking them away. In utter surprise, her eyes sprang open, and she found green ones staring at her warm and tear-filled.

"I'm so sorry," Jam whispered over and over again until Aly couldn't help but shake her head. He shouldn't be with her; as much as she had wished he'd be so she could make things right with him, he needed to be back in Townsend with Alessandro.

"You left our son... your son alone back home? With no one to watch over him?" she screamed, starting to beat her fists against his chest in a rapid succession. He caught her wrists, pulling her close so she had no room to move.

"Greg will check on him, and so will Phil and Dorly. They'll figure something out. Your lawyer called my lawyer, which, by the way, is the woman in the picture," he said carefully, still holding onto her wrists as if he was worried she'd hit him again. Just then, she remembered who stood in front of her and instant regret took over her body. *She had hit him.* As if he hadn't suffered enough. Appalled at her own actions, she stepped back, raising her offending hands to her mouth.

"I'm so sorry, Jam. I shouldn't have hit you. I just didn't... I was so upset, but it's no excuse to hurt you like that! I'm so sorry!" She stepped back farther, but another time, he reached for her hands, making sure she met his eyes.

"In contrast to what you might think, you aren't that strong, Aly. You couldn't hurt me with that. I've known much worse. I understand you're upset, and you have every right to be." He caressed her knuckles and then raised her hands to his lips to kiss her palms before pressing them against his cheeks. "I could even understand if you tell me to get lost after all I said to you the last time I was here. I felt cornered, so I attacked. You didn't deserve that."

She heard the words but couldn't believe he was apologizing.

"Stop it, Jamison! Just stop it! I had no right to say the things I did. I had no right to push you as I did. It was my fault you lashed out. And by any means, I have no illusions about your sex life. And while it maybe didn't mean anything to you what we shared, it—" He hushed her with his fingertips on her lips. She had missed him so much; this little touch gave her tingles like none had in a long time.

"Aly..." he just whispered, shaking his head in disbelief. She could see it all on his face—worry, regret, longing—and it made her weak. Looking at him, she knew he could make her forget her pain just for a little while.

"Jam," she gave back, just holding his glance while taking a deep breath. She had imagined what it would be like to make love to him for the last decade, but ever since he'd been with them, every night he slept innocently next to her, her heart had been racing and she had wondered how it would be. Now, she needed to find out, and nothing short of her son returning would keep her from it.

~

*J*am saw the change in her posture, and it made his breath hitch.

"Do you have anywhere to be?" she asked, her eyes getting dark as she let her gaze roam over his body. They had everywhere to be, but Jam couldn't care less. Shannon was meeting that Lenard-guy, and maybe it wasn't the worst idea to let the two lawyers talk it out first. They could do without them for a few hours, right? Besides, he had wanted to make it up to Aly, and he was more than glad he had the chance now. No one knew what would happen once he and Shannon returned to Townsend. He had an uneasy feeling in his stomach, a sense of foreboding hanging over his head like a cloud in a stormy sky.

Without an answer, he drew her close, kissing her as if his life depended on it. Even though that was not the case, she could very well affect his sanity.

"Good," she breathed against his lips, and he picked her up, carrying her back to her own house. He didn't bother locking the door. He didn't even bother making sure that it had fully shut before carrying her up the stairs. He had expected this to be a frantic thing—tearing off clothes, nibbling on lips—but suddenly, she looked as if she was afraid of him.

"What now?" he asked, frustration making him sound whiny. Amusement had entered her eyes before she sobered again.

"You didn't like it much when I undressed you. In fact, I had the feeling you didn't like undressing. Period," she explained carefully, not meeting his eyes any longer. He placed her on the bed and then leaned over her, one hand on either side of her beautiful face.

"For the things I have in mind, and the ones you obviously have been thinking about, I kinda need to get out of my clothes."Even if it made him feel uncomfortable. Especially since he couldn't cloak the room in darkness. She must've seen something in his eyes since she reached out and then moved to kiss him gently. With her movements only, she forced him to sit back on his heels, making his whole body accessible to her. She cupped the back of his neck, drawing herself closer to him while intensifying the kiss. It was crazy, but his whole body instantly stood at attention. Her lips traveled down his jaw line, brushing the slight shadow of a beard he kept carefully trimmed. Her reaction to his other scars had been enough; he didn't need her to know he had more than just the cut on the lip on his face.

Tentative, yet without taking her mouth from his skin, she brushed her hands under his shirt and he involuntarily tensed. If she realized it, she didn't let on, just pushing the material higher and then pausing long enough to pull it over his head and throw it to the floor. Her eyes stayed on his face as she leaned in and then kissed him again, letting her hands touch his skin. He watched her until her fingertips brushed his chest and then his nipples. He hissed, sensations exploding in his body. It was as if for years he had kept himself from feeling the little things, making him feel the way her nails teased his skin, the hot trail her lips were leaving on his neck, or the way her shaky breath zigzagged over his shoulder every time she exhaled all the more intense.

He let his head fall back, deciding to fully enjoy her sweet torture for now. He didn't mind her taking over control because he knew she was nothing like Collene. With Aly it would be a kind of giving and taking; raw desire reflected in every one of her movements.

She nipped and bit lightly wherever she liked until Jam was ready to come in his pants. She knew exactly how to be gentle yet tempting. When she pointed him to lie down, he swallowed. She instantly went for the buckle of his belt, her hands brushing the erection straining against his jeans, ready for her to worship.

"Aly, Aly, Aly," he forced out, his voice rough with need and longing while he grabbed her arms, trying to stop her. "If you touch me one more time, this is not gonna take long for both of us," he promised, but the glint in her eyes told him that she didn't care.

Pants and boxers were gone at once, and he was naked on the bed while she looked down at him, licking her lips. She was the sexiest thing he had ever seen, and he needed to get her undressed *pronto*!

Crawling to where she was standing at the edge of the bed, he felt strangely liberated. No matter which scars he had, she didn't mind in the slightest. In fact, he almost felt handsome with the way she looked at him. It was something no one else had ever been able to give him, and Jam suddenly wanted to propose to her right there and then because, rain or shine, he wanted her tied to him. Somehow, though, he figured asking her to marry him naked with his cock hanging out in the cold air probably wasn't what she expected or deserved. Besides, Alessandro wasn't yet safe. Going down on one knee would have to wait until after they'd solved this situation.

"You're looking at me funny. Don't get me wrong, I don't mind staring at your absolute divine sight, but this kinda makes me nervous," she said in a hushed whisper, and Jam grinned, having her under him before she had even realized he had reached for her.

Her delighted giggle made him take a deep, calming breath, especially since he wanted to wipe that smug smile off her face. He pushed her shirt up and pulled the cups of her bra down until they didn't cover her breasts anymore, but supported them, making her nipples jut out to him. He leaned down, sucking them between his teeth until she all but writhed underneath him, her fingers digging into the sheets. He let his tongue tease the sensitive peak before switching sides and applying the same treatment to her free breast. Aly panted, goose bumps covering her body as he gently blew on the skin he had just worried with his teeth. Another time he leaned in, now cupping one breast with his hand while taking care of the other. It was a game he enjoyed playing until she cried out his name in a desperate plea.

She wanted more, and he was definitely ready to give it to her.

~

*A*ly was sure Jam meant to kill her with anticipation. She wanted them to become one, but instead, he kept teasing her skin until she was ready to take matters into her own hands. As if he had felt the direction her thoughts went, he finally kissed his way lower and lower until his handsome face vanished between her thighs, making her panic. It had been forever since she'd been close to a guy, but never before had she allowed anyone to kiss, let alone do other stuff, where Jam was heading right now.

"Jamison," she started just when he put his mouth on her and deliberately swiped his tongue up and down slowly. "Oh, my God," she moaned, her body tingling in all the right places.

"Still want me to stop?" he asked, his eyes shining with mischief. So he had known exactly what she intended to say.

Her thoughts were jumbled, yet she tried to collect her wits enough to reply. "Well," she started just as he lowered his lips again, flicking the tip of his tongue over her sensitive nub in a few quick successions until she bowed off the bed, drowning her hands in his hair. He pulled her closer, holding her hips still while varying between letting her have his whole tongue and just the tip. She couldn't say what she liked more, but there was no question that both brought her close to a very intense orgasm. Just then, he started to suck her sensitive nub between his teeth, biting down ever so slightly. It was enough to make her call out his name as she came. He didn't stop, drawing her pleasure out until she was a shivering mess.

He looked too damn self-satisfied when he came up to meet her lips, and she absolutely didn't like that. They both should be on the same page.

He actually was cocky enough to smack his lips and rest back against the headboard in all his naked glory; looking like a man who had just cured an incurable disease.

"You feel pretty good about yourself, don't you?" she asked, moving slowly, realizing her voice was huskier than she thought.

He just gave her another grin, and she leaned over him, biting her lip while he was watching her.

Jam just popped an eyebrow, looking a lot less smug as she wrapped her fingers around his erection, gently moving her hand up and down, actually lowering her eyes to the task at hand. "Aly?" he inquired quietly and then made her meet his gaze again.

She crawled closer, still holding onto him before positioning herself right above his cock. His eyes widened as she lowered herself down on him. It gave her intense pleasure to watch the way he drew in a sharp breath and then threw his head back, his fingers digging into the same sheets she had gripped not ten minutes prior.

She rode him slowly, set on driving him just as crazy as he had done to her. The problem was that she hadn't exactly considered how much it would turn her on, too. She placed her hands flat on his chest, staring into his eyes while she made sure that neither of them was able to think further than those four walls that surrounded them right there and then.

~

*J*am kissed Aly's forehead, knowing they couldn't stay away from reality forever. She was somewhere between sleeping and being awake. "We need to leave," he mumbled, and she shook her head against his chest.

"If I get up now and you get up now, we need to deal with the fact that our son—"He loved how she now called him that. "—is gone, and that we shouldn't have spent the last hour..." He hushed her with his lips on hers because the way that sentence would have ended wasn't right.

"We did exactly what we should have done. I'd even let you sleep for a few hours because I don't think you've had much sleep over the last days, but there are lawyers to tend to and solutions to find," Jam whispered against her hair, then kissed her another time before getting up. He pulled his boxers over his hips, glancing back at her. She looked like a mess, and he missed the happy glow from just a few minutes earlier.

"Lenard told me that there's no legal scenario where I can get Alessandro back. He's not my son by blood nor by law. Besides, I will go to prison if you try to get your son, Jamison. Do you even realize that?"

Jam knew it, but he was determined to find a loophole, and the way he saw it, so were Lenard and Shannon. Which was exactly why they needed to move now.

"If you stay where you are, they've won. Don't let them win," he pleaded, and she shrugged; a movement so small he knew how little hope she had left.

"They already did, Jamison."

Suddenly, he knew exactly what Dorly and Phil had talked about when they had sworn Aly needed him. She was worse off than he had guessed. "Alessia, when in the world did you turn into someone who had no hope?" He knew he shouldn't be challenging her, but he couldn't help it. She had been Miss Optimistic for as long as he could remember. He wouldn't deny that things looked bleak, but giving up the battle before they even started? No, he wouldn't let that happen. Sitting down on the bed, he cupped her cheek, seeing how she closed her eyes.

"Jam..." He leaned in and kissed her until they were both breathing hard, and then he pulled back.

"Move that cute ass off the bed now and get pretty. We'll fix this. Somehow, we'll fix this," he promised, and Aly watched him for a long moment before nodding and getting off the bed.

∾

*A*ly sat next to Jam in silence, letting him drive her car because she wouldn't be able to focus enough. It was crazy, but she didn't look forward to hearing anyone tell her how many years in a federal prison she'd get. Or what Jam would get for having kidnapped his son. At least he hadn't brought Alessandro over state lines. Alessia had made the mistake of looking up penalties on Google, and even though her knowledge of legal speech was very limited, she had read enough to shut down her browser immediately and break out in cold sweat.

She hadn't told anyone that she had dared to look it up, but the way Jam was acting, she was sure he hadn't.

They parked in front of her café, and she was startled. "Spencer opened up for us. It's just for private business, seriously. I didn't want to do it in your house. I think there are enough bad memories there now. We don't need to add any more," Jam explained quietly. Obviously, Phil had told them where to find her key. She couldn't help but be glad since the café alone usually offered her solace.

"Let's do this," Aly said, getting out of the car. Spence welcomed her in the door and hugged her tight. She could tell it was for Jam's benefit, and it made her shake her head slightly. "Don't start anything with him today, Spencer," she pleaded in a low voice, and he sighed.

"I'm sorry. Of course, not," he promised and then shook hands with Jam. It was obvious the two guys didn't like each other much, yet Spencer proved how grand a man he was by telling Jam how sorry he was about this whole situation.

"So am I," Jam replied, placing his hand on the small of her back to lead her inside. Just a second later, Aly understood his need to mark his territory because the redhead from the pictures was sitting at a table across from Lenard. It made Aly ready to kiss Jam smack on the mouth. Obviously, she must've tensed because he leaned in and kissed the side of her head.

"Just a friend," he promised, not really easing her worries. She had never known herself to be that jealous; then again, Jam had never been hers for the keeping before, either.

Shannon got up and instantly pulled her in a hug. "Hi, I'm Shannon, Greg's girlfriend and Jam's lawyer," she explained, but Aly didn't like the way she called him Jam. It didn't matter that everyone else did, too, she felt as if the right should lie with her only.

"Hey, I'm Alessia," she replied and then focused on the people she actually knew in the room—Lenard and his mother.

"Mrs. Cleo." Aly smiled, being a lot warmer toward those two than she had been toward Shannon. Behind her, she could hear the woman whisper with Jam, but she tried to ignore it.

Eventually, they all settled down, and Jam reached for her hand again. The grave expressions on the lawyers' faces told her everything she needed to know. It took everything within her not to burst into tears at their sight.

"It's legally not possible to get you and Jam out of going to prison unless a mistake is made during the trial," Shannon started.

"It's legally not possible to get you and Jam out of going to prison. Period," Lenard corrected, and Aly pressed her lips together, let go of Jam and fisted her hands. She felt her nails biting into the soft flesh of her palm. It didn't help much to ease her heavy heart. Faintly, she heard the key being turned in the lock and looked up to find Spencer by the door.

"There is, however, a possibility you will only have to spend a few days in there, but for that, Aly needs to return to Townsend with us," Shannon whispered, lowering her voice in secrecy.

"I can't. Alesandro's grandmother made that quite clear," Aly replied.

"She threatened you, that's right. She will have the police take you in. This town's as corrupt as it gets. We need to hope for a mistake by the police," Shannon went on, and Aly got up. She couldn't possibly sit.

"So you are saying you count on a mistake by the police to keep Aly out of prison? Do you even hear yourself?" Jam asked, and Aly saw how Shannon threw Lenard a glance.

"I'm going to be frank here. The mishandling of cases happens more often than you think. Miranda rights forgotten, the subject handled too roughly, or evidence not properly processed—those are all things that make it necessary for a judge to dismiss a case.

Aly would be in prison for no more than a week at max, and she could never be tried for Alessandro's kidnapping again," Lenard tried to soothe Jam, but Aly could tell it wasn't working.

"She didn't kidnap him. I won't let her go to prison for something I did. You're hoping for a technicality to keep her out of prison. The Karmisons will make sure that everything, and I repeat *everything*, will go according to law. They'll be eternally happy if Aly and I are locked up. While I don't give a shit what happens to me, I'm not gonna let her suffer for me!" he cried out, the rage obvious in every rigid line of his body.

Aly moved back to him, placing her hands on his shoulders. "If you go to prison, Alessandro stays with Collene. Do you really want that, Jam?"she inquired, and he let his head drop forward, his shoulders slumping. Defeat had never been written more clearly across a man's body than it was right there at that moment with Jam.

"As it is, Collene has every right to her son, and Jam barely has any. If he wants a chance at sole custody, he can't be tied to the kidnapping," Shannon explained carefully, and Aly felt her body go cold. "Even then, we need to prove that Lesso has an abusive mother or chances are slim to non-existent regardless of his participation."

"So let me do a quick recap," Aly mumbled, making everyone shut up. "If I go to prison, saying I did it all by myself, I'm going to be tried by a federal court since I took the child across state lines. I can be sentenced up to a death, depending on what they think I did to him. Either way, Jam will *not* get custody of his son unless Collene beats the child so bad she's taking him to a doctor. Let's face it.That won't happen. Absolutely no outcome will result in Alessandro being fine, right? Because if Jam takes some of the blame for this kidnapping and we can prove Alessandro was being abused, he's not gonna go to his dad, but end up in foster care, which is probably equally as bad as Collene having him," she concluded, watching for the reaction of the lawyers.

"They never said anything about a death sentence," Jam said the same moment Shannon reached out to grab her hand.

"Not many states have a death sentence for a case like yours. They'd most likely sympathize with you and reduce your sentence. We could always try to negotiate a deal or something," she remarked, and Aly hugged herself, before starting to pace. This wasn't just bad; this was worse.

~

*J*am felt frozen to the spot. No one had ever bothered to mention there was a chance they'd die over this. How had Aly known, though?

"I Googled," she replied, and Jam realized he had spoken out loud. "I needed to know what I was facing. I don't know. I guess I was hoping it said *Blackmail the bitch and you'll get the kid back without problems*," she then admitted, and Jam finally got up to walk over to her. He needed to hold her, touch her, feel her. She evaded his arms, though, and it pissed him off. Didn't she understand they were in this together?

"This, of course, would only happen if there'd be a kidnapping case to begin with," Mrs. Cleo suddenly interrupted the silence, and Aly spun around almost smashing into Jam.

"What?" she asked, and when he reached for her another time, she actually let him draw her close.

"Tell them, son," Mrs. Cleo insisted, and Jam almost growled at the suspense.

"Well, let's say Jam had full custody of his son. Then he could take him wherever he wants, whenever he wants... like, for example, to raise him with his girlfriend out of state. No one could press charges on anyone for anything because it's totally legal for Aly to raise him then. Plus, maybe one day she could actually adopt him so he'd be legally hers if the real mother would be willing to give up her rights," Lenard mentioned, looking at them as if it wasn't a big deal. Only it was.

"I don't have sole custody, and we just settled I won't get it, either," Jam stated while Aly turned in his arm, hiding her face against his chest. She was giving up, and he was tempted to follow close behind, even though the lawyers seemed to look pretty confident.

"How? How in the world should that work?" Spence asked, throwing his hands up. Jam almost liked him then and there. Almost.

"Well, for that we would need leverage on the Karmisons," Shannon whispered as if she feared someone would overhear them.

Jam raised a brow at that. "Leverage? That doesn't sound exactly legal."

Lenard shook his head. "It doesn't even end there. We'd need a judge in this, too," he allowed, and Jam felt how Aly took another deep breath against his chest.

"I'm pretty sure the leverage isn't the problem at all, but the judge would be," Shannon whispered sadly, shaking her head. "That's the only flaw of the plan we developed now... and why we didn't mention it before. We need to legalize Jamison's claim to Alessandro, and for that, I fear we'll have to go a not so legal way, but..."

Aly suddenly jumped away from him. "What would the judge have to do?" she asked almost breathless.

"Sign a custody form that was backdated to when Alessandro was born. It basically means he would have to do something illegal, and we'd have to risk outing you to him. There's a good chance he'd have you arrested, after all," Lenard explained.

"Especially if we consider that the Karmisons probably bought everyone who matters," Shannon injected, and suddenly, Aly was laughing. It was crazy. Jam worried she had lost her mind fully now.

"Alessia," he whispered, cupping her cheek. "Are you okay?"

"If I get the form, can you get the Karmisons to sign it?" she asked, her eyes bright as if she had caught a fever. It made him swallow.

"How?" Shannon interrupted, but Aly just spun around, holding a finger out.

"It's better if you know as little as possible. What would we need to have the document legal? Besides the judge's signature?" she questioned, her breath exhilarated.

Jam wished he could read her mind because she was just not making any sense.

"Well, the mother would have to sign in the presence of either said judge or a lawyer," Shannon announced, and Aly clapped her hands together, laughing again.

"There's hope, Jam! There's hope! You can get your boy back!" She was pinching his cheeks in a moment of total excitement, and he grabbed her wrists.

"Calm the fuck down, Aly," he demanded, but she just shook her head, her dark waves flying excitedly from one side to the other.

"Get the dirt, Jamison Loane. We need to get our son back."

chapter

$\mathcal{A}$ ly didn't want Jamison to go back, yet she knew he had to. He and Shannon had a flight booked late morning the next day, and it hurt her not to know what would happen next. She had a plan, and before she told everyone else, she wanted to make sure it worked. There was a judge she hoped would help her, but if, against everything she believed him to be, he turned her down, she didn't want to involve anyone else.

"I can feel you thinking, Alessia," Jamison mumbled. She laughed as he combed his fingers through her curls.

"How am I supposed to stop when tomorrow you'll go back to Townsend while I have to stay here?" They had decided it wasn't worth taking the risk of the Karmisons having Aly prosecuted just because she couldn't stay away. "I'm not gonna see you, or Alessandro, for quite a while. I miss him so much, but right now, I'm trying to focus on taking it one day at a time. You being here helps, but…"

Jam grabbed her chin and made sure she met his gaze. "You'll get him back," he promised, and she rolled her eyes. She knew he didn't deserve her doubt, especially since the hardest part was on her, but still, she just couldn't help it. Jam actually sat up, almost looking hurt. "I mean what I say," he insisted, and she sat up, too, hoping to soften the anger on his features.

"I don't only want Alessandro back. I might have gotten greedy in the last weeks," Aly admitted, and even though she had been sure it was obvious to Jam, he looked at her with a questioning expression.

"What else could you want?" he asked.

"Nothing less than your heart and soul," she whispered because it *was* what she wanted. She wouldn't agree to take less than everything when it came to Jam. Secretly, she hoped this whole thing would offer Jam some kind of closure. If somehow, by luck or fate or whatever you wanted to call it, they'd get Alessandro back, Jam's business with the Karmisons would be over. They'd no longer have anything on him.

"Aly…" he started then stopped himself. His eyes left her face, going down his bare arms and the scars visible there. For a very long time, he was quiet, almost making Aly wish she had shut up.

"I'm sorry, Jam, you don't…" She broke off as he lifted his haunted eyes to hers.

"No, you're right. You need me whole and not broken. I'm not ready to go to a psychologist, but I want you to know… understand how…" He breathed deeply a few times, and Aly wasn't sure if she should be touching him or not.

As it was, he took the decision from her by getting up and pulling over a long sleeve shirt and his jeans. She noticed he didn't button them up, and even though she shouldn't think about anything but his pain, she couldn't help but lick her lips.

Shaking her head, she focused on him while he walked over to the window. The sun was setting, sending a red glow into the bedroom. Jam's blond hair looked as if it was on fire, his eyes having an almost dangerous hue. The light made the green appear almost black.

He leaned his hands against the window frame, taking a deep breath.

"Jamison," she whispered, not exactly sure what she wanted to say, but he only shook his head.

"It was a party. Collene wanted to show off how well we worked together…"

Aly sat back on the bed, pulling Jam's sweater close. She had a feeling this was going to be a story she wasn't ready to hear naked.

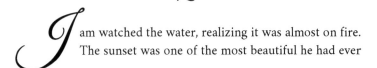

*J*am watched the water, realizing it was almost on fire. The sunset was one of the most beautiful he had ever seen, yet it was almost telling. Aly was going to hate him after this. His world would go down in flames, and he was the one putting the match to the gasoline.

"I usually didn't drink when I was around her, but that night… God, Aly, it was too much. I think I was drunk before most of her friends really showed. She made me wear a suit, or better just the tie and the shirt, dress pants… you know." He shrugged, his throat feeling clogged. He suddenly wasn't sure he could tell the story anymore. Or that he should. Luckily, Aly had decided to stay away from him. He wouldn't be able to deal with her touching him. Just the memory of that evening made him feel dirty.

Pushing away from the window, he thought about how he shouldn't be telling her the story there, in her bedroom, her sanctuary.

"We should go somewhere else," he stated, panic making his voice sound high-pitched.

"We're staying right here, Jamison. Pace all you want, maybe even stop telling the story, but don't run away," she pleaded, and Jam swallowed. He couldn't look at her.

"Aly, you and I shouldn't be together. I'm darker than dark, and you are the brightest star out there. I…" He trailed off, rubbing his hands over the sleeves as if it made the dirt go away.

He needed to get it out now or he was never going to finish.

"She was pissed I was drunk, but her friends loved me. Everyone wanted me. I was the best trophy she had. I guess she figured it was time for punishment. I guess *I* figured it was time for punishment. Either way, I took a girl to her bedroom. I thought maybe, just maybe, Collene would be tired of me if she found me with someone else…"

Her gasp made him pause. "Jam, if the scars on your body are any indication, she was likely to kill you for disobeying like that," she cried, and he slowly nodded. She knew pretty well the most likely scenario.

"I didn't care. You see now how weak I am? I thought it would have been the easy way out." Oh God, he had never admitted that out loud.

"Weak? You stayed with her because of me. Thea Karmison told me when she left. All the people she would've hurt when instead hurting you…" She shook her head, and Jam turned away just enough so he could see her face in the mirror without being obvious about it.

"The girl tied me up. Handcuffs on the bed." He rubbed his wrists, remembering too well the burning he had felt the next morning. "That girl… shit, I don't even remember her name. She went over to the door and said she'd just turn off the light. Next thing I know, Collene is kneeling over me. Of course, I was naked. How else can you get kinky?"

Had he ever hated himself more than he did at that moment, seeing Aly shudder? His voice dripped with sarcasm. Getting into some extra-special sex had *not* been on his agenda that night. He grabbed her dressing table, worrying that his tight grip would splinter it.

"I was drunk. I thought maybe nothing would happen. Hell, how often do you hear that drunk guys can't manage to get it up? Of course, it was just my luck that my body decided it needed some action. After all, there never had been any up until that point. At least not from the moment I started dating that bitch. Frankly, she knew how to do it right, too. I guess she didn't stay abstinent the way I did. Anyway, she…" He gritted his teeth until his ears were ringing.

"I get the idea. She abused you sexually. You were drunk and cuffed to the bed."

"I pretended it was you." His voice was barely a whisper. "It was the only thing that helped to get me through it. You were my happy place. You've always been my happy place even though you never deserved my mess. Alessandro is the result of that night. As much as I hate what she did, the moment I knew she was expecting my child, all I wanted was to make sure the baby would be okay." It had been the only thought driving him from the second she had presented him with the result. She had even blackmailed him, but that was something Aly didn't need to know.

As it was, she was crying silent tears, no longer looking at him. He just saw it through the mirror, her hand pressed against her forehead, the dark hair hiding her wet cheeks. He needed to scrub his skin clean even though he wanted nothing more than to walk over and take her in his arms.

Walking back, he hit the wall next to the door and then turned, stumbling into her bathroom. Tearing the shirt off, he threw it on the floor.

Jam was breathing hard, not able to control his body's reaction. It always ended that way. Every time he thought about that night, he started to shake until he almost wanted to throw up. Sometimes, he wondered if that was how women felt after they had been violated. Only he should have been stronger than that.

He turned the water in the shower on until steam filled the room then he grabbed the nailbrush, rubbing his lower arm under the hot water. His skin burned almost instantly, but in contrast to all the other times, it didn't soothe the feeling of hatred.

"Fuck," he growled, not being able to wash the images from his mind. "Fuck! Fuck! Fuck!" The steaming water turned colder and small hands wrapped around his, halting his movements.

"Jam," Aly whispered, her voice thick with tears. He couldn't look at her. There was no need for her to tell him to get out. He knew he didn't deserve to be with her.

"Just a second," he pleaded, but her hands just turned him away from her, placing his hands against the cold tiles. The jeans he wore stuck to his legs uncomfortably, and he could feel the sweater she still wore was getting soaked. Closing his eyes, he rested his forehead against the cooling porcelain.

The water was falling on his shoulders, running down his back in calming rivers. Suddenly, a soft sponge pressed against his skin, never ceasing to draw slow circles until his ragged breath evened out.

"Turn," Aly ordered quietly. He did, looking at her face while she focused on his skin, cleansing him more thoroughly than he ever had been able to.

"You're amazing," she said loud enough for him to hear over the running water. "You are brave." She kissed his chest, dropping the sponge. "You are incredible." Aly let her hands roam over his chest, his shoulders, down his arms. "And you are mine. This wasn't your fault. None of this was." She gave him a slow smile.

"You still want me?" Why the hell was his voice so rough?

"Are you kidding me? You wear jeans in the shower. They're molded to your body. There's nothing more sexy than this!" She winked and Jam grinned, reaching out to cup the back of her neck and draw her in. Wet and soaked as she was, she still was the most beautiful woman he had ever seen.

"Besides the jeans, though," she mumbled, pulling back until he was looking at her, "I love you, Jam. I never stopped. So please, whatever you will have to deal with, whatever comes, don't be afraid I'll leave or resent you."

He watched her face for a long moment and then picked her up, kissing her with as much love and need as he felt. They stood under the shower, both half-dressed yet fully bare, but he didn't care. Obviously, neither did she as she grabbed his shoulders, his hair, whatever she could reach and hold onto. He wanted to have her just that bit closer, feeling the need to become one with her. It was there, at that moment, Jam decided to make this right eventually. Once the dust had settled and their lives had calmed down a little, they needed to make adjustments. Big adjustments.

"What are you suddenly smiling about?" Aly asked, nibbling on his jaw while softly humming in appreciation.

"I should've known you're the most amazing person in this world, Alessia. I just... ten years is a long time," he whispered against her lip and then felt his heart double its speed as she broke out into a happy laughter.

"Ten years is a lifetime for your son, but for me, it's just another decade I wish I could have spent with you. None of this was your fault. None of this was mine. It just is what it is, and we can't change it. We can decide, though, where we are going from here, handsome. The way I see it is you decided to go forward, so let's make sure there's something to walk to."

She brushed her fingertips across his cheek, down his neck, and along his shoulders. He shivered without really being able to help it while the water still ran down their bodies.

"Let me make you happy," he pleaded, and she smiled, only nodding.

Together, they left the bathroom after getting rid of the wet clothes. Aly looked at him over her shoulder, the dark hair almost black after the shower. Her eyes were shining with hope as she winked and then dropped the terry cloth to the floor, moving forward to the bed.

Jam couldn't help it, reaching out to pull her from her crawling position back against his body. She stretched against him, leaning her head back as he cupped her breast from behind while gently bending her head back a little further, kissing the side of her throat. She moaned as he teased her nipples; hard little pebbles against his palm. They were a perfect fit for him, and he couldn't even begin to comprehend how much this woman meant to him.

He had sacrificed it all for her, and now, she was ready to make it all worthwhile.

∼

*A*ly could finally put a name to an emotion she had always seen on Jam's face, but never once had been able to name —self-hatred. As much as he should know that none of this was his fault, he thought he had deserved every bit of the treatment Collene had reserved for him.

Aly couldn't wait to get a word in with that abusive bitch, yet she knew that had to hold out just a little longer.

The moment Jam pulled her back against him, cupping her breasts, all thought fled her mind, though. He was gentle with her, just like the first few times they had been intimate, but something about his movements was different. It was as if he had a purpose suddenly, and Aly loved it.

She could feel his erection probing her back. As much as she wanted to turn around and grab onto it, Jam had her in a body lock, almost wrapping his body fully around hers. His fingers teased her breasts before wandering lower, and his tongue and lips nipped the side of her neck, her earlobe, and then her lips as she turned to him.

She spread her legs just a little farther for him, knowing she wanted him like a starving woman wanted food. His left hand found her mound, cupping it before gently letting his fingers part her lips and stroke her clit. She instantly shivered, holding her breath to fully enjoy the sensation.

"Aly, you're so wet for me," Jam mumbled next to her ear. "Don't you wish I could push a finger into you and find that exact spot? You know, the one that will make you writhe under my hands? Don't you wish I could push my cock into you deep and give you that orgasm you are heading to?"

Who knew the man could be a naughty talker? Aly certainly wasn't going to complain about his newfound dirty mouth.

"How about you stop talking and let actions follow?" she asked, breathless. She was trembling all over while Jam's index finger kept a regular rhythm, teasing her clit until her knees threatened to give out.

"Just a few more minutes," Jam promised, now placing one arm around her middle, holding her to him when she couldn't hold herself up any longer. "Place your arms around my neck," he whispered and she did, feeling how he pushed two fingers ever so slowly into her before letting them glide back out and across her tight little bud.

"Jamison," she gasped, somewhere between a plea and a protest.

"Right here," he replied in a husky voice that tickled her nerve endings as if it was something tangible. "How about we bend you forward now and I let my cock slowly push into you until you can feel me everywhere inside you?" he asked, and she instantly wanted to move, but he just chuckled, holding her back. "Kiss me first," he pleaded, and she did, turning her head enough so she could lick his tongue with her own, tease and taste him at least a little bit. He was hard against her, so hard, but his patience didn't seem to wane.

Another flip with his fingertip against her clit, another dip of his fingers into her… it just didn't stop. Eventually, she reached the point where she started to move her hips against him just to get a little more friction. She needed a tiny bit more and her world would shatter.

Finally, Jam bent her forward, pulling her hips back against him. She closed her eyes in anticipation, but all he did was lean in to kiss her spine and run his hands up and down her sides. She wiggled her body against him, hearing him chuckle.

"Impatient much?" he asked.

"If you don't hurry, I'll finish myself," she grumbled, finally feeling how he lined up with her and then moved his hips ever so slightly. She wouldn't have it, trying to take over, but he instantly held onto her.

"No, Alessia, this is my dance. I'm leading," he fussed, and she let her head hang in resignation. This anticipation was killing her. Jam lowered his body to hers until he could kiss her neck, being fully buried in her now, withdrawing as he licked his way down her spine, only to push back in and gently let his chin and, therefore, his scruff tickle her skin. The sensations exploded in her body as he repeated the procedure again and again. Eventually, she reached between their legs, finding his balls and gently cupping them. Instantly, he hissed, freezing in position while she gently massaged her newfound treasure.

"You're not playin' fair," he gritted out, and she laughed a throaty laugh, not stopping her movements.

"Stop torturing me then," she answered, and finally, he began a rhythm she liked. Reaching around her stomach, he pulled her up again, her back pressing against his stomach. His movement didn't cease as he brought his attention back to her breasts. Aly was ready to burst.

"Jam, please," she whimpered and then felt how he kissed her shoulder and her neck before gently biting her earlobe. "Do it, Aly. Make yourself come," he ordered, and she gasped, bringing a shaking hand between her legs. She felt his erection against her fingertips, slippery from her own arousal, and it was almost all she needed.

"Shit, Aly," Jam grunted, taking her just that bit harder while she alternated between brushing her clit and his cock with her hand. "I can't hold out much longer," he admitted, and she exhaled.

"Come for me, Jam," Aly whispered, and he did, giving one hard thrust that made her cry out, too. The world came apart in a shower of sparkles and black dots. It took a moment until she remembered where she was, actually finding herself beneath Jam on the bed, his body pressing her into the mattress.

"You know, if we get Alessandro back, we can't do these stunts anymore," he mumbled against her skin, kissing her back before moving away to get a washcloth. Aly didn't move, waiting until he returned. Just like the gentleman he was, he cleaned her up, too, then drew her into his arms.

"We still can. You just can't be that loud anymore," she teased, and he poked her stomach.

"Me? I think it was you screaming my name there at the end." He grinned and Aly laughed, but then took a deep breath. She wished her son was home now already. It wasn't exactly easy to forget that he was gone, but with Jam around, she sometimes had moments where she felt as if she could finally catch up on what she had missed out on when taking care of Alessandro. Maybe things would have been different for her if Jam's child really were hers, too. Maybe she didn't deserve a boy like Alessandro if one handsome man made her forget him, but Jamison wasn't just anyone.

He'd always been the only one for her and, with the way she felt, this would never change.

chapter
Ten

*J*am drove the streets he knew too well, his mind back on the coast with Alessia.

"You've been awfully quiet," Shannon commented, and Jam only nodded. He felt as if he was a different guy from when he had left less than a week prior. He couldn't believe he had told Aly about Alessandro's conception, and she hadn't thrown him out. In fact, she had done everything right, and he felt free. It was as if he had been suffocating without even realizing it, and she saved him.

"Aly knows," he announced, and Shannon waited. She seemingly didn't know what exactly Aly knew.

"Good," she answered diplomatically.

"She still loves me." That was probably what worried him most. He felt as if the second shoe was gonna drop. No way in hell was it okay for Aly to love someone so tainted. Now that they were apart, she probably would rationalize and reconsider. It scared the hell out of him.

"Good," Shannon said again, more softly this time, pulling him from his thoughts. She sounded genuinely happy for him.

"You think so?" he wondered, and she nodded.

"Alessia is an amazing woman. There's a whole little town ready to take the fall for her. They want to lie until no one even remembers the truth if push comes to shove. Jamison, that woman was sent from heaven to make things right for you," she insisted, and Jam shrugged.

"She feels guilty." There hadn't been any need for Aly to say it since it had been in her eyes whenever she thought he wasn't looking.

"Thea Karmison did a great job fucking with everyone, didn't she?" Shannon mumbled, hatred protruding from every word she uttered.

"Did you draw up the contract? The one that will make Alessandro my son?"

"Zack. That's the name they gave him, and therefore, we need to have this paper signed with his original name, Zack Karmison. And yes, we did, but Aly has it." She got quiet toward the end, and Jam sighed. He had waited for some warning since they had left Sunrow.

"There's a ninety-nine percent chance that the next time you'll see Aly, she'll be in prison. Approaching a judge to do what she will ask him to do is bad. Seriously bad. It's bribery, and that is a crime. Another one she's committing."

Jam knew that. He and Aly had actually talked about it, but she said she'd end up in prison either way, so she didn't care any longer. They had agreed they could at least try, and that was what they focused on for now.

"Jam, you need to get used to the idea that this will not work out. You need luck, and on top of that a little more luck, and then just a tiny bit of convincing, but mainly... luck. It's almost impossible."

He parked the car as they reached his home. "Let me do a quick recap. We need a judge to not call Aly in, and then we need the same judge to sign illegal papers. After that, we need to get the Karmisons, who own about every person in this town, to sign the paper. In order to get them that far, we need something we can blackmail them with. Once we get that lucky, we need to have the judge, who hopefully signed the papers, witness the signing of the papers." He let that settle for a moment. "I don't see the problem." He winked and then got out of the car.

It was a lie. This whole thing was crazy, but it didn't matter. They wouldn't win unless they tried because if you didn't fight, you had already lost.

≈

*T*homas Fairchild still lived in a big plantation home. In fact, nothing had changed about the exterior. Ever.

Aly stepped up to the porch and rang the doorbell, her hands shaking as she held onto the manila envelope that meant everything to her now. This little thing held all papers people needed to make or break her. It was a scary thought, but Aly didn't mind. She no longer had anything to lose because she knew if Jam wouldn't manage to get Alessandro back to her, he'd hate himself even more than he had before coming to her door after ten years.

The judge opened the door himself, and Aly couldn't deny that she liked knowing he wasn't too proud for that.

"Mr. Fairchild." She smiled, trying hard not to run in panic right away. Maybe the old man wouldn't remember her. She had been eight, maybe nine at the oldest, when she had first seen him. She remembered well how fond her mother had been of him. Aly wasn't sure if anyone besides her knew that her mother had been there almost daily for a few years, but right now, that didn't matter, either.

"Little Aly," he called out in surprise, opening his arms for her. She didn't hesitate for a second, letting him pull her into a hug. She couldn't help but worry about how fast his mood could change.

"I heard what happened to your mother back then. I wanted to drop by, but you know how she always wanted to keep this a secret," he mumbled sadly, and Aly squeezed his hand.

"My mother loved working in your garden. It gave her peace of mind, but she never wanted my father to know that the money she made here helped around the house. He felt bad enough for hardly being able to provide for a family, and she didn't want to add to his unnecessary guilt." It had been some stupid, backward notion on his part since women sure could help with money, but Aly guessed it had something to do with the grandparents she never met. Obviously, long before Greg was born, they had a fallout, her parents and theirs, and the siblings had never bothered to get back in contact.

"Exactly, which is why I decided to respect her wish and just keep it under wraps. You obviously haven't forgotten, though," he remarked and then made room so she could step into the house. Instead, she shook her head.

"I haven't been by the house in way too long," she started, but the man interrupted her with a shake of his head.

"You moved away. I heard all about it. The town is proud of you, little Aly." Mr. Fairchild smiled, and she swallowed hard, wondering what the town would think of her if they knew.

"I don't think there's much to be proud of. I opened a café and live a quiet life," she replied and then started to walk around the house, wanting to see the garden. "Mr. Fairchild, I'm so sorry I wasn't here when your wife passed away," she continued, and he touched her arm, making her look up.

"Please, you were always meant to get out of this town and as far away from here as possible. A corrupt town is nothing for the softhearted, especially not if they are anything like you and your mother."

Corrupt town... he had given her the perfect in, but suddenly, Aly couldn't find any words to start. Tears were spilling over her cheeks, and she wished there was just a hint of how this would end. Maybe, just maybe, she'd find the right words to say then. Trying to hide her wet face, she turned toward the roses her mother had once tended to and that now looked a little bit wild. There were weeds everywhere, and she took a deep breath, kneeling and starting to pull them out just because she needed to keep her hands busy.

"Oh, sweet girl, I have a feeling you didn't come here for a social call," Mr. Fairchild mused, and she shook her head, her throat too clogged to bring any words out.

Aly worked in silence for a few minutes while he vanished and then reappeared with a chair and some lemonade. He took a seat next to her so he could see her and still wouldn't be in her way, but she just couldn't look at him. Suddenly, she wasn't sure she should be there any longer.

"You stayin' at your brother's place?" he inquired, and Aly cleared her throat, figuring she might as well get this over with.

"Mr.—"

"Oh please, would you stop that? Call me Thomas. There was a time when you used to call me grandpa just because you didn't have one," he announced, and she cringed at the memory. She had been so young and innocent, in dire need of *more* family just because everyone else had grandparents so she had started calling them that one day. They never bothered to correct her and it stuck. It hurt her heart now because she finally knew that whatever family you had, you should appreciate.

"Yeah, you never stopped me," she remembered and then sat back on her heels, looking up at him. There was a wistful expression on his face, and he even smiled.

"My wife was never able to conceive a child. When she heard that your mother had a daughter, she asked her to bring you along. We might not have been quite that old, but we didn't mind you calling us that. It gave us a purpose of sorts. We lived to spoil you." He winked, and Aly chuckled. It was hard to believe her mother had been able to keep their trips a secret.

"I loved being here. I always imagined that one day I'd be living in a big house like that. It used to be my biggest wish," she explained, lowering her eyes back to her now soil-covered fingers.

"And now?" Thomas asked, and she took a deep breath, turning her attention back to the weeds in the roses.

"Now, I wish I could change the past." Oh, and wasn't that just the truth? In fact, it was what she had come here for.

"We can't do that." Thomas laughed, but he sobered quickly as she looked up. She could feel the tears ready to spill from her eyes again.

"Well, to be honest, I hope we can."

≈

"*J*talked to some friends. You know a couple of the guys who went away to college and came back changed men. We no longer ignore what's going on in the town. They are terrified out there in the streets, or they are corrupt. Either way, the Karmisons have almost everyone in their pockets. It wasn't easy trying to get a feel for the people," Greg explained the moment Shannon and Jamison had entered the guys' house.

Jam wasn't sure he wanted to hear that. Maybe, if he pretended to be oblivious to all that was coming in the next hours and days, then he'd be able to take a shower and relax a little. He no longer understood why they tried to rush things.

Dorly had made it more than clear that Alessandro was fine. In fact, she had seen him out in town with his grandmother, and he was taking his promise serious, it seemed. He was avoiding trouble and that was all Jam had asked of him. Frankly, that gave him a false sense of security that allowed him to worry about Aly.

Where was she? Whom exactly did she want to talk to? Maybe he should have stayed with her and tried to convince whoever she hoped to draw over to their side.

Maybe he should have just tried to keep Aly out of it after all.

"Hey," Dorly said quietly next to him, and Jam shook his head, trying to clear his thoughts. "Did everything work out for the two of you?" A sparkle in her eye indicated she knew exactly that things were fine between Aly and him, but he couldn't help the curl of his lips. It wasn't really a smile, but it came close.

"She's pretty forgiving," he admitted, and Dorly gently patted his arm, her papery skin cold. It made him worry. He and Greg never froze, but the house maybe was a little too air-conditioned for an elderly woman. "Do you need a blanket? A sweater?" he instantly asked, ready to jump up, but she just pulled him back, stopping him in mid-movement.

"No, I'm fine. I always have cold hands. I'm old. My body can't pump the blood like it used to." She winked at him and then turned serious again. "You look different."

He gave her a questioning look, and Dorly reached out to touch his face. "You look more relaxed. The lines on your face are no longer as deep as they used to be. And while you look worried, you don't constantly frown. Something changed you," she explained, searching his face as if the answer would be written there.

Aly had changed him from the core, but telling Dorly that would mean to admit to the rest of the story as well. He didn't want to go there yet.

Maybe never.

"Aly is my salvation. She is my one shot at the perfect life. I don't know how I ever deserved someone like her, but I'm ready to make this right. That's all I can say."

"She knows exactly the right words to say, doesn't she?" Phil asked, and Jam realized the silence had spread in the room so everyone could follow his whispered conversation with Dorly.

"Which is why we need to say the right things," Jam announced, hoping to bring everyone back on track.

"As I was saying," Greg continued, giving him an annoyed look, "I found two officers who I trust. I didn't tell them what I might need them for, but I made sure their cards got into Alessandro's hands."

"And a weird little lady may have made sure that Alessandro knows to call one of those numbers if anyone should hurt him," Phil quipped and then beamed proudly. Jam had no doubt that she could pull off the weird woman. It made him grin, and he bit his cheeks to keep it from showing.

"What are you smirking about?" Phil wanted to know, her eyes now narrowed in suspicion.

"Shut it, Phil. He just knows you aren't exactly normal," Greg teased, and Jamison realized that those three had gotten close in the last days. Then again, he guessed that an extraordinary situation could cause this.

"How much do you trust those two?" There still was the unsolved problem of getting Aly back into town if she came down here to talk to that mysterious judge. They hadn't spoken about where she would stay, but Jam guessed she'd need a base from where she'd be able to operate and complete her mission.

"If you're thinking about getting Aly back here, forget it, buddy," Shannon instantly cried out, and Jam decided to ignore her, just raising an inquiring brow at his friend.

"Jam, Aly won't come back," Dorly said quietly. "She'll stay as far from here as she can because otherwise she could risk it all."

Jam finally pushed to his feet. He couldn't stay seated if he thought about the fact Aly was there all by herself and everyone else was here with him.

"Whenever she's ready to meet that guy—"

"Jam, sit down. She won't tell you. You won't find out unless it either worked or not. In both cases, she will call you, just the location will differ a little," Philomena pointed out, and even though he knew she tried to lighten the mood for his sake, he couldn't get himself to appreciate it.

"When is she planning to come down here?" Maybe one of the women knew something since Alessia had refused to tell him anything.

"Whenever she's ready," Phil repeated, and he didn't like that at all. It could be now, a week from now or a whole month. He just wanted this to be over. Rubbing his face and then drowning his hands in his hair in frustration, he growled, ready to kick the table aside. There was nowhere to go with his rage, and it pissed him off even more.

Everything depended on a tiny, soft female who held his heart.

"That tiny female held everything once before in her hands, Jam. Remember?" Greg asked, making it clear Jam had spoken out loud against his intention. "The night she took your baby boy away, she did the same. And look how well she did that job. Maybe you should trust her another time?" Aly's brother suggested.

Before Jam could say something, the doorbell rang. He pointed at everyone to stay seated and that this would take just a second then he went to the hall and opened the door. His heart stopped almost instantly.

"Thea," he growled, holding on tightly to the door just because otherwise he was tempted to do something he'd regret later on.

"Zack has been such a good boy, and I know he misses you, so I promised him he could see you today," she stuttered, and Jam's jaw almost hit the floor as he realized that Thea actually cared about his son. Something in her eyes pleaded with him not to make a scene. Jam's mind was one-tracked, though. Lesso was there.

Looking over the shoulder of the tiny woman, he saw his son in a car. Without hesitation, he pushed past Thea Karmison and walked barefoot down the little driveway while Alessandro already scrambled from the car, squealing in delight. Jam knelt, catching his son as he all but flew into his arms.

"I missed you so much. I wanted to see you so much, but a crazy lady said I needed to be good or the family would hurt me. I don't wanna be hurt. I wanna go back home, Dad," the boy sobbed, and suddenly, he seemed so young, so broken. Jam squeezed him a little tighter, breathing him in. He would give everything to have Aly there and let her hold Lesso, but that was impossible.

"Your mom really misses you," he choked out, and Lesso pulled his arms closer around his neck, obviously not wanting to let go. Jam got up with him in his arms, wondering what best to tell his son. He was getting heavy and definitely shouldn't be carried around, but Jam didn't care or mind. This was his son and he needed to know he was okay.

"I need to see her, Dad. She probably thinks I don't love her anymore. I should have stayed with Mom and not left with grandma," the boy mumbled and then sobbed some more. "I didn't know it would be like that."

He was crying now, and Jam just whispered fake assurances about making everything all right. He only needed to soothe his son's hurting heart. "Just a few more days," he promised eventually as Alessandro had calmed down.

By God, Jam hoped that was the truth.

～

"*A*re you still a judge?" Aly hadn't even thought about the fact that Thomas Fairchild could be too old for the job and that would mean they'd need to find someone else.

"As long as Townsend doesn't get a new judge who's ready to fight against those damn Karmisons, I won't retire. They need someone like me, little lady. Trust me," he grumbled, anger clear in his voice and on his face. That was at least good news.

"Good," she decided, moving on to another row of flowers, finding the task of weeding oddly settling.

"Why don't you tell me what you came for, Alessia? You're not a girl easily frightened yet you seemed to stop smiling whenever a certain thought crosses your mind. Care to share?" Of course, she wanted to share, but somehow, she just couldn't. This was too nice.

Get a grip. This is about your son, not you, she scolded herself.

"Do you know Jamison Loane?" It probably was the safest way to start and guess what the judge thought.

"That poor boy. Of course, I know him. I've been at the hospital a few times when he was admitted for one football injury or the next. Never thought it was accidents causing his bruises and bleeding, but no matter how hard I tried, he wouldn't talk. Someone was beating that boy up, and I couldn't do a thing about it." Regret shone in his old, watery eyes and Aly hated herself for it, but maybe she would be able to use his guilt for her cause.

"He's a broken man today, and it's the Karmisons' fault. Thea Karmison's husband beat their daughter until she didn't have any other choice than to stay a victim all her life or become an abuser like her father," Aly explained, wondering how far into Jam's past she'd have to go to convince the judge.

"I knew something was wrong with them. He conveniently always collapsed at their residence after another football injury. They always brought him in from what I hear."

Alessia nodded, wiping a dark strand of hair from her forehead. He was surprisingly well informed for someone who surely had kept out of the loop on most things in town on purpose.

"Why did he allow it? He was taller than her, wasn't he?"

Aly had feared that question and had turned possible answers over and over in her mind.

"Why does any man allow it? They don't. They get belittled, beaten with objects, humiliated and controlled until they come to the point of thinking they are exactly what the woman accuses them to be. He was trying to make her happy and do the right things, but he couldn't." Aly almost gagged as she spun this so it turned out to be more a love story than what it really was. Jam's sexual abuse was something only he had a right to share, and Aly knew Thomas wouldn't judge her for that little white lie in the end. After all, there were greater sins to reveal.

"You've read up on the topic?" he asked out loud, and Aly shook her head. There hadn't been any need to. Jam's body said it all, even if the man himself had remained silent. Plus, she knew Collene's behavior.

"Jam and my brother, Greg, are best friends. I won't lie. It took Jamison ten years to tell me what had kept us apart back then, but that doesn't lessen the scars." And it was true. Jam carried them around like a shield and while Aly hated it, she could understand him.

She took a few deep breaths, wondering how to approach the next part of the story.

"I don't know if you ever heard about it, but Collene Karmison had a baby that vanished."

The sentence hung in the air for quite a while, and as curious as she was, she didn't dare to look up and check for Thomas' reaction.

"They didn't want people to know, but I saw the file on the local station. It was a tiny investigation really," he finally said, and Alessia breathed a little easier. He knew at least. "I always guessed something happened to the boy and that they just tried to cover it up."

It was now or never. "Something did. His father gave him to a girl to get the boy away after Collene almost killed him."

The old man sighed, sounding like a broken tire that lost all air while Alessia continued.

"The girl took the little boy over state lines and raised him as her own." Her voice broke at the end, and she saw tears hitting the grass she was sitting on. This was it, the end of her story and, if the worst-case scenario came, it could be the end of her life as well.

*J*am didn't want to let his son go again and still, once Thea announced that they were leaving, Jamison knelt down and touched his child's cheek. "You need to stay strong. If you keep being a good boy, we'll see each other again tomorrow. You heard that, right?" Thea Karmison had promised it earlier, and Jam counted on it to be true. That way he could check his son each and every day for injuries. He knew not to be obvious about it, touching the boy wherever he figured bruises could have built, but not once had his son winced. Alessandro was still safe and that was all that really mattered to Jam.

"I don't wanna go with her, Dad. I don't wanna be a good boy for them. I want to see Mom," Lesso insisted, not ready to let go of Jam after hugging him.

Prying the little arms away from his neck and feeling his heart break with every damn inch, he pushed his son away from him, making sure Alessandro listened. Only after his son's blue eyes focused on him did he lean in as close as he could without crawling into the boy.

"Your mom's doing everything she can to get you back. I promise. Stop worrying and just play along a few more days. I'll come by tomorrow and check on you. We'll have some fun then. Promise." He didn't know how often he had said the word now, but Jam didn't care. He meant it. He would not leave his son hanging, and they were so close. He just *had* to believe this would work.

"Okay," Lesso mumbled, his lips turned down as Thea took his hand.

"Eleven tomorrow at our home. If you are late, I'll not allow the meeting. If you are early, I'll never again allow any meeting," Mrs. Karmison announced, and Jam just nodded. He'd ring the doorbell at exactly that minute. Whatever was needed, he'd do it.

The two left and still Jam remained in the kneeling position he had taken. Letting his son go was harder every time, especially because he worried it was the last time he'd ever see him.

"Come on," Dorly whispered softly, placing a hand on his shoulder while he pinched the bridge of his nose, trying hard to stop the tears from falling.

$\sim$

"*L*et's go inside and settle in the living room. I'm too old to sit in a garden chair for long," Thomas remarked, but Aly didn't miss the way he looked around his enormous garden as if someone could have possibly overheard them. She knew he was trying to take her back inside to talk some sense into her. It made her hold her breath to calm her heart down. Maybe it meant that even though he wouldn't agree to help, he wouldn't report her, either. It was more than she could really wish for.

Nodding, she gathered the lemonade glasses he had carried out earlier. Hers still sat untouched even though Aly's throat felt parched. She just didn't trust her stomach to hold anything in until she knew where they stood.

Until Thomas voiced an opinion in any direction really, she was not willing to relax or settle. Already, she knew he'd be angry with her for pacing once they were inside, but since he had taken the weeding from her, she felt the need to occupy herself somehow.

"Why don't you start at the very beginning?" Thomas asked as they were in the living room. He had even turned on some quiet music, hushed enough so it wouldn't bother them while talking yet loud enough to distort the voices for anyone outside of the room.

"It's a long story, and part of it is painful, but not my history. I don't want to pull Jam into this more than I already did, so—"

"He's in it, all right. He kidnapped his son," Thomas injected.

"That's out of the question. But some of it doesn't belong to our story, so I'll skip it."

"Can you skip on to why a guy would have a baby with a woman who abuses him if he doesn't love her?" That was the main question, wasn't it really?

"I need to call him and ask. I won't decide what I can and can't tell."

"Oh boy, little Aly, what happened to you that you got into this?" Thomas asked, and only then did Aly realize she was crying. When had *that* happened?

"I think I just fell for '*the one*' way too early in life," she admitted and then excused herself. It took a moment until Jam answered, and he sounded devastated.

"Loane?" he said, and his voice was rough as if he had been crying.

"It's Aly." There was silence for a long moment at the other end, followed by muffled noises like deep breaths and throat clearing.

"Hey beautiful," he greeted her a lot more cheery, and Aly wondered if he was trying to lie to her or just make it easier for her.

"Tell me," she pleaded. She wanted them to be a couple, and couples shared their worries, right?

"Alessia, just don't. Why don't you tell me why you're calling and where you are?"

"Jam?" she inquired again, and he sighed.

"When we're together, I'm sure we can do it all. Seriously, as long as I hold you close, I know we can get all this sorted out in the best way possible, but then I'm alone and see Alessandro, and I have to let him go, reminding myself that you can't come here. It's just a little much."

Setting her jaw, she steeled her voice, trying to be strong for both of them.

"Okay, I'm going through the things I have to tell the judge. I promise I'll try to keep you out of this as much as I can, but Jam, what if I am asked how you can have a child with a woman you fear? I know it's your story to tell, but what if it comes up? And what do I say if I get asked about why you let all that happen?" She knew the answer to the last one, and it made her ready to cry again. This was all because of her.

"Aly, I know what you think, but trust me, once in the circle, it's hard to get out of it again. There was a point after probably half a year where I thought I deserved it because I was just that bad, that karma didn't want anything else for me. It wasn't you driving me any longer, but my self-hatred. Her punishments seemed the thing I needed. I wasn't good. I couldn't make her happy, or you, or my mother. Whenever you all looked at me, I saw the devastation. Not that I ever wanted to make her happy, but you couldn't even do it right with her," he whispered, and she could see him shrugging in her mind.

"She's abusive. Of course, you can't make it right with her. No matter what you try. And me... I loved you and couldn't have you. If I had known what you went through because of me, I... don't know." She couldn't have changed anything. If she had known, she probably would have gone and talked to Collene, demanded her to stop treating him the way she did.

"No what-ifs or buts, Alessia. It's done, and we can't take it back. At least, I started the healing process and all because of you. So if you need to tell the judge, tell him that abuse sometimes includes more than just beating, even for men." It was all the permission she needed, yet she wished she could've seen his face while he gave it because it was so much easier to lie over the phone.

They both stayed silent for a long moment while Aly tried to imagine where she'd find Jam now, and how he'd look.

"Tell me you really have a plan, Aly. Tell me you know a judge who could possibly help us," he eventually pleaded, and Aly looked through the open doorway at the old man she was visiting, seeing him stare blankly at the wall.

"Maybe," she conceded, not wanting to keep his hopes up. "I won't end up in prison though for now," she then added, knowing somewhere deep inside her that was true. Thomas wouldn't do that to her.

"I wish I could see you."

She had it on the tip of her tongue to tell him that he could because all he'd have to do was drive out there. The problem was, the more contact they had, the more likely it was that things went down the drain.

"I wish that, too. Just give me a little more time, Jam."

He took a few deep breaths, and Aly wondered if he had reached his breaking point.

"Soon," she promised, hoping and praying she could keep it together enough for both of them. "I love you," she whispered as a way of good-bye. Jam gave the sentiment back, but as much as she knew it was true, his statement lacked heat and that was what made her get up. Thomas needed to know and decide because if he wasn't helping her, she had more people on the list she was going to try to convince. There had to be someone who would help them.

"So here's the whole story," she said loudly, pulling the old man from his thoughts. She started at the beginning and ended where they were now. It took a while, and they relocated to the kitchen at some point so Aly could cook, but she didn't leave anything out and Thomas didn't say anything until she concluded her story.

For a long time all that was between them were two wine glasses, filled to the brim since nothing less would suffice.

~

It was freezing on the floor where he sat, his cell rested against his lips as he considered calling Aly back. He should have been the one to calm her down; instead, she had assured him they'd work it out. Only now, when thinking back and analyzing what she thought did he realize that her voice had been thick with tears. She had been crying, too, and he had been too self-absorbed to realize it. Darkness was descending into the rooms, bringing more cool air with it.

Jam had dark moments before; so bad, he had wanted to die

without a second thought, but while sitting there in the hallway, he thought he hadn't known darkness until that moment. He couldn't ease his son's worries because that would maybe forever exile him to his grandparents, and he couldn't stop Aly's tears because she was too far away. He couldn't make it right without causing her more harm. Not for the first time, Jam wondered if there had been a point in life where he should have gone the other way.

There was one. Back when he had given the boy to Aly. He had thought that this was his only true way out, but that wasn't right, was it? He could have found a prosecutor some towns over to press charges the Karmisons. He could have tried to run away with the child without pulling anyone else into the dark web of the kidnapping. He could have gotten a doctor's certified proof that Collene had been abusing their child. Either way, it would have kept Aly out of this. She would be happily living with another man, having her own child without a care in the world. After all, she wouldn't have to keep a secret like that. It was hell.

Jam pulled his knees up, trying hard to ward off the cold and make himself as small as possible. It was all that mattered right now. He wanted to vanish, go back, and get another chance to redo it all.

Resting his forehead against his bent knees, he gritted his teeth against the pain that came at him from everywhere. He felt like tearing his own skin off.

Jam lost track of time, and only the moving moonlight was an indication of how far the night was moving along. Greg, Phil, and Dorly sat in the living room, and by the sounds of it, they were sharing a bottle of whatever. Maybe Jam should have joined them, going for a few glasses to ease his pain, but he hadn't. No one had come to check on him, either, and it probably was for the best.

He didn't deserve their compassion. He had turned them all into accomplices, just by handing Alessandro over to Aly.

His thoughts were an abyss, threatening to swallow him whole, and the only person who'd be able to stop the downward spiral was out of reach. He wouldn't call her, begging her to ease his pain when she hadn't seen Lesso in longer than he had.

The phone in his hand vibrated, startling him. The display lit up with Aly's smile, giving him a chance to glance at the clock. It was past two, and she should be sleeping.

"Al," he whispered, wondering if the quieter he spoke, the less she'd hear his desperation.

"You know I adore you, Jam, right? No matter what comes, what happens, you're the only guy I will ever love. There can't ever be anyone else for me. There wasn't back then, and there won't be any time in the future. You're all I need, Jamison. Always. Don't give up hope yet," she pleaded as if she was privy to his thoughts.

"What if I can't, Aly?"

"Don't you dare give up! We're so close, Jam, so close to success," she begged, and he felt a hot tear run down his cheek. He hated crying, tried hard to avoid it, but that night it didn't work.

"I gotta go, Aly," he replied. He didn't even wait for her to answer before just hanging up. He needed only a few more hours to collect himself. As soon as the sun would rise, he'd be proud and strong again. All he had to do was get through those hours.

Movement on the stairs caused him to grit his teeth, hoping that whoever had come up wouldn't see him. He was out of luck as Phil sank down on the floor next to him, entwining their hands in silence. He squeezed hers, hard, but she didn't wince. He knew that Aly had sent her, and it was somehow as if no matter how far away Aly was, she was guarding him from the darkness.

❦

*A*fter she finished her message to Philomena, Aly couldn't keep her sobs in, burying her face in her hands. Thomas had offered her a bed for the night, and she had gratefully accepted since it was way past midnight and she didn't have the energy left to look for a motel. She dropped the phone, and it silently bounced off the heavy carpet.

Jam couldn't give up now.

Thomas had kissed her forehead and had told her good night after her story. She didn't know what to make of it, but then, for now, she didn't care, either. She hadn't been able to find any sleep, her heart racing in her throat as if she was running a marathon being followed by a serial killer and he was about to catch up. There was no chance for her to close her eyes, so she had sat back up, the impulse to call Jam overwhelming.

She never had thought about how deep Collene's marks would reach into Jam. The episode in her bathroom had been an indicator, but she had been naïve enough to think that they'd be able to solve that with a little love and affection. After all, hadn't Jam been much happier after his confession?

Hearing him now, though, she knew he needed professional help, no matter how much she wished he could get through it without reliving it all anew.

Starting to pace her bedroom, she wondered if she maybe should get outside and just wander the garden aimlessly in the moonlight. She needed to get away from herself and out of the room that seemed to be suffocating her since it contained all her worries.

Wearing just a long white tee that she still had left from Jam, she ventured outside, her bare feet hitting the dew-covered grass. Looking up at the clear sky, she could see a million stars, missing home yet feeling oddly close to her little house by the sea.

The moon stood full and high, easing her mind. The night was beautiful, filled with only a few soft noises here and there. Feeling her naked toes on the wet grass grounded her somewhat, making her spread her arms and breathe deeply.

"You look like a fairy, little Rhyme," came a voice from the door, and Aly flinched, spinning to face the porch.

"I didn't mean to wake you," she explained, looking at Thomas. In the pale moonlight, he looked even more breakable than she had thought during the day.

"It's hardest at night for me. I still miss Brenda in those hours because there's no getting away from your thoughts at night, is there?" he wanted to know. "Frankly, I followed the open doors until I found you here, standing in the garden. Did it help?"

She giggled a little embarrassed and then nodded. "Jam is in a bad place, and it's hard being strong when all you really want is to curl yourself into a ball and cry. He has been strong for me long enough. I need to be strong for him now when he can't be. Being out here helped. A lot. I don't know why, but something about the silence of the night is soothing. And you still have the moonflowers. I always regretted that I never got to smell them because they were blooming only in the dark. Your garden is an escape. Exactly the one I needed. I'm sorry my mother stopped tending to it at some point. I probably should have continued her work just because you've always been so generous to us, but by now, I can't change that. Thank you for letting me stay and... finding peace in an impossible situation," Aly explained, watching in surprise how Thomas Fairchild, county judge and lonely widower, took off his slippers and walked down the stairs to join her barefoot dance on the lawn.

"I haven't taken the time to enjoy the flowers in years. Without Brenda, I just didn't see a reason. Now, though, I think it might have soothed my soul before, too. After all, she always loved every plant here. I should feel closer to her here than I should anywhere else," he admitted, taking slow, deliberate steps across his own property as if he had never before seen it.

"The only thing you need to feel close to someone you've lost is the memory in your heart, Thomas. No matter where you go, what you'll do, they'll be by your side if you keep them inside of you. Every smile, every word you remember makes them more vivid. Only when we start forgetting are they truly gone from us. That, too, is the reason why at night you miss her the most. Your head can't stop your heart from going down a path you're too afraid to follow during the day. In dreams, we are unguarded. In dreams, we are free. In dreams, they are alive. Always."

Greg used to say that to her when she worried about forgetting her parents. It was crazy that even now she could recall the words so clearly.

For a long time, Thomas just kept walking in silence, his feet digging into the earth as if he was trying to grow roots, but then he looked up and Aly saw emotions race across the old man's face like pictures crossed a movie screen without a break.

"You're a smart, little lady," he finally commented, and Alessia laughed.

"Greg told me those exact words when I was younger. They just came back to me a few minutes ago, and they're true. Scary but true." She shrugged her shoulder and then hugged herself. "I think I'm calm enough now to find some sleep," she then added, and Thomas nodded, a surprisingly satisfied smile on his lips.

"Sleep tight. I think I'm going to walk a little longer out here under the stars," he decided, and she kissed his papery cheek.

"Make sure you rub your feet warm before you go back to bed. And I hope you'll have sweet dreams," Aly said softly then walked up the porch steps and into the house, making sure to clean her feet on the doormat before walking up the stairs and snatching the phone from the floor. Out of habit, she lit the screen, not expecting anything since it was so late, but to her utter surprise, there was a message from Jam.

Always and a day, Aly. That's how long I'm yours.

She read the words over and over, her heart becoming much lighter, eventually calming down enough to help her find some sleep.

chapter Twelve

$\mathcal{I}$t was early when Alessia made her way down the stairs. She had decided to make Thomas some breakfast for everything he had done for her, even if he now would send her packing without her being any closer to solving her problem.

The kitchen was huge, all state-of-the-art appliances. It reminded her how much she loved cooking, even though her own kitchen wasn't half as modern or big. For a few moments, Aly wondered how an old man like Thomas could feel all right living in a house like that all by himself, but then she guessed he simply enjoyed being so far away from a town he equally seemed to hate and love. Aly hoped that one day Townsend would be free of the Karmisons. It was a far-fetched wish, she knew that, but there was nothing worse than giving up.

Opening the fridge and getting out all she considered necessary for a great breakfast, she smiled. Resources were vast, making Aly reconsider what she wanted to cook every ten seconds. Should she go for French toast? Or pancakes? Or maybe bacon and eggs? She literally started drooling as she thought about all the food, so she put on the coffee and then just decided to prepare it all. Pancakes could be eaten cold, too, and Aly sure wouldn't mind taking something that felt like home when she had to leave the house, searching for other possibilities.

There was no radio in the kitchen, and it struck her as odd since she always had music on, but then she just figured she could hum whatever song she still had stuck in her head. It was a pop song, and most likely, it was the last one she had heard. Not that she was able to name it, but then, it didn't matter.

Getting lost in the task of cooking, she didn't even notice she had an audience until a laugh made her jump, causing her to drop a fork. It clattered to the ground, filling the kitchen with noise. She rested one hand on the counter and the other over her heart, trying to calm down the racing in her chest.

"I'm sorry, sweetheart." Thomas laughed, and Alessia gave him a smile.

"It's not your fault. Lesso always complains that I forget the world around me when I'm cooking," she admitted, her heart starting to hurt at the thought of the boy she hadn't seen in so long. For a mother, it always felt like an eternity when she was away from her child for any amount of time. For her, it was worse, since she didn't know if she was going to see him again or not.

"I guess he wouldn't have complained about the smiling faces on the food, though," Thomas mused, and Aly looked down on her pancakes, bewildered. She hadn't consciously decided to make them just the way Alessandro loved them.

"I'm so sorry! That wasn't on purpose," she mumbled, embarrassed.

"You do realize there's no way you can get Alessandro back to live with you, right?" Thomas asked, obviously realizing how important Alessandro was to her. She couldn't even be mad at him for starting the topic she hadn't known how to approach.

"I needed to try," she admitted. "Giving up was not an option. If you turn me in, I'll understand. In fact, I know it's what you have to do. If you don't, maybe the next judge will. I'm not gonna stop. I can't. It's not only me. This also concerns Jam and Lesso. I'm sorry to have put you on the spot like that." She meant it, but she was desperate.

"You committed a federal crime, child. One some states consider worthy of the death penalty."

Again, it wasn't news to Aly. She still waited for Thomas to go on. "Don't go to other judges. In fact, if things are quiet, you might want to keep them that way. The Karmisons are not people you wanna fight," Thomas insisted, and Aly looked at him, her vision blurred by tears. Not because he was turning her down, but because he was worried about her nonetheless.

"I don't care who they are. They have my son, and they ruined

Jam. I cannot stand back. They'll never stop if people don't stand up to them." She meant every word yet knew she wasn't exactly in a fighting position. One word from the Karmisons and she was faster in prison than she'd be able to pronounce the word.

"Goddammit, child! Are you so willing to lose your life over this?" Thomas screamed, and she reached out to touch his arm.

"They took Alessandro. I have nothing to lose."

Thomas stared at her for a long time and then pushed the manila envelope, which Aly had successfully ignored ever since placing it on the counter upon her arrival, back toward her.

"Take that thing away. And either then you can eat with me, or you can hate me forever and leave. It's your choice," he challenged, and she took the envelope, putting it into her bag before returning to him. She wouldn't leave after he had been so nice to her, especially not for turning her down. She had known that his was the biggest possibility, and therefore, would act grown up about it. She'd have time later to break down and consider a new course of action.

"Food is fine. I'm starving. And you need to tell me how you deal with this huge house all by yourself," she prompted and watched as the old man's expression softened. After a moment of slight hesitation, he started to tell her about all the crews that came in to help, about poker nights and movie dates with old friends. The tension left soon after, and Aly decided to give herself until after lunch, then she'd leave and think about what best to do next.

∽

Jam had spent most of the night on the floor with a silent Phil next to him, and it was all he had needed. Talking wouldn't have been an option without hurting people who didn't deserve it. Now, he had showered and felt halfway human. He badly wanted to talk to Aly and apologize because he had scared the hell out of her, but she wasn't answering and he decided not to worry. She was a grown woman and maybe she was driving. It had to be something, or at least that's what he told himself. He had scared her probably more than he could imagine, but again, he couldn't do anything until he heard her voice.

"Hey champ, you look like shit and so does Philomena. Next time, do the manly thing—get drunk with your best friend and spill your worries to him instead of camping out in the hall," Greg called as soon as he entered the kitchen. Jam knew it was Greg's way of trying to lighten the mood, but Jam couldn't even force a smile. Joining Greg at the kitchen counter, he took out a mug and poured himself a black coffee. He most likely would need more than one, but it was at least a start.

"Did she call?" he asked brusquely and knew there was no need to define the woman they talked about.

"You cannot be stupid, man. Aly won't survive losing you and Alessandro. I know that you've been through hell and back, but don't stop walking when it's just three more steps to success. She's trying everything to make this right for you, too, you know? Alessandro needs his dad."

Alessandro needed more than that, but Jam just didn't say anything.

"Jam, man, how often do you have moments like last night? And how have I never noticed them?" Greg looked guilty and worried, probably only now realizing that maybe he should have noticed something was wrong.

"It wasn't your fault. You couldn't have known," Jam mumbled, trying hard not to sound annoyed and totally pissed off. He shouldn't have sat in the hallway, but somehow, that had been as far as his feet had carried him.

"You'll see your boy later on, Jam. Aren't you excited?" Greg asked and finally the tight fist around Jam's heart eased a little. He actually did look forward to seeing him because he already knew that just one tiny smile would remind him of all the good he had in life.

"She's never gonna leave you alone again, you know that, right?"

Jam knew that it was only half a joke, and finally, he could actually crack a smile. As it was, he was more than aware of the fact that if he ever got Aly and Lesso back the way he hoped he could, she'd watch him like a hawk. He wouldn't deny that this was something that didn't bother him at all. After all, she was his woman, and if someone could make him better, it was the little brunette.

"I know. I'm taking that as confirmation that she called you, too," he then groaned, realizing it meant Aly had probably contacted everyone in the house after he had rather rudely hung up on her.

"It's incredible how much she knows you really. Phil was the best decision to send to your side since I would have failed. And I won't lie. You break her heart with a comment like that at any other time, and I'm gonna personally help you over the edge."

"Not exactly the right thing to say, but yeah, I get it," Jam replied, clearing his throat and then lowering his gaze. It was weird, unusual really, to have to think of someone else when being in a mood like that. For ten years, it only had been him, and suddenly, he had a family.

The thought made his vision blurry again, and he had to breathe through the tears to keep them from falling. Until that moment, he hadn't thought of what all this meant, all the implications the other two brought into his life, and frankly enough, it was as if he suddenly saw the light.

They were his family, and he couldn't think of anything that would make life more worthwhile than that.

$\sim$

*L*ess than twenty miles were between Aly and the Fairchild mansion when she stopped on the side of the road near a field, opening the convertible and sitting down with her feet on the backseat. She tried hard to hold things together, but it was almost impossible.

Arriving at Thomas' doorstep, she had been sure that she successfully quenched every last bit of hope that this plan would succeed. Only now, she realized she had been lying to herself. She was devastated Thomas had turned her down; even while she knew she should be glad she was still walking around without cuffs around her wrists and ankles, it hurt. Not wanting to break down, she reached for her handbag on the passenger seat. She needed a new plan, and if she wanted to keep the tears at bay, she needed to focus on what was to come, not dwell on the things that hadn't worked out.

Her fingertips grazed the envelope, and it was as if it felt extra cold against her skin, reminding her that what was inside was evil, illegal. Pulling the papers out, she noticed that the envelope was bigger than before. Earlier, when she had stowed it away, she had been in such a hurry to get it out of Thomas' sight that she hadn't focused on it. Now, she was in a haste to open it.

A lighter fell out, and she caught it in her hand, then she pulled out a paper that was tinged brown and looked elegant.

It was a letter in a hand that clearly hadn't written more than its name in a long time.

ear Alessia,

our dilemma breaks my heart. I hate nothing more out there than the Karmisons, especially since they obviously pulled you into their drama without you being close enough.

As it is, by now I will have given you an ear full about your illegal actions. How could you... save the life of a child against everything that came with it? You are brave and outstanding and selfless, walking up to a judge like that. I don't even want to think about what would have happened if you hadn't remembered me. Do you have any idea about how prisons are these days? You can't because, despite everything, you are an innocent soul.

As I write those lines, I can hear you crying next door. Nothing is worse than hearing someone you consider family cry. Then again, you currently are away from yours, knowing that the devil could do whatever to them. I guess that's even harder.

I'm never going overcome the awe I feel for you, even though personally I think Jam should have taken different actions. I can see, though, why a boy the age he was when the baby was born wouldn't see any other chance. I hate what this city has turned into, and I'm glad I'm living so far out that you could come and see me.

As much as I wish I could offer you a place to stay until all this is solved, I can't. I signed the papers, and it's better if no one sees you around the house. Not for me, but for you. You want the boy back and even though step one is taken (frankly, as you pointed out during our talk, the hardest step), you and Jamison need patience now.

When you are done reading this letter, burn it. Not because I don't want you to have it, but because the more proof someone can gather that this wasn't done the right way, the higher the chances are that you'll just lose your boy again.

Needless to say, I won't be there to witness that, but in the end, that doesn't matter. All you need is the Karmison signature on the paper and then stow it away. Once it's signed and you have the boy back, I'll vouch for you any given day—or nighttime. After all, I clearly remember the day Jamison came into my office with Collene, holding the baby boy and telling me that they needed to solve the issue.

You get the drift. Just make sure she signs in the right spot. As soon as you can, get an adoption paper on him. Collene signed all rights over to Jamison, not wanting any participation in the boy's life. Or at least she will have done so by the time you apply. Once that's settled, there are even more legal documents making him yours, and if something should happen to the boy's father, you'll get him, no matter what. It's the best way to handle this.

Now, once you have your family back, maybe you'll have time to visit an old man.

Sincerely,

T. Fairchild.

*A*ly lowered the lines, her heart squeezing tight as she realized what this meant. With a lump in her throat, she checked the papers—the ones that would change her life for the better—and saw Thomas' signature at the bottom, perfect ink and his seal making this the most valuable thing in her possession. Her heart thundered against her ribcage, making her hold her breath, but nothing could change the pattern. They were closer, so much closer, and it made her heart light. The talk they had before breakfast was just for show, and if push ever came to shove, he could always deny any involvement. He had to think of himself, and she could always pretend to have stolen his official seal. If they brought her to prison, she didn't have anything to lose anyway. She couldn't and wouldn't be mad at him for trying to do her a favor, yet save himself.

She hopped out of the car, the lighter heavy in her hand, and walked out onto the empty country road. Looking left and right, she didn't see anyone so she held out the one page and lit the corner on fire. She wouldn't ever forget what she read on there, but if she wanted to save her son, those words had to go up in flames. Evidence was bad, that much she knew, and she did not intend to leave any behind. After the wind had blown away the ashes, scattering in all directions of the sun, she got back in the car and started up the rental. She knew she wouldn't find any good motels on the route, but now, she didn't care any longer. She could spend a few nights in a bed that wasn't hers or exactly clean, as long as in the end, she would get to hold her baby again.

~

*J*am couldn't get out of his funk. The dark was walking around the edges of his consciousness more clearly than it had in years. He didn't know what had changed, but maybe it was all the memories flooding his mind ever since he had told Aly all he had dared to tell her.

No denying he needed help, but for now, Jam hoped that getting rid of the immense anger he was feeling would be a start.

"Carl." He greeted the guy from the junkyard. He knew him well, and Carl was already there, a hammer in hand. To Jam's luck, the place was far out of town, and no one had ever seen him there, meaning he didn't mind parking his car and spending hours there.

He had seen Alessandro that morning, ringing the doorbell exactly at eleven, not a second later, and then had been allowed to be with his son under supervision for an hour. Even though that time didn't feel nearly long enough, Jam itched to get away. Lesso had most likely caught on to his mood because the boy had been unnaturally quiet, begging for Aly. That was probably what Jam had done most of the time—holding Lesso and trying to soothe him.

"You're lucky, son," Carl announced, handing over a mechanic's jumpsuit, too. It said a lot that Jam had brought his own protective glasses.

"Is that so?" Jam asked while pulling on the protective gear. His skin was crawling with anxiety as if a million ants had made it their home.

"We just got a new one in. Perfect piece. The engine gave in, though." Carl took the lead and Jam followed him, already feeling better the moment he lifted the sledgehammer.

They rounded a few piles of metal junk and then Jam's eyes fell on a perfectly fine red car.

"What the hell? They could've sold it, for fuck's sake. Someone probably would have been ready to buy a new engine," he stated in disbelief, and Carl shrugged.

"I thought about selling it, but I think it'll satisfy you a lot more than any of the crap pieces I have."

Jam wouldn't even deny that. He knew that the shinier the surface, the more he could ruin the thing. Just as it was with him.

"Radio's working. Find a heavy metal station and get on it, boy." Carl came over and placed his hand on Jam's shoulder. He looked at the older man, seeing the sadness in his eyes.

"When you didn't return for nearly a decade, I thought your horrors were over finally. Now, I can see they're not. You need to get on that shit. I saw your whole body trembling the moment you stepped out of your car." He shook his head, and Jam gritted his teeth.

"She has my son."

If Carl was surprised that his abuser had been a woman, he didn't let on. "I think I should gear up as well and join you," he growled, and Jam saw his eyes blazing as he looked up.

"If I ever find out who did all that bullshit to you, I'll probably need a whole squad of cars," he growled and then turned away.

Jam thought about foregoing the music, but heavy, angry sounds always had been crucial to his soul's healing. Even though he hadn't needed any of it in forever, he needed it now.

The moment he had found the right station, heavy screaming filled the air and he raised the hammer. Pausing for only a second, he then let it crash down on the windows. The shattering sounds mixed with the music eased his mind, giving him a rush like a cutter probably felt when he saw the first drops of blood well from a fresh mark. It wasn't anything good, or healthy, but it sure gave a person relief as nothing else ever could.

Jam turned the destruction into a symphony. The raining down of the sledgehammer against the metal came at regular intervals, accentuating the music, pushing it higher and higher until the echo of Jam's pain filled the whole junkyard. For weeks in a row, he had been here to express his anger the only way he knew without hurting people or himself, and it had always done its deed. He wouldn't stop until his arms were shaking and his knees threatened to give in.

It was what he needed—mental and physical exhaustion. He knew tears were streaming down his cheeks, leaving tracks in the dust that was flying through the air with every step he took and settled on his cheeks because of the sweat running down his skin.

He didn't care. This was his escape, and he needed it.

Losing track of time and space, he focused on ruining everything about this car that once had been shiny. He started in the back, making his way around until reaching the front, closing his eyes as exhaustion started to set in. He raised the hammer, waiting for a moment, testing his emotions and his body. He was so concentrated that it took him a second to realize the music had changed.

He let the hammer go down again, only to whip around as he saw movement out of the corner of his eye. He dropped the hammer, too afraid what he'd do with it otherwise when he realized it was a dark-haired angel. That was the only explanation Jam had for the vision standing in front of him.

She wore black heels that were dust-covered yet sexy, leading the eyes up long, bare legs that vanished beneath a skirt that was a lot shorter than he knew on her. She wore a white blouse that was pretty much giving a perfect idea what was hidden in the black bra showing at the neckline.

"Holy fuck, Aly," he mumbled, wanting to rub his eyes, but the dirt on his hands wouldn't be the best thing for his vision.

She didn't reply. Instead, she pulled some pins from her hair, making the dark waves tumble down her back, then she walked closer to him, pulling him with her until she was almost seated on the hood of the red piece of trash.

Jam didn't hesitate, leaning in to run his tongue along the edges of her bra. She instantly moaned, and he pushed the cups aside, finding her nipples, sucking one while gently twisting the other between his fingers.

Her hands were between them, unzipping the jumpsuit and then unbuttoning his jeans. Jam growled against her skin as she wrapped her hand around his cock and started stroking.

His touch left her chest, pushing his way beneath her skirt, finding that she had obviously forgotten her panties. When Jam met her eyes with an inquiring expression, Aly just drew him in for a kiss that was almost rough while she aligned them with her other hand. He could feel her hot and needy, and it made his body tremble again; only this time, it was something entirely different from when he had gotten here.

She wrapped her legs around him, and he reached around her back, cupping her cute ass in his hands before pulling her close and drowning himself in her in the same instant. He actually had to pause for a moment, feeling overwhelmed with need and lust.

"Hell no," she just whispered and then started to move against him, not giving him a break to collect himself. Her kisses were hot and heavy, leaving him breathless as she sucked his lower lip in before sweeping her tongue into his mouth, pulling herself closer to him, using her legs to urge him to move.

"Aly," he gasped.

"Harder," she said in return, and he knew his fingertips were already bruising her hips, but he still followed her order, taking her faster, rougher, until he was soaring high, brought there by her moans, her whimpers, and pleas. "Yes, Jam, fuck me just like that," she mumbled, and he couldn't stop it, coming deep inside of her. He knew she hadn't come yet, and once he regained his wits, he pulled his shirt off, cleaning her up before replacing his shirt with his tongue, positioning her legs over his shoulders.

He licked her clit, hearing her nails scratch over the metal as she tried to find something to grasp.

Eventually, her hands found their way into his hair and he pulled her closer, licking her harder. He could feel her heels digging into his back, and it was obvious that while being half-crazy with lust, she still tried not to hurt him. He just knew that she held back.

"You can't hurt me, Aly."

"Lick," Aly ordered, and he had to laugh at her husky tone, getting serious again, though, the moment he lowered his lips back to her. "I'm so close," she whispered, and he slipped two fingers into her raising the intensity. He knew how close she was, he could almost feel it, and then she came apart under his hands, calling out his name. He drew out her orgasm, before he stood again, looking at the woman who owned his heart. Her dark waves spilled over the red paint, her white blouse, now gray with grime, giving way to tanned skin and a black bra that supported but did not hide her rosy nipples. Her skirt was high on her hips, and she looked up at him with her eyes shining.

God, Jam could never thank heaven enough for having given him this woman.

chapter
Thirteen

$\mathcal{A}$ly never wanted to move again. This definitely was a lucky coincidence that she had seen Jam's car out front while being on the way to talk to some people at a bank. She had been dressed up, but without needing to talk to him, she could guess what he was doing there. Not thinking long, she had lost her panties, opened her blouse, and walked into the junkyard.

"Back," an older guy only told her, pointing a certain way, but it wouldn't have been necessary. She could hear the music and the destruction.

She had walked there and then... she'd say the rest would go down in history.

Pulling her skirt down and trying to rearrange her clothes at least a little, she watched the angry, dirty, yet in her eyes perfect, man in front of her.

"I ruined your blouse," he whispered while buttoning his jeans and tying the jumpsuit around his hips. God, he was sexy all dust-covered and sweaty. She never had been into sweaty guys, but seeing Jam like that... man, a woman quickly could get weak. She drew him close by his belt, making sure he was between her legs again.

"Hey," she said over the music, and he groaned, leaving her to silence the air around them, then he took the spot again that she had assigned him. "I think *we* ruined my blouse." She laughed and then reached out to brush her hand through his hair, resting her forehead against his.

"Alessia," he breathed and then pulled her close to hug her gently. The way he was holding her was such contrast to his touches just moments ago.

"Feel better?" she asked, her lips moving against the skin of his shoulder as she spoke.

"So much," he confessed. "I can't believe you are here. I thought my exhausted mind conjured you up because there's nothing more healing for me than you."

She gently let her fingertips glide up and down his back, and she could feel his muscles react to every little touch. "You need help, Jam," she mumbled and held her breath as she expected a huge fight to come.

"I know," he surprised her by saying, and she had to pull back to look at him. He meant it. Oh, dear God, he meant it! She wanted to sob in relief and swallowed a few times before nodding.

"Good. Jam, I'm so happy you see it that way."

He gave her the smallest of smiles. "I'll find someone once we have our son back. I'd love to move up there with you, and I want to have a life with you, Aly. I've never wanted anything more. Just be patient with me," he pleaded, and she knew she could do that. After all, he had been patient with her for a decade and more.

"Jam, I have news," Aly burst out. She had been ready to tell him right away, but somehow, other things had been more important.

"Good news, the way your eyes shine." He laughed, and she nodded.

"I got the papers signed."

The silence that followed her statement wasn't at all what Aly had expected. "Which papers?" he finally asked, and she grinned.

"The ones stating that Collene hands over all rights of Alessandro to you."

The disbelief on his face made a giggle explode in her chest. Man, she was so happy they had managed that hard part already.

"You're lying, right?" Jam asked, and she shook her head.

"I mean it. All we need now is something to use against her. I need you to be patient, okay? Just a few more days. Jamison, can you promise me you'll keep it together for that long?" She wouldn't lie; last night had scared her like nothing else.

"I'm okay. I come here when I feel I can't go on. Trust me. It always helps me. Nothing's more liberating than ruining something else when you have been ruined." He started to grin then, and she could almost hear his next comment before he made it.

"That is, I think nothing's more liberating than trashing a car and getting to take your woman on it afterward."

She laughed and then kissed his lips quickly. If she lingered too long, they would most likely go another round.

"Tell me about Lesso." Her voice broke at the end of the sentence, and she realized she needed to get a grip. Aly lowered her eyes, letting her fingers go over his abs and then his chest. She had missed him so much.

"Did you think about what all this means to Alessandro? What it might do to him?" Jam asked, and she shrugged. Of course, she had thought about that, but then it was too late now to change anything.

"I know they've told him by now I'm not his mother. I don't know if he understands it or not, but Jam, did he give you the impression he hated me? That he didn't want to be back with me?"

Jam couldn't meet her eyes, and her heart stuttered in her chest. If her son would refuse her, this was all for nothing in the end. "Oh God, Jam, don't start lying now. I've been lied to enough, and so have you. Let's be adult about this," she pleaded even though she didn't want to be.

"He asks for you every single second we're together. Every. Damn. Time. It kills me. But that's not what worries me. What if he starts hating you, hating us both, down the road? You pretended to be his mother," Jam remarked, and she gritted her teeth.

"I *am* his mother," she protested, walking away from Jam. She just needed to be out of reach.

"I know, but Aly, you need to consider the possibility."

God, his serious moods got him thinking too much. She hated it. With everything they had to think about right now, the future beyond adopting her boy wasn't exactly on her radar.

"I'm not sure I can. How about we cross that bridge once we get there?" she asked, and Jam reached out for her, but she dodged his hand.

"Don't, Alessia Rhyme. We're in this together, and while I might not exactly act like it, I know it. Don't lock me out. Let me hold you. I know it'll ease your pain," he whispered, and she knew he was right. Just as he had told her last night, she too had the feeling they could conquer the world only when they were together.

With a nod, she went into his arms and then leaned into him. She didn't mind that she'd have to shower in that shabby motel room of hers. She didn't mind that they stood in a junkyard. And most of all, she didn't mind that for a few seconds, her world again shrank down only to them, making her envision a time when things would be perfectly fine.

*F*our days.

That was how long Aly was confined to a run-down motel room without any chance of getting out or helping Jam. He called her almost daily, gave her updates on her son, yet she couldn't get any closer to them because they still had nothing to make the Karmisons sign. Collene wasn't around, which was the best they could wish for, yet it had made Shannon realize they needed someone else to sign the papers, preferably Thea.

It was crazy that they hadn't seen Collene's absence as a problem back then, yet there had been so much to think about; no wonder they had overlooked that 'little issue.'

She was going crazy. TV did nothing to ease her mind and taking the car to aimlessly drive around just made it worse. She never had been without a purpose and while there was an endgame and a goal she was working toward, she still was the one who had to sit back instead of taking action.

Checking her watch, Aly realized Jam was just about to go see Alessandro. How she wished she could be there, too. She wanted to hug her boy and assure him that she was still his mother, no matter what people said.

To her utter relief, Jam had collected himself again, taking charge of his own life instead of letting his doubts win. But that meant, too, that he was getting restless because he also had to sit back and wait, letting worries take over as he had nothing else to occupy his time with. With him being at the Karmison's beck and call, he couldn't really take on jobs, either, leaving his hands idle.

Aly had spoken to the two officers in town who were on their side, just to ease her mind, but since they also had to fly under the radar, they couldn't offer anything new. One of them said they saw Alessandro around town and was happy he looked fine. The way she got it, he had lost weight, though, and it made Aly worry. She knew he wouldn't eat if things bothered him, but the Karmisons didn't know that.

She considered talking to Thea again, maybe make an offer, and tell the woman she could see Alessandro regularly if only he could live with her, but then she remembered Thea still belonged to an abusive family that made you obedient one way or the other.

There was also the fact Thea's husband seemed to be suspiciously absent. Jam hadn't seen him around once, and while he was glad about that, Aly started to consider that a bad sign, too. Then again, she was locked away for now and had too much time to go over the facts again and again. Suddenly, finding a judge to help them seemed as if it had been the smallest of their worries.

Her phone rang, and she jumped, surprised.

"Phil, hey! Are you ready to go home?" Aly smiled, knowing it was just a matter of days now that Phil would return to Sunrow.

"Aly," Phil just replied, and Aly already knew something had happened. She wasn't sure she could take any bad news, but at least something was moving.

"Tell me," she demanded and then nearly crushed her phone when her best friend did.

~

*J*am watched his son draw a picture of what Lesso considered a race car. Jam would call it a truck with too small wheels, but he didn't say that.

The boy was in a surprisingly good mood and that was all that mattered to his father. Jam leaned back, watching. They were in one of the Karmison's sitting rooms—a wide, open space with a fireplace to his left. It was so big Alessandro would be able to stand inside it with no trouble at all. A seating group in the middle dominated the rest of the room. While the whole area held cream-colored tones, the furniture was kept dark, making it contrast perfectly with the walls and the tiled floors. The windows were framed by red velvet curtains the color of Bordeaux. It was an elegant room, opening up to the terrace and the huge gardens. Thea had opened the doors to get the stuffy air out of the room, and Jam didn't mind. It was a nice summer day with a light breeze going. There was no doubt that back in Aly's house this would have been a cause to hang out at the beach all day.

"Do you want it green or blue, Dad?" Alessandro asked, and Jam focused back on him, picking up the green pencil.

"Green," he decided, and Lesso nodded.

"Wanna help me color it?" he asked, and Jam leaned in.

"Oh, my... what a sight!"

Jam's insides went ice cold. He had hoped to never hear that voice again, yet while not having seen Collene for years, he felt her harsh tones crawl up his skin, making him want to calm her down, to satisfy her need for control. Old habits clearly died hard.

"Keep coloring, buddy," Jam ordered, tousling his son's hair. Luckily, Lesso didn't even look up while Jam moved, so he stood, hiding their boy from Collene's view.

"I'm out vacationing for a few weeks and bam, look who shows up. With my kid!" She lowered her sunglasses while walking closer, dragging luggage behind her.

"Collene, hey," Jam greeted her, wondering which was the best cause of action. He had no idea if assaulting her would keep her away from Alessandro or if playing nice would do the trick.

"How about a kiss as a welcome, lover boy?" she inquired, and Jam's insides churned.

"He loves my mom," Lesso injected, and Jam looked up to the ceiling, wondering if someone up there tried to punish him for something.

"*I* am your mom," Collene protested, moving so she had a visual on the boy they were talking about.

Jam felt how Lesso took a spot next to him, grabbing his father's hand.

"Alessia is my mom," his son stated, his voice hard, his expression the same.

"I carried you and then you were taken from me," Collene

replied, and Jam wondered if she realized that she was discussing with a ten-year-old. He did notice the way her eyes glazed over with anger though at the mentioning of Aly's name.

"People in town say I was saved from you."

Shocked, Jam stared at his son. He couldn't believe someone in town had been brave enough to say that to the little boy. "Grandma says my mom... Alessia was my salvation."

"You don't even know what that means," Collene hissed, leaving her luggage behind as she came closer.

"Grandma said it meant I couldn't swim and was in water I couldn't stand in, and Mom taught me how to swim so I wouldn't die." Jam wanted Alessandro to stay quiet, but the fight in his son was obvious. He had not the slightest idea what Collene could do, and if Jam had any say in it, that wouldn't ever change.

"That's not what salvation means." Collene's eyes went from the little boy to Jam, and it was the best thing Jam could wish for. "Salvation means you are close to dying and someone comes to rescue you. There's no salvation for people like you and your father, Zack."

"Wrong, Collene. He has been saved before, and I don't care what you'll do, touching my son is not an option." Her face froze, and Jam realized that this was probably the harshest he had ever spoken to her.

"Dad, can we just go?" Alessandro finally seemed to pick up on Collene's aggressive mood, and it was good that his instincts told him to run.

"You can go. I need to talk to that woman for a few more minutes," Jam replied, kneeling down to tell his son good-bye properly. His stomach felt heavy as if his whole body knew something that his mind hadn't realized yet.

"Come with me, Dad," Lesso pleaded, wrapping his small arms around Jam's neck.

"Don't cry," Jam whispered. He didn't mind, but he knew it would cause Collene to be even more of a bitch. She had a thing about tears.

They turned her on, gave her a feeling of power. She had a hard time letting her victim go once she spotted the first tears. "Go, and don't come back. If you meet someone, tell them you got lost and you need to find Greg Rhyme. You know your uncle. That's who you are looking for." He said it so quietly, he hoped that Collene wasn't able to hear him. "If I say go, you need to start running." Lesso nodded slightly against his shoulder, and Jam prepared mentally for keeping Collene's attention on him when his son was torn from his side.

"Stop the whispering, you pussies." Jam cringed at her words. Lesso didn't belong in a world so crude, so brutal.

"Let him go," Jam demanded, getting back to his feet to have the advantage of height. Not that this had ever helped him.

Collene didn't. Instead, she shook the little boy until Jam could hear Alessandro's teeth clatter.

"I see how it is," Jam taunted, his voice cold even though he was feeling anything but. "I'm too much for you to handle, huh? You are getting old. Thirty is right around the corner, and you don't have enough strength to push me around anymore."

The grip on his son's arm tightened, but Collene's eyes were on him.

"Shut up," she almost screamed. Jam wondered where the rest of the household was, but then he guessed that the staff was used to screaming and even more to looking the other way.

"Why? Don't you like being talked to as if you're worthless?" he continues, stepping toward her even though his heart beat an erratic tattoo against his chest. He had never been so scared in his life and the imprint of his fear would probably be visible on his skin.

"Jamison, be quiet," she shrieked, and then pushed Alessandro away so hard the boy stumbled. Jam wanted to kneel down next to him, but he couldn't. He needed to keep Collene occupied.

"I really was a bad boy if you call me Jamison." He laughed. It came out as a choked sound, though.

"I can still take you on," she replied, and he felt the blow before he saw her hand moving. She had hit him right below the ribs, and she still had a lot of force in her arm.

"What was that?" he asked, blinking as if she had merely tickled him even while the pain was radiating from his side. She hit again, higher this time, and he had to hold his breath in order not to double over.

"Run, Lesso," he ordered, for a quick moment looking at his son, whose eyes had widened in utter disbelief.

"Zack! His name is Zack!" she screamed and then kicked Jam in the knee, making him go down. It was the last thing he had wanted, but he couldn't change it.

"Dad!" He could hear his son, but all that mattered now was letting him get away.

"You definitely got weaker, girl," he sneered, and she punched him right in the face. He felt his nose breaking, knew the feeling too well. The next minute, Collene howled in pain, kicking Lesso. He had thrown himself at Jam's attacker, biting her in the leg. Now, he was crumpling on the floor in pain. It made Jam see red. Before he could say or do anything, though, a fourth person joined them and it was then that Jam realized he had never before felt true fear in his life. With a trained eye, he took in all the 'weapons' in the room, everything that could be used by Collene. There were too many to name, among them a bottle and a fire poker. He knew Collene to be able to do immense damage with both. It settled like lead in his stomach.

Someone was going to die that day and the way luck had been playing him, it definitely wouldn't be Collene.

~

*A*ly was seething. She had broken every speeding law out there once she had heard that Collene had been sighted in town. Ringing the doorbell most likely would have been a stupid idea, so she had walked along the property until she found a door on the garden wall. It was slightly ajar, obviously having been thrown closed yet not with enough force. Following a path leading away from there, she had found a rose garden and then heard screaming.

The first thing she saw was a bleeding Jam then her son on the floor.

"You fucking bitch will die for that!" She held onto her handbag as if her life depended on it. She had the papers in there, the ones she needed to have signed, and as much as she didn't want to let go of them, she feared it was better to separate them from her body.

"Mom!" Alessandro pushed himself off the floor, clearly in pain, but nevertheless eager to get to her. She embraced him only slightly, too worried to hurt him further.

"Go, there's a police officer outside, the one you met before, the one who handed you his card, remember?" She knew because she had shot Phil a text to get them out just in front of the property, waiting for something to happen. Now, she just hoped they were ready to take Lesso away.

"She's hurting Dad," he whimpered, and she kissed his hair, time running out quickly.

"I know. I won't let that happen. I never let anyone hurt you, right? Now, you need to go. I'll be right out with your dad," she promised and then made him leave, walking by his side to keep Collene's eyes on her. It wasn't hard. The crazy woman watched her like a hawk.

"You! I had totally forgotten about you after that little party," Collene remarked, and Aly shook her head, knowing exactly which one she referred to.

"Go, Alessia," Jam demanded, his breaths coming short; his voice sounded stuffed due to what surely was a broken nose.

"Don't you hate her, Jammy? It was her who caused all that pain after all," Collene asked, her voice taking on a soft, compassionate tone.

"It was you, not her," he forced out, the hatred so visible in his emerald eyes that Aly cringed.

"No. It was her. She was on my list. A girl with too bright a smile, too good a character. She needed to be broken. But then you came and I forgot about her. I forgot about everyone." Bile rose up in Aly's throat as Collene touched Jam's chin in a caressing gesture.

"Take. Your. Filthy. Hands. Off. Him." Aly spoke slow, quiet. She was set on not letting Collene hurt Jam any more than she already had.

"Alessia, stay out of this," Jam ordered, starting to stand. It was obvious how much pain he felt.

"I'm not. It's time I carry what was supposed to be my burden."

"A lover's quarrel! How adorable," Collene snickered, and Aly walked until she stood between Jam and his abuser. It couldn't be more obvious how powerful Collene was even though she seemed to be so tiny. If Aly hadn't known Jam as closely as she did now, she wouldn't have seen the fear etched into his eyes each and every time his gaze fell on Collene.

"I wonder if maybe you'd hurt more if I…" Collene trailed off and then kicked Jam in the knee again, making a crack reverberate throughout the big place. Jam groaned quietly, holding a scream in while Aly stormed toward the woman who had turned her life into a nightmare.

It took only a few seconds and Aly realized that whatever she thought she could do with her anger didn't outweigh Collene's decades of causing pain. The woman knew what she was doing, hitting Aly in the throat right away, raining down punches until Aly couldn't do anything but cover her face with her arms. She stood in front of Jam, ready to take on whatever Collene would bring, but her body was starting to scream in pain.

No matter what she had thought, Aly hadn't been prepared for the blunt force Collene used. When the woman suddenly turned away, Aly sobbed in relief, only to notice the bottle Collene was grabbing. It was a typical wine bottle, half of the red liquid still inside. Collene didn't care, spilling it onto the floor right next to the empty wine glasses that stood on a tiny table next to the seating arrangement. Then Collene came for her.

"No," Jam moaned next to her, and she looked at him for a

quick second. It was all she needed to straighten her shoulders again.

Aly was empty-handed and usually against violence. How in the world did she think she could do anything against Collene?

"How did you manage it that he loves you like that?" Collene asked, the bottle in her hand lazily swinging. She sounded curious, and it caught Aly off-guard. Then again, she could talk, so maybe if she occupied Collene long enough, Jam had a chance to get away.

They had moved away from the seating area, and Aly was glad about that. It was somewhere behind her now, but at least there were no direct obstacles between her and the garden or her and the way to the front door, even though Aly remembered the way only vaguely. Jam would know better. That was what mattered.

"I never beat him into submission. I gave him my heart and that was all he needed. He'd walk to the end of the world for me," Aly answered casually, blindly trying to reach for the man in question. He was somewhere near. She could hear him breathing heavily.

"Leave her alone, Collene. You never enjoyed beating anyone as much as you enjoyed beating me," he said, and suddenly, he was so close, he squeezed her hand.

Aly spun around to glare at him, positioning herself between Jam and the Karmison daughter.

"Shut up. Get out of here. Let her get whatever she thinks she'll get out of this situation. But you need to go and grab my bag. If something happens, something serious, it's the leverage you—"

She didn't get to finish as stars exploded in her vision and blood filled her mouth. She heard Jam call her name, but it was as if cotton packed her ears.

She emptied her mouth of the metallic tasting liquid and then turned back to Collene, seeing the green bottle shine with something red.

Her blood. And Collene was swinging again.

She couldn't think, her natural instincts kicking in and making her back up. Collene aimed for her head again, but this time Aly raised her arms, the pain from her head making her numb to everything else. She walked blindly and heard Jam call out, but she didn't care. She didn't stop. Then she was falling, tumbling over something in her way. Collene was the last thing she had seen before her head hit the coffee table.

She must've been closer to the table than she had guessed. It was the last thought she had before darkness claimed her.

~

"*T*his is almost too easy." Collene dropped the bottle, and Jam heard it shatter on the tile floor, the glass splinters jumping all around them, but his eyes were trained on a lifeless Aly. Her head wounds were bleeding, covering the tiles with what looked like velvet and truly was hell.

He could hear the clatter of the fireplace instruments, and he knew she was going for the kill. Collene was in a murderous frenzy, and he couldn't even say why. Then again, something as small as him being back or Lesso talking to her the way he had was enough to make Collene's sanity turn off.

Jam crawled over to Aly, making her as small as he could so the crazy bitch behind him had nothing to aim at but his body.

"I'm sorry, Aly," he whispered into her sticky hair, not caring that he got her blood all over him.

"Step away. She ruined my life. I could never own you because she did. Every single day we were together, right? That's why you never loved me!" Collene demanded to know, and Jam ignored her, cradling Alessia close.

"I am talking to you," she screamed in outrage, and Jam closed his eyes.

"I'm not talking to you," he replied, his voice calm. He was no longer afraid of her because unless Aly would open her eyes again, he had nothing to live for. "Alessia, open your eyes. Look at me, beautiful. Don't let her win," he pleaded against her clammy skin.

"Shut up. I always win!"

"Aly, I love you," he whispered, ignoring Collene even though he knew this would only make her angrier.

"You should love me!"

Collene's anger echoed throughout the room and Jam knew the moment she fully snapped. He anticipated the first blow with the heavy metal, even knew the ribs she was breaking. After the first two blows, numbness took over his body. His arms were getting heavy, and he was hardly able to hold onto Aly. Lowering her back to the floor as gently as he could, he bent over her, his eyes trained on her face. If he'd die, it would be with her face in mind. He wouldn't look back at the object of his torture because it would give Collene too much power.

Suddenly, hot white agony raced through his veins. She didn't hit him; instead, she stabbed him with the poker.

"You don't deserve to live." She laughed, sounding like the true maniac she was.

Jamison's vision turned blotchy, black taking over most of what he was seeing. He knew that once Collene had finished him, she'd return her attention to Aly. All he had wanted to protect her from, all he had endured for her had been in vain in the end.

chapter Fifteen

*A*ly became conscious with a start. She sat up, feeling something restrain her, and she started screaming. Her mind was fuzzy, shattered memories appearing and disappearing without a warning. She heard voices; screaming, sobbing, low discussions, hurried words. It all blended in a nerve-racking hum.

"Stay where you are, Miss Rhyme," someone said, and she turned her aching head. A paramedic. Someone was injured or paramedics wouldn't be there.

"Jam!" She tried to sit up again, this time even managing to. Her eyes searched the room, finding Thea Karmison and Collene sitting on a sofa, both pale while Shannon sat in front of them, waving papers and making gestures. Then Aly's gaze landed on the bloody floor and the body which two more paramedics crouched over, working hurriedly. A doctor gave instructions, his white gloves and clothes covered in more blood. How much blood could a single person lose before they'd never get up again?

"Jamison," she called out, trying to get off the stretcher. Why the hell was she on a stretcher and Jam on the damn ground?

"Miss," the paramedic pleaded, but she still stumbled away from him, strangely aware of the fact that all eyes were on her while silence descended over the room. Aly's heart stopped. There was no movement from Jam; a mask covered his face, cuts and purple bruises covered his body where they had cut open his shirt.

"He's not dead. He's not dead. He's not dead." She repeated that sentence over and over again before breaking down next to his body. "No," she sobbed, not even daring to touch him.

"He doesn't feel pain," the doctor offered gently next to her as if he could tell how badly she needed to feel Jam.

"That makes it better, right?" she snapped and then still leaned over, covering him with her body while she held onto him, resting her forehead against his chest. She could feel the pads stuck to Jam's chest to monitor his heart as they pressed coldly against her face, and it only made her cry more.

"We need to get you to the hospital," the doctor told her. Her mind took the words in, yet her heart was oblivious to them. She didn't feel anything but the cold of Jam's skin under her hands and the way his heart was beating so weakly; she felt as if she should press her body against his just to make them both beat in one rhythm.

"He tried to save your life. I'd even say he succeeded." Someone stepped next to her, and in her daze, it took her a moment until she realized it was Greg. He was the one reaching out for her, pulling at her shoulders. God, why was she hurting so bad?

"At what cost?" she asked and then looked up. Her brother looked as if he, too, had been in a fight with them, his eyes bloodshot, meaning he had cried.

"How long was I out?" She wanted to know, sitting back on her heels.

"Let those guys take Jam to a hospital, Aly. They are the only ones who can save him," Greg whispered, and she tried to get to her feet, but it was nearly impossible.

"She nearly killed you, too, Alessia Rhyme! What were you thinking coming here?" he asked as he had her in his arms, leading her away.

"She had them both. I couldn't let her win. I couldn't let her hurt them. And I failed Jam," she cried, her chest hurting with more than physical pain. "Will he be okay?"

Greg didn't look at her another second, his eyes finding someone across the room. He nodded after a second, his expression grim.

"Mr. Rhyme, I need to take your sister away. We need CT scans, MRT, and some blood work from her," the doctor said, obviously having left Jam's side. He was talking right over her, and Aly wouldn't have it.

"I'm awake and listening. Talk to me if you need something," she ordered.

"Mom!" The cry pulled her from her anger, and she knelt as her son came running but stopped a few steps away from her. He looked pale, but other than that fine.

"You're bleeding," he whispered, his eyes filling with tears.

"I'm fine," she promised and then opened her arms for her son. He smelled of fabric softener she'd never use, clean air, and male perfume, most likely Greg's, but that didn't matter. Holding him felt like coming home.

"The emergency guy told me to take your hand and get you because we both need to go to the hospital. You're hurt, and I'm hurt, and they want to make us stop feeling the pain," he explained, and Aly nodded.

"Then let's go." If her son were hurt, she would go anywhere with him to make it better. Plus, there was only one hospital around and Jam would be there as well.

She got up from the floor, insisting on carrying her son despite her body screaming out in pain. She needed him close.

"Miss Rhyme, this... I'm... so sorry." Thea Karmison had the balls to step in Aly's way.

"You're sorry? For what? Not knowing that your daughter would kill someone one day? For making sure you ruined three lives in one day just because you didn't think to talk to me about visiting rights? I'm sure once your husband comes back, he'll make you feel sorry."

"My husband will never return," Thea promised her with a certainty that would've scared Aly if she could feel anything but pain.

"The way the doctor looks at me, neither will Jam, and that goes on your conscience. Each and every day of your life you can get up with that thought. You're the reason Jamison Loane might no longer be on this Earth."

With that, she walked away, sitting down in the ambulance until she got a dizzy spell then lying down next to her son, letting sleep take her over. *Just a few minutes*, she promised herself. She needed to escape the pain and the loneliness for just a little bit.

~

*I*t was night by the time she regained consciousness. A noise had woken her, and when she looked up, it was a woman wearing a doctor's coat.

"How is Jam?" she instantly asked. She knew Lesso would be okay and most likely asleep, so the guy she loved was Aly's first priority.

"Still in surgery." The curt answer told Aly more than the woman probably intended to.

"How likely is it that he can see his son again? And don't lie to me. I'm most likely on my way to prison sometime soon," she mumbled, her head much clearer again and her body burning less with pain than earlier.

"Do you realize that Jamison's and your story actually is the thing people talk about behind closed doors? The story is made of epic," the doctor replied instead of reacting to her question.

"Head injuries?" Aly inquired, not ready to give up.

"Extensive. They had to drain the swelling."

"Broken bones?"

"Multiple."

"Internal injuries?"

"Yes. A torn lung, some bleeding. A lot of pain. And a coma."

"Thank you for not lying or trying to ease my pain," Aly mumbled, meaning it.

"If he ever wakes up again, we can't be sure he'll be the same man you fell in love with. There's a high chance he'll be forever changed and in need of assistance. Miss Rhyme—"

"There's a higher chance he's dying right there, right?" she asked, and it took a few seconds before the doctor nodded, sitting down on her bed.

"I looked at him. This wasn't the first beating he had gotten, right?"

She was a young doctor, probably about their age, but Aly didn't know her. Clearly, she was someone from out of town.

"How in the world did you come to be a doctor in hell?" Aly asked, and the woman shrugged.

"I didn't know, but I learned pretty quickly who rules the town. Look how far it has come. We have a man dying because them now."

"He was dead inside long before that. Jam was a broken man when he showed up on my doorstep some weeks ago, but I thought we could make it all better. I knew he needed professional help, but I figured we could get him there with a little coaxing. I wanted him to overcome his past. Instead, his past won." She felt a tear slip down her cheek and then took a deep breath.

"Where is Alessandro?" she asked and the doctor leaned back enough so Aly could see the bed at the end of the room. Her son was sound asleep.

"Is he okay?" she then inquired and the doctor looked up. Aly couldn't believe that she hadn't even cared enough to wait for a name or ask for one.

"He's bruised and battered, but I think all that matters to him is you," the doctor admitted, and Aly ached to touch him.

"What's going to happen now?" she asked quietly, and the woman got up from her bed.

"I think it all depends. A few people want to see you in the morning. Try to get some sleep."

"Doctor...?"

"Johnson. I'm Lucy Johnson." She smiled, and Alessia nodded thankfully.

"Can you free me from the machines? I need to touch Lesso, and then..." She shrugged, guessing that the doctor knew pretty well what she was trying to say.

"He's not out of surgery, Miss Rhyme," the doctor reminded her.

"Call me Alessia. And I know, but I wanna be prepared and not cause a riot if I get up."

"Well, then I'm Lucy. It'll be bad. I'm not sure you want to see that," the woman mused, and Aly met her eyes.

"He gave his life to save mine. I think I can handle anything for that guy," she assured her, and Lucy nodded.

"Very well then. I'll send a nurse to unplug you and if I have news, I'll let you know."

Aly gave her a smile and then watched as the doctor left, basically being replaced by a nurse. The moment she could, she got up and walked over to Alessandro's bed, lying down next to him. She cuddled him, and he instantly turned into her embrace, coming closer.

"Love you, Mom," he mumbled sleepily, and Aly kissed his hair.

"Love you, too, son," she replied and then hummed until she was sure he fell back asleep. No matter how hard she tried to keep her eyes open, waiting for Doctor Johnson to return with news about Jam, she couldn't stay awake for anything in the world.

≈

*J*am wasn't alive. He was in a world of pain. Groaning, he tried to open his eyes. There was no way for him to take inventory of all his injuries because there wasn't one part of his body that didn't hurt.

"Jamison, are you awake?"

"You need to leave right now!"

"I need to make sure that his son will not go into the system if he dies. Otherwise, Jam's sacrifice was for nothing."

"You need to leave. He is not in a frame of mind to make a decision like that and any judge would fight that!"

"Doctor Johnson, excuse me, but you aren't from here. You don't understand what—"

"Oh hell, I understand well."

"Stop." Jam's head was hurting with the low discussion at his bedside. His throat ached and bringing the words out was torture. He did recognize one woman, though, and that was Shannon.

"Jam!" He felt someone touch his left hand, and he turned toward the woman.

"I got the Karmisons to sign over custody. It's all done and well now. But you might die." At least she had the decency to cry while saying that. Not that the mentioning was needed. The pain was subsiding, and Jam had a hard time keeping the threatening blackness at bay.

"Papers. Pen," he ordered, using what little control he had left.

"Mr. Loane, I'm..." He groaned and the male voice trailed off. Time was limited. "You are right. Screw this. Here."

Something long and slender was pushed into his right hand, something cold placed under it. "Just one signature, Jam. Write your last name," Shannon urged, and he took everything together that he had. For Aly. For Lesso.

"That's it," the guy coaxed, and after the last 'e,' Jam dropped the pen, all strength having left his body.

"Alessandro is now officially Alessia Rhyme's son, as well as yours," the guy stated, and as much as Jam wished he could smile in triumph, he couldn't.

"Tell my son I love him. Tell Aly to marry Spencer. He's a decent guy. Tell her to be happy."

"Hell, no, Jamison Loane, you marry that girl. Don't you dare die after everything we reached," Shannon fussed, her voice filled with despair.

"You all need to leave finally," Jam heard, but then the voices already got further away.

"But..."

Unconsciousness claimed him, owned him, and Jam guessed, never would let him go again.

∼

"*M*ommy. Mommy! You're squeezing me too tight!" Lesso moved in her arms, and she slowly blinked. Waking up was hard and her body demanded more sleep.

"Morning, you two." Shannon came in; followed by a guy Aly had never seen.

She sat up, combing out her hair with her fingers. It took her a second to realize that it was all stiff and that her blood still coated it.

"I need to take a shower," she announced, getting up. Her legs were hurting, but so were her arms and her whole body really.

"Let me get a nurse," Shannon offered, and Aly glared at her.

"I can do it myself. If I don't, they won't let me see Jam," she protested, and Shannon slowly nodded, looking like hell. She clearly had seen Jam already.

"Before you go, you need to sign papers. That's Kent. He works with the adoption agency. I've been making sure everything was ready in case the plan worked out." She raised an eyebrow and Aly understood that the guy didn't know what she talked about. Aly did, though. Shannon had somehow managed to get the signature on the custody papers.

"You mean us coming down here. Too bad we got in the middle of a fight," Aly replied calmly. She didn't mind lying any longer. Alessandro would never return to the Karmisons and that was all that mattered.

"Jamison Loane signed the papers to agree on you adopting his son. You need to sign, too, so that in case—"

"Don't." Aly gave the guy a sharp look and then nodded at Alessandro, who was listening intently, then she arched a brow, holding out her hand.

She was handed a pen and the papers, and her eyes fell on the second line, the one holding Jamison's name. It was shaky and not nearly as masculine as she had seen previously, but it was there. He had been awake. It gave her hope.

"Congratulations. Zack Karmison is now officially your son," the guy said and then stepped back. Shannon was crying silently, and Aly thought about the fact that this probably was as hard for her as it was for Alessia. They all had hoped Jam could've been among them to enjoy that moment.

"Thank you. For everything. For being here last night and getting his signature. For waiting for me to wake up." The agency worker nodded and then left, telling her that he'd have the papers along. Shannon told him just to get everything to her and she'd deal with it. Aly didn't mind, even though she knew she'd be in town until either Jam walked out of this hospital or... the second possibility she wasn't even ready to consider.

She vanished in the little bathroom then, glad that someone had brought her clothes. They didn't exactly fit, but once she got out of the shower, she didn't care any longer. Phil was there and so was Dorly. God, she had missed her friends.

They stayed a few feet away, and she silently thanked them. Any hugs and she might start to scream.

"Look, Mom, Phil's here! And Dorly!" Alessandro held onto the two as if they were part of his home, and he couldn't wait to be back there.

"I know, Lesso." She smiled, but with all the people that she loved in one room, she knew one person was missing. She had to see him now, had to say all that she wanted to tell him in case he... in case he never woke up again.

"Philomena, can you maybe..." Was she really ready to go there?

"Lesso, you can stay with Dorly for a few minutes, can you?" Aly asked, and Lesso looked at her, looking suddenly so much more grown up than the last time she had seen him. It scared her and made her worry that he had lost his innocence. It would be another loss she'd heavily mourn.

"I wanna see Dad, too." Aly gasped, bringing her hand to cover her mouth. "They said he'd never wake up again. Can I say good-bye? Isn't that what you were going to do?" he asked, and she hesitated a moment before nodding.

Taking his hand, she followed Phil out of the room. Her best friend definitely knew where she had to go, and Aly had a hard time ignoring how everyone looked at her. God, they knew. Hell, did everyone know? It wouldn't be long until the handcuffs would click, that much she was sure of.

"No, Dad…" The broken sob of her son pulled her mind back, and she gritted her teeth before turning to the open doorway of the intensive care unit. He was bandaged. Every little bit of him seemed to be covered one way or the other.

Lesso didn't care about hurting Jam; he just threw his little body over his father's bed, sobbing hard. "I'm sorry for being a bad boy, Dad. I didn't want you hurt. But they say you saved my mom. You're a hero, Dad. My hero!"

Aly was pissed at herself that she had been out enough that people obviously could say many things to her son. She under-stood that they all were trying to help, but she'd feel better if she could just shield him from all pain and the reminders for it.

As if.

She knew that was a dream, but it was all she had left.

She and Phil stood in silence for a long time until Alessandro's sobs ebbed away and he started to breathe regularly. "He fell asleep," Aly whispered, and Phil nodded.

"I'm gonna take him away. Be prepared to have nurses come in all the time. I'll make a mention to give you some time, but he's under strict supervision," she explained. Aly didn't care how many people would witness her misery. As it was, the whole town seemed to know about it anyway.

She waited until her son and her best friend were gone, then she moved toward the bed, her knees giving out just as she reached it. All the tears, sobs, and fears she had held in over the last couple of weeks finally broke free until Aly was almost choking on her heartache. She clung to Jam's hand—the only thing obviously not destroyed by the monster—and pressed it against her cheek.

"Forgive me. I should've left when you told me to. I thought I'd be ready to protect you when all my life you've been protecting me. You deserved it. I was sure I'd be able to bear the pain for you. I failed." She paused, trying to collect her thoughts. "Our whole ride has been ridiculous. Jamison, I just got you for the first time in my life, and now, I'm supposed to let you go again? How can I when I'll never find out if maybe, just maybe we'd make pretty babies? I will never have the chance to show you how amazing you are. I've seen the doubt in you, but Jam, you would've been an amazing dad. I don't want to say good-bye. This is not good-bye." She had to stop again, her voice breaking. She wanted to get up and kiss his cheek since a mask covered his lips, but her body wouldn't move. She was kneeling in front of his bed as if she needed absolution and maybe that was exactly what it was.

"You gave your life for me, and I wasn't prepared. I'm still not. Come back to me, you stubborn idiot. See what you managed! See how the people react to you. Jamison, don't leave me. This can't be good-bye."

She had no idea how long she was there on the floor when a hand landed on her shoulder. She was too scared to turn around. If they took her away now because of the lies she had been telling, they all had been telling, Jam's death seriously was for nothing. It couldn't be.

"I can't go to prison," she mumbled, not turning.

"You won't." That voice sent shivers down her spine, and Aly jumped up, standing protectively in front of Jam. Not that anyone could harm him much more than he already was.

"You need to leave," Aly snarled, but the woman across from her shook her head.

"I came here to tell you that we took it all back. I retracted the missing person's case from back then. I told them we only filed that since we hadn't had any idea about Jam having sole custody. As well, my daughter will be going to prison. With my husband God knows where, I think it's time to do the right thing. There's no real need for any of you to make a statement because if Jamison Loane should really die, it'll be murder, but I still wanted to tell you that whatever comes, I will back you up. *You*, and not the monster my husband raised. She has no funds whatsoever whereas you and Alessandro…" Aly actually saw how Thea Karmison swallowed while saying that name, "will get all the assistance you need."

"I don't want anything from you. You had your chance."

"I wanted my grandson. I thought you'd never allow me to see him because you know I'm a Karmison," Thea admitted, and Aly couldn't help but think she looked like a broken woman. And in so many ways that was probably true.

"How sure are you that your husband won't ever return and that your daughter will be locked up while I will walk free? Can you guarantee that?"

A small smile played over Thea Karmison's face and Aly had the hint of an idea how beautiful the woman once must've been. A trophy, without a doubt, in her husband's collection of riches and awesomeness. "I'm so sure that I'd bet my entire fortune on it."

Aly couldn't deny that she liked that answer, but since she was standing by the deathbed of the only man she had ever loved, she wasn't yet up to generosities.

"Maybe, in six months or so, you can call Alessandro up and talk. And by a call, I mean via phone and nothing else."

Thea slowly nodded, her eyes going to the blanket-covered body behind Aly. She wouldn't step away from his head, wouldn't give a woman who had allowed his abuse to go on to look at his broken form.

"I hope he comes out of it. He deserves to be thoroughly loved without reservations," the woman mumbled thoughtfully.

"He is thoroughly loved," Aly assured her, crossing her arms in front of her body.

"How are you?" Thea asked, and Aly wanted to give a pert reply, but then she reconsidered.

"I have a broken son thanks to our family. He cried himself to utter exhaustion on his father's lifeless body. I have a concussion, and while I'm heavily medicated, I can feel all the bruises your daughter caused me because they serve as a vivid reminder of what Jam has gone through for years. A man I loved all my life protected me, and I didn't even know it. The way it looks, I won't have a chance to make it all up to him, so what do you think? I'm alive, and for now, I guess that's all I can ask for."

Thea nodded and then turned just as a nurse came in. "You need to leave, Miss Rhyme. Your body needs rest and your son is awake, asking for you. That crazy woman told him to stay where he was."

Crazy woman? Aly arched a brow. It had been a while since she'd heard Phil called that. "I'm going," she promised.

"Yeah, he won't go anywhere anyways," the nurse replied nonchalantly, and Aly felt like committing murder.

"I think we need another nurse to watch over Jam," Thea decided from the doorway, and Aly gratefully looked at her. For once, they were on the same page at least.

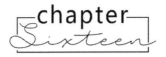
"*A*lessia, you're still here." The young doctor came back in, and Aly looked up. She had lost track of time, but she didn't mind.

"I'll be here until he either opens his eyes or his heart stops beating," she replied. "Hey, Lucy."

The woman came over, her straight dark blonde hair falling down her shoulders, making her small face look even slimmer. "I brought you food," she told Aly.

Alessia just nodded. "Thank you."

"I brought you a Chai Latte, too," Lucy continued and this time Aly's head whipped up. "Honestly?" she asked, craving the sweetness.

"You'll get it under one condition," Lucy replied, settling down in the chair across from her. It was for whoever else visited Jam. Most of the time Greg sat there.

"What's that?"

"Tell him good-bye and start living your life again. You are wasting away in front of my eyes, and I will not and cannot ignore that any longer."

"Keep the Chai. He's here because of me, and I left him once before already. It's never going to happen again," Aly insisted, her head whipping up just as Lucy jumped.

"He reacted to your promise," she announced, and Aly quickly quenched all hope that was threatening to rise up.

"Watch," she said, taking Jam's hand. "Always and forever. That's how long I'll be yours," she whispered, and there was a series of spikes in his brainwaves.

"Does that happen every time?"

"Every time I promise to stay with him," she agreed, and Lucy turned to her.

"Okay, so you know it means nothing, right?" she asked and

even though Alessia had tried hard to tell herself the same thing, it made her angry to hear it from Lucy's lips.

"Forever, Jamison, right? You promised me." Another irregular wave.

"Alessia," Lucy started

"Always." It was nothing more than a hushed whisper.

Utter silence spread in the room as the cardiogram registered an increased heart rate. Jam coughed between them, and Lucy jumped into action while Aly stood frozen.

"Mr. Loane, you're awake," Lucy exclaimed, and Jam coughed again then cleared his throat.

"I promised," he rasped out, and Aly couldn't do anything but stare. His head turned, his green eyes finding her.

"What? Disappointed now?" he asked, forcing a smile even though it was clear how much pain he felt.

"Fucking idiot," she fussed, feeling hot tears streaming down her face.

"Doc?" he asked, and Aly watched as Lucy paused.

"Mr. Loane?" Lucy inquired.

"Is it okay for me to be kissed?"

"Can you breathe?" she asked and then took the mask from his face. It sounded harsh, but at least he was drawing the air into his lungs all by himself, holding out a shaking hand to her. Aly wanted to weep with happiness. Maybe, just maybe, they had gotten a lucky break.

~

$\mathcal{H}$e hurt everywhere. Even the tip of his little toe hurt. But Jam felt it all. Every little bit. It made him want to call out in triumph, but then, his throat hurt, too. What he still needed to do, though, was to hold Aly just to make her realize he wouldn't go anywhere.

Fighting against the darkness that had been ready to keep him under had been everything but easy, yet she had been his guiding light. Her voice had been present in his mind, and some words reminded him why he needed to fight the darkness.

Forever.

He had wanted that with her and nothing would ever be able to keep him from that.

"Aly," he whispered, and she came closer, ignoring his hand while reaching for something that doctor woman held out. Ever so carefully, Aly reached out and lifted his head. Boy, it hurt like a bitch, and she instantly apologized as he winced. Holding a cup, she carefully let him take a sip from the straw, and the cool liquid eased his aching a little. His eyes never left her face, and his heart swelled with how much he loved her.

"You were really ready to sit by my side until it went one way or the other?" he asked, and she looked at him.

"I was ready to take you home and take care of you if you woke up and weren't your smartass-self."

"I didn't want that for you," he whispered. Talking hurt, but he wanted to speak to her.

"I wanted that for me," she said decidedly, and he reached out with his good hand, the one that wasn't in a cast, and cupped the back of her neck.

"One kiss," he pleaded, and she wrinkled her nose. It was too cute.

"You don't smell too good," she teased, and he was about to protest when she lowered her lips to his anyway. "But I still love you," she promised, and he couldn't help but smile until he remembered why he had ended up here.

"Did I... did everything work?"

"Well, I officially am Alessandro's mother now. Only we still need to have him renamed. And Thea Karmison swore that her daughter would be locked away. You saved your son and me," she replied, and Jam couldn't help it as a tear slipped down his cheeks.

"I hate to interrupt, but we need to run tests now that you are awake," the doctor interrupted, and Jam noticed that she was blushing. Obviously, she wasn't used to that much open affection. Oh, if Jam could do as he wanted…

"Sure," Aly mumbled, stepping back. Jam wanted to protest; instead, he looked at her, keeping his eyes trained on her face. He knew they'd be together forever now, just as he had promised her.

*A*ly took a deep breath, looking at the snow-covered beach.

"Mom, are you coming?" Alessandro stuck his head out of the backdoor and rolled his eyes at her. "Terra will eat all the pudding if you don't come," he fussed, and she laughed.

"You can start without me," she answered, and he came closer, easily towering over her. He leaned in to kiss her cheek, hesitating while watching her face.

"What is it, Mom?"

Twenty years of age and Alessandro didn't mind the slightest to show his soft side. He had so much from his father that sometimes Aly wondered if he had any of her traits.

"It's Christmas, Lesso," she mumbled as a way of explanation, and he drew her to his chest. Would she ever get used to the fact that he was a muscle-packed, almost grownup man?

"Everything worked out. We are fine. Dad is here. You got a beautiful little daughter that I adore to pieces. And you have me, your son. You'll always have me, Mom. Everything you've been through for me, all you've done... no one else can say that about their mother."

She wiped away a tear, not stepping away. She wouldn't ever cut a hug short, especially since Alessandro was ready to move out and live with his girlfriend. Aly loved her like a daughter, but still, letting Lesso go was hard.

Very hard.

"Mom, can we eat? I'm starving," Terra called from the inside.

"Brat," Lesso called back, his tone loving.

"Cut it out, you two," Jam's voice came just before he appeared in the doorway. God, Aly loved him now more than ever. She wasn't sure if that was really possible but still.

"Hey, beautiful," Jamison greeted her, and Lesso let her go.

"Ugh, I rather go back inside. I feel PDA coming." Lesso shook his head as if he was still ten years old and found kissing disgusting.

"Are we gonna do that melancholic thing every year, babe?" Jam asked and gently framed her face.

"I won't ever stop reminding myself of how close I was to losing everything, Jam."

"Things turned out perfect," he reminded her, and she nodded. As her son had guessed, he leaned in and kissed her deeply, making her whole body tingle. She would never tire of the feeling of his lips against hers. "Come on."

He grabbed her hand and drew her inside to the totally overflowing living room.

"Ah, beautiful Mrs. Loane," Thomas greeted her, winking at Dorly. The two had hit it off the first time Aly had invited the judge to her house by the sea, and it made her heart swell that they both had found one another so late in their lives. Aly guessed they'd now live forever; that was how happy they seemed to be.

"Mom!" Terra jumped off her chair, and even though she had Jam's green eyes, the girl looked every bit like her mother. Aly loved it.

"Let's get started," she decided, and everyone started to clap. Across the room, she caught the eye of her brother, and Greg slightly nodded at her. They finally had a huge family again, and while their parents probably were watching from heaven, she knew that everything was finally good.

Turn the page for a sneak peak at

Tagged For Life
(Tagged Soldiers Book 1)

Prologue

29th Nov. 2014

*T*essa,

My beautiful, amazing Tessa.

It's kind of scary knowing that you are close to me and yet so far away. But then, close is always a question of definition, isn't it?

I've had a lot of time to think over the last couple of days, and frankly, all I really worried and wondered about was how to start this letter. 'Hey' doesn't seem to cut it. 'My love' might scare you off, right? And everything else wouldn't be enough. I figured your name was the best thing to express what I wanted to convey. I can still feel it on my tongue. I can remember the way it would roll off and how it always filled me with such warmth.

That moment before you'd look up at me, was always filled with anticipation because I had a feeling every time you raised your eyes to mine, you were more amazing and I was falling just a little bit more for you.

I know what stands between us in the sense of distance and trouble, but I won't lie, when I think of you I feel tall enough so I can look over it all and see you.

There's nothing I want more than to tell you I hope you flying back home hasn't changed any of the things you felt for me. You just... Remember? We both know how that sentence should have ended. You just love me. I can't wait to hear the words from your lips. You keep me going right now. Do you even realize that?

We never exchanged contact details and I don't know why.

Maybe things had been just too head-over-heels in the end? Maybe you didn't want to because you thought that I needed to focus on other stuff. Maybe you thought I wouldn't contact you. Either way, I figure I need to fight for this harder than I have ever fought for anything. That sure means something because I am a soldier. Anyways, I got your address from the front desk. Remember that you needed to sign it? Well, technically the solider did that for you, so maybe it slipped your mind. It certainly vanished from mine. Either way, thankfully Tank reminded me of protocol.

It's too funny how he suddenly changed his tune about you because he thinks you are what will keep me sane. Little does he know that sane is not what you do to me.

When I think of you I cannot help but feel all warm. I want to be rough with you even while I'm soft. I want to mark you mine even while I hope you'll mark me yours. I want to own you while I want to be owned by you.

I've never been one to write letters. I always hated that there was no response or no chance to see what the person reading thinks while doing so. With you I don't mind. I guess it's because I can always tell myself the letter got lost.

Or someone kept it from you.

I don't know how good I'll be with writing, or how often, but I want to try, because the need to pick up the phone and call you is overwhelming. Not that I have your number or anything...

No matter what's coming our way, Tessa, remember that I'll always be your soldier. Remember that you are the woman who cracked my heart wide open. Remember that you are all I want. There are moments when I think that you are maybe MORE important than anything else. Does that scare you?

It sure as hell scares me. And proves one thing:

I love you.

Jazz

Chapter One

OCTOBER 2014

*T*essa Rowan checked her list for the hundredth time. It wasn't every day that she traveled to the US to meet all her crazy online acquaintances. Aimie, Hilary and Emma were going to be there once she arrived. Three weeks of fun, friends and festivities. She hated that her best friend wouldn't be able to join them, but Evy had just been promoted at work and wasn't ready to leave yet.

"What if we don't get along?" Tessa asked again, hearing her best friend sigh. She had come over to help her pack, but really didn't offer much useful advice. Instead though she seemed distracted, her eyes straying to the window or staring at the wall without really seeing anything.

"It'll be fine. The good thing is none of the girls have met before. I mean this will be new for all of you. Imagine how I'll feel next time I come along. You already know each other and I will be the outsider," she complained and Tessa turned back to her, placing her hands on her hips. As if she'd let her bestie feel left out. She cocked her head, eyeing Evy for a long moment.

"Please, as if I'd ever give you the chance to feel unloved," Tessa mumbled, grabbing a pair of jeans. For some reason, she was nauseous. In less than twenty-four hours she'd be sitting in a plane, getting away from everything at home. For years she had thought about that trip and finally it was becoming reality.

"I know you'd never do that, but still… Besides, I want to go with you," Evy fussed and Tessa rolled her eyes.

"And I want your ten thousand plus pay check every month," she replied. Evy grinned, sitting up. That definitely was something she liked as well. This was probably one of the few moments since she'd arrived where her best friend didn't look pensive.

"Okay, so I checked you in online. You'll have a window seat throughout almost every flight. In LA you'll have to hurry since I'm not able to reserve a spot from there to Monterey. Not that it will matter, because by then you'll be ready to drop."

Evy was damn good at her job as a travel agent, therefore making it easy for Tessa since she didn't have to do anything. All she'd done was pull out her credit card and pay for whatever Evy had gotten her.

"Thank you, I can't say that enough," she muttered, feeling emotions bubble up.

Her best friend just waved her off, giving her a hug before finally starting to fold Tessa's clothes and doing what she had come over to do: help Tessa pack. She had so much stuff that she would need six very strong guys to carry her bags. Half of everything would stay in the US, since Tessa had agreed to bring chocolate and other goodies with her, but somehow she was sure she'd fill the space with new items in no time.

"I want you to message me once you've landed and found Wi-Fi. Remember, roaming costs are enormous. You want to avoid them, trust me," Evy explained and Tessa felt a little as if her mother had gotten a twin. Between those two it wasn't hard to feel twelve years old again: "Wear a sweater. It's California, I know, but it'll be October nonetheless." Her mother was worried out of her mind, and Evy wasn't far behind, even though her best friend would never officially admit to it.

"Keep an eye your bags. You'll most likely have them checked in all the way, but your handbag and carry-on definitely need watching. There's a lot of pick pocketing in LAX, but I'm sure you can keep your stuff together. Split your money. Everything you have should be in four different bags. It's safer for you. Plus, the credit card; keep it where you can reach it and not lose it. I don't know, sew a pocket into your bra or something," Evy went on and Tessa turned, cocking her head.

"It's not my first flight. Even though my last trip to the States was more than a decade ago, I still know overall what I need to be aware of. Besides, I plan on keeping my credit card with me at all times. It's the only thing that can save my life after all," Tessa winked, hoping that once she'd start her trip, her calm would finally return.

Thinking about which handbag to take for the flight, and which to pack for use in the US, she threw her favorite black one into the luggage since it was too small for a trip like that.

With combined forces they closed the two suitcases and then sat down on them, sighing. This was it. She had her clothes ready and all she had to do now was wait for morning and her trip to begin.

≈

The moment it was time to say goodbye, tears started streaming down Tessa's cheeks. It made her realize that life could be over in a matter of moments. Even though airplanes had amazing statistics when it came to delivering their passengers safely to their destination, there were enough crashes to bring Tessa to remind Evy that she loved her more than anyone on this earth. She was the sister heaven had refused to give to her.

"I'm going to miss you like hell. No matter what'll come, you're the best friend a girl can wish for. I'm gonna text you whenever I can. And I'll Facetime you every night. You work forever anyways, so we'll have all the time in the world. Please, try to get out of work earlier than you did the last few days though. Actually, don't. It might make you regret not coming, and regret is something you shouldn't be feeling. We'll make sure the next get-together is here, at our home," Tessa promised, seeing how Evy wiped away her own tears.

"Stop making it sound like we'll never see each other again. I want you to get out, clear your head and have fun. I know you need it."

And it was true. Tessa's life had run in circles for the last three years and her usually calm demeanor had changed into a short-tempered, frustrated one.

Besides, Tessa knew she needed to get away from her monotone routines in order to find out what she was missing. Hanging with the girls seemed to be the perfect way to get her head back in the game and think about where she wanted to go in life, because even though she always used to have a plan, it seemed to take an entirely different turn. Twenty-nine was by no means old, but she wasn't the exactly a teen anymore, either, and kids seemed to be a fantasy that didn't belong in her reality any longer. After all, just the timeline already was difficult: finding a guy and getting to know him enough to maybe plan a baby... that could take years. And then you never knew if you'd even get pregnant right away... nah, children most likely weren't in her cards anymore, especially since finding a guy seemed impossible. Once burned, twice shy; that was definitely Tessa's motto since her ex-boyfriend had managed to crumble her self-confidence into little pieces over and over.

Perfect, none-cheating guys existed only in books. Romantic gestures were a creation of the female mind because they were deprived of the flowers-and-candles-reality. Maybe all stories had spoiled Tessa for any real man out there. She had no idea and didn't want to think about it any longer.

"We both know I do," she agreed, picking up their topic again, kissing her best friend's cheek another time before hugging her tight. Her luggage was checked in, her tickets were safely put away in her handbag and her credit card rested between her Starbucks-and her health-insurance-card.

"I want postcards. A million. And pictures. A million-and-one," Evy whispered before releasing her.

"Everything you want, I promise," Tessa laughed and then

stepped back, knowing she needed to go now or she wouldn't ever leave without stowing her best friend away in her handbag.

Passing through security, Tessa thought about the last time she had been so excited and obviously it had been too damn long because she simply couldn't remember it at all.

Interested?

Buy Tagged For Life now!

Acknowledgements

Thank you to my best friend Yvi and her little boy, who has the best mom ever. You two inspire me and make me feel the love! ;-)

Thank you to my betas Erica, Lucy, Staci, Aimie and Ewelina who always rock my life with their feedbacks and comments.

A huge shout out goes to my CS Chicks, as always. I love how well this thing between us works, because whenever I need encouragement, I know I can find it with you. Thank you.

Jenny Sims, your editing is very thorough and I'm super impressed and grateful I found you. Keep on rocking, girl.

Danielle, thank you so much for giving Aly and therefore AJ a face that makes it as beautiful on the outside as I hope the story is inside.

Terra, you crack me up, and have my back every damn time I need it. You are fun and tough and I wish I'd be just a bit like you.

Last but not least, the biggest thank you goes to all of you readers. Thank you for buying this book. Thank you for buying the rest of my books. Thank you for being the best readers in the world, because just one sentence from you makes my day. Come and talk to me if you want to. Tell me what you thought while reading. There's nothing more fun. Thank you.

xoxo,

Sam

about the Author

Once upon a time there was a young girl with her head full of dreams and her heart full of stories. Her parents, though not a unit, always supported her and told her more stories, encouraging her to become what she wanted to be. The problem was, young Sam didn't know what she wanted to be, so after getting her A-levels she started studying Computer Science and Media. After not even one year she realized it wasn't what her heart wanted, and so she stopped, staying home and trying to find her purpose in life. Through some detours she landed an internship and eventually an apprenticeship in a company that sells cell phones. Not a dreamy career, but hey. Today she's doing an accounting job from nine-to-five, which mainly consists of daydreaming and scribbling notes wherever she can.

All through that time little Sam never once lost the stories in her heart, writing a few little of them here and there, writing for and with her best friend, who always told her to take that last step.

Only when a certain twin-couple entered her mind, bothering her with ideas and talking to her nonstop did she start to write down their story - getting as far as thinking she could finish it. Through the help of some author friends, and the encouragement of earlier mentioned best friend, little Sam, now not so little anymore and in her twenty-seventh year, decided to try her luck as an Indie author. She finished the story of the first twin, Jaden, and realized she couldn't ever stop.

So, it really is only after five that the real Sam comes out. The one that hungers for love, romance, some blood, a good story, and, at the end of the day, a nice hot cup of Chai Tea Latte.

And if the boys are still talking to her, she'll write happily ever after.

Contact the author:
Website: http://www.samdestiny.com
Facebook: https://www.facebook.com/SamDestinyAuthor
Instagram: https://instagram.com/authorsamdestiny/
Pintrest: https://www.pinterest.com/samdestiny/
Goodreads: https://www.goodreads.com/authorsamdestiny
Twitter: https://twitter.com/SamDestinyAuthr

20881081R00149

Printed in Great Britain
by Amazon